FLOWERS IN HER BONES

A TROUBLED SPIRITS NOVEL

J.R. ERICKSON

DEDICATION

For my star sister, Audra.

AUTHOR'S NOTE

Flowers in Her Bones is inspired by a true story. To avoid spoilers, that story is briefly retold at the end of this book.

PROLOGUE

June 22nd, 2012

"Come on, we've got to get away from the lights if we're going to see the meteor shower. There's a trail off this one that leads up to a little overlook."

Wren followed me away from the Dancing with the Dead festival. The music trailed us, the Kirk Bender Band crooning about the ache of lost love.

The moon revealed herself in pale slivers through the silhouettes of trees that lined the path. We walked in darkness.

I'd done many night hikes and my eyes easily adjusted to the contours of the Porcupine Mountains forest, the poke of roots from the ground in front of us, the dark masses of foliage. Wren walked slowly, staring at the ground, careful not to lose her footing.

"Gloria, I can't believe you talked me into this. I could be sipping apricot brandy and dancing and instead I'm following you into the dark woods."

"For a meteor shower," I reminded her. "Instead of wishing on candles for our nineteenth birthdays this year, we're wishing on stars. Way more powerful."

She laughed. "When you put it that way…"

The leaves shimmered silver when the moonlight struck through the dense canopy, but most of the forest colors had turned to black. Here nothing had distinction, it all merged into a singular mass, and if Wren and I stood very still we'd be as indistinguishable as the saplings.

The trail started to climb.

"Look," Wren said. "A falling star."

I gazed up at the night sky, caught a glimpse of the white streak falling toward Earth then fading out.

"What did you wish for?" she asked me, looping her arm through mine.

Behind us on the trail a twig snapped and then another.

We both turned to look back. I studied the shapes. Something or someone approached us.

A beam of light ignited, shining directly at our faces.

"Dude, turn that off, you're blinding us," I said, shielding my eyes from the stab of light.

"Yeah, seriously," Wren echoed, cupping a hand over her eyes.

But the light didn't lower. The silhouette of the man behind it loomed large.

"Don't move," he said, moving closer.

I took a step toward the light, irritated.

Wren spoke so softly I almost didn't hear it. "Gloria, don't."

Her tone stopped me. I tried to see what she saw, but the light was blinding and then I caught the glint of metal in the man's opposite hand.

He held a gun.

My stomach dropped and I took an automatic step back.

"Don't move," he said, and this time his voice had an icy edge and something… carnal.

Wren grabbed my hand. Hers was trembling, cold with sweat.

I wanted to shout, "Run!" If we split up, he couldn't shoot us both, but he could shoot one of us, drag the other into the dark woods. Make us both disappear…

No, it was too risky. We had to stay together, wait for the right opportunity.

1

———————

Two Years Later

"Hi, Gloria. How are you today?"

"I'm tired."

"Are you having trouble sleeping?"

"Am I ever not having trouble sleeping?"

Dr. Fry smiled. "You had a few weeks not so long ago where you slept pretty soundly."

"Yeah, when I was drugged, but then..." I shook my head. "I don't feel like I ever wake up. The days pass in a haze. I can't take that stuff."

Fry wrote something in his notebook. "Shall we try something else, then? An alternative sleep aid."

I tugged at my hair, scratched at the skin peeling off my lip. I wanted to go lie down, but I felt wired. "I had a nightmare last night."

"Tell me about it."

I closed my eyes, the lids heavy, my eyes beneath sticky. If I let my head slump forward, chin resting on my chest, I could probably fall asleep. The dream stole in. Dark forest, rough hands shoving me to my knees. Wren whimpering, begging. 'Please don't hurt her,' she'd said.

I snapped my eyes open and jerked my head up so fast my neck twinged.

Fry watched me through the video screen, his eyebrows knitted together. "It was just a dream. You're in your apartment, a safe place. You're talking to me, Dr. Fry, a safe person. We can examine this without reliving the experience. Right? So let's tell it in the third person. You're not Gloria now, you're a detached observer watching someone else's dream, Gloria's dream, play out on screen. Tell me what's happening in that person's dream."

I swallowed, rubbed my eyes. "I'm—"

"Third person, remember?"

I nodded. "Gloria... is... she's in the woods and it's dark. Her wrists are bound and Wren is on the ground, crying. The man is behind her and he pushes Gloria onto her knees. Wren is begging the man not to hurt Gloria and then... that's all. There's nothing after that."

"Okay, good, very good. And that's a dream we've looked at before, isn't it?"

"Yeah."

"But it's been a while. Why do you believe you had that dream last night? Did you watch anything yesterday that might have triggered it?"

I tugged on my eyelashes, pulled a few free and placed them on my desk.

"You're doing some picking tonight, Gloria."

"I am?" I realized I was scratching my earlobes. In my mind's eye a particular earring arose, a silver leaf. I tried not to see it, which made it loom larger, and now it wasn't just an earring. There was also a hand, and the earring was ripped free, the lobe split and bleeding.

I cradled my head in my hands and shook my head. "No... no... no."

"Let's breathe back from ten, shall we? Look at me, Gloria."

Eyes closed, I continued to see the earring, the bleeding lobe.

"Gloria." His voice was stern.

I looked up, stared at his eyes.

"There, good. Big breath in, hold, and now release to the tune of ten... nine... eight... seven... six... five... four... three..."

I let the last of the breath out at three. I never made zero.

"Better?" he asked.

"A little."

"Okay, let's talk about the dream. Did something happen? Something that triggered the memory?"

I thought back to that day. "I ate a frozen turkey dinner, knitted for a while, and watched *Gilmore Girls.*"

"Were there woods in any of the *Gilmore Girls* episodes?"

"Yes." I fiddled with my shirt and then, realizing it, picked up the matching kitty stress balls on my desk and worked them between my hands. Squeeze and release, squeeze and release. The kitties' faces shrank, distorted, then expanded out, eyes big and blue.

"Perhaps the scene in the woods brought some things back... some memories."

"I shouldn't have watched that one."

"I think it's okay that you watched it. Remember what we talked about? Tiny safe exposures. Over time, you build new associations with those triggering symbols. There was a time in your life when you loved the forest. Remember? You told me about going on long hikes. You hiked the Appalachian Trail by yourself."

The summer after I'd graduated from high school, I'd hiked the Appalachian Trail. Not the whole trail—it's over two thousand miles long. I would have had to devote six months to a year of my life to such an endeavor. Instead, I hiked a section that took nearly three weeks.

I met a woman on that hike. She was in her sixties and told me it was her second time doing a thru-hike, meaning hiking the entire two-thousand-plus-mile trail. We camped together one night, sat together by a bonfire and ate oatmeal from metal mugs.

When I met that woman, I imagined I too would someday be silver-haired, my face grooved and tan, my legs spindly but strong, meeting some young woman on a trail and imparting my wisdom. I naively assumed I had a million hikes ahead, adventures that I'd yet to fathom.

Despite the passage of only three years, my current reality seemed eons from that former vision of my future. Now I lived as a recluse in my safe little apartment. Most days I felt like the oldest twenty year old who'd ever lived.

I shuddered. Hiking the Appalachian Trail had been a fond memory, a happy memory. I'd felt so brave. Now the idea of such a journey made my guts twist, made me want to yank on my hair and feel the pull deep in my scalp. I should never have done it. It was crazy. Anyone could have come upon me out there, done anything they wanted. I'd been armed with little more than a box of matches and a flashlight.

I squeezed the kitties, released them. My hands ached, but I didn't stop.

"That was before," I said. "Now…"

"Now the woods are scary."

"Yes."

"And having the nightmare about the woods affected your sleep the rest of the night."

"Probably."

"But you're not sure?"

The night had stretched, weird and foggy. I'd thrashed in bed, got up and flipped through TV channels, moved between the couch and the bedroom a dozen times. I'd peeked out the curtains around midnight, saw two girls walking down the sidewalk alone, illuminated by the dim streetlamps. I'd wanted to scream at them to get off the street, call a cab, run. Run before he got them too.

"I was thinking about a lot of things and nothing. Nights are weird."

"They can be," Fry agreed. "Especially when you've been suffering from insomnia. Sleep deprivation is linked to a host of unpleasant symptoms—confused thinking, hallucinations, mood swings, just to name a few. There's even, in extreme cases, sleep deprivation-induced psychosis."

I worried at the stress balls, frowning at the word he'd uttered—psychosis. It was an ugly word.

"I wonder," Fry continued, "if the approaching two-year anniversary of the attack is bringing things up for you."

"Two years?" I murmured, glancing at the calendar on my wall. I wrote nothing on it, rarely even looked at it, but dutifully flipped the page every month on the first. The image that went with this month, June, was a sunrise. The motivational quote in big block letters stated: *The cave you fear to enter holds the treasure you seek. — Joseph Campbell.*

My father had given me the calendar at Christmas, though I suspected Janice had purchased it.

"My dad and stepmother want to come visit," I said, glowering at the calendar before shifting my attention back to Dr. Fry.

I'd opened the email from my dad requesting a visit, but had not responded. I'd not even allowed myself to consider it, but immediately shelved the message to talk over with Fry.

"How do you feel about that?"

A trickle of dread swam down my throat. "Not good."

"The last visit went well. Remember? Your dad brought your dog Hercules to visit. That was nice."

"Exactly. He brought Hercules and left Janice at home."

"Janice is coming this time?"

"The email said, 'Janice and I would like to come visit.'"

Fry nodded. "Okay, so how can we best prepare you for that visit?"

"I think I should just tell him no. I'm not up for it."

He cocked his head. "You could do that, but Gloria, your father is the only family you have regular contact with. It's important to maintain a relationship with him."

"Janice is not my family, though. She doesn't like me. I don't like her."

Fry folded his hands on his desk. "I know you're uncomfortable in her presence. I know you've said she pushes too hard for you to return to your before life."

"God only knows why. She didn't like me then either."

"Relationships with step-parents can be difficult."

"Tell me about it."

"But you want a relationship with your dad. Sometimes we have to accept less than ideal conditions to maintain our relationships. It's simply part of life."

I brushed my hands back through my hair, cringed at the oily strands. When had I last showered? An hour ago? Two? It didn't matter. I felt dirty. I needed another shower.

"Maybe Dorian could be there when your dad and Janice visit? It helps to have a"—he made air quotes—"'safe person' with us to help ease the internal tension."

I sighed. "Dorian already comes over practically every day. His whole life revolves around me, his dead sister's best friend. It's not fair to ask him to do anything else."

"I understand your reluctance, but remember, you never asked Dorian to show up for you. He did it. He was the one at the hospital every day. He stepped forward and took on the role. Has he ever implied that he resents it?"

"No, but..." My throat grew thick around my words. "I'm so sick of being helpless."

"You're not helpless. Look at this lovely and very useful coaster I have to set my coffee on." He held up a coaster I'd knitted in shades of orange and blue. "My wife loves these, by the way, and she loves the sweater you knitted for our dog, Honey. You have a job, you have hobbies, you have friends. You have a very full life. Yes, you don't currently leave your apartment, but that's temporary."

"You said yourself it's been nearly two years."

"And what you went through, lived through, is more than most of us will ever have to process in a lifetime. We cannot know how our nervous system, our minds, our bodies will react to such a thing. This is your healing process. Process, in its very definition, is a series of steps. Those steps take time."

"Okay," I said. There was no use arguing. Dr. Fry would never affirm my negative thoughts.

"I'm going to be in town in a few weeks. Would you like if I stopped by? I could bring Honey again?" he asked.

"Yes. That would be nice."

Other than Dorian and his daughter, Rylie, Dr. Fry was the only person I could easily invite into my apartment. Because I'd disclosed everything to him, the darkest moments of that terrible night and the darkest moments since, there was no risk of being further exposed in his presence.

I'd had panic attacks in front of him. I'd crawled under beds and hid in closets and screamed like someone had lit me on fire. There was nothing I could do or say that would shock him. He'd seen it all and continued to work with me anyway.

"I'm not going to advise you one way or another on the visit with your dad, but I challenge you to think deeply on it. Move past the impulsive response. Let's shift now to what we talked about last week, imagining life in the future. Gloria, what does your perfect day look like?"

"I haven't left my apartment in nearly two years. I don't think perfect days are part of my life anymore."

"Agoraphobia aside, imagine one year from now. Pretend you no longer suffer from the condition. You're healed. You're able to leave your apartment. Imagine your ideal day. Not a fantasy, not sipping a margarita in Bali—unless, of course, that's your perfect day. I want you to envision a day that encompasses the life you want to live. What does that look like?"

I stared at him on the screen, frowned. "I don't know. To leave, right? I mean, isn't that what people like me want? To leave my house without ending up as a puddle on the sidewalk, without blacking out or screaming or tearing out my hair?"

He tilted his head, gave me the 'is that what you really want, Gloria?' look. "Think on it, okay? Journal about it. Daydream about it. I want to see it when we talk next week. I want to be able to close my eyes and visualize walking in your shoes on your perfect day one year from now."

2

———

After the call, I showered and dumped the previous night's clothes into my washing machine. I threw in a few more pairs of jogging pants and t-shirts—my wardrobe of choice—and added soap.

I plucked a notebook from my bookshelf and sat at the kitchen table, determined to give Fry's advice a try. I'd always been a consummate student, and it was no different with my therapist. If he gave me homework, I did it, even if begrudgingly.

At the top of the page, I wrote: *My Perfect Day.*

The words struck me as funny. I might have written this very essay in third grade. My perfect day would be playing in the woods with my best friend, Wren, looking for bugs and salamanders and trying to catch chipmunks. Those would likely have been my words. For so many years my perfect days included Wren.

Now…

I closed my eyes and tried to see it, to see anything other than the eggshell walls of my apartment, the clunky thrift-store furniture, the art prints of beloved books.

Originally, Janice had adorned my walls with the ugliest paintings on Earth: Victorian ladies lunching, bowls of fruit—all of them in similar shades of drab. I'd hated them, but my father had told me they were neutral, not triggering. The doctor had recommended choosing art that blended in, didn't catch the eye.

Eventually Dorian had arrived with prints of classic books: *The*

Adventures of Huckleberry Finn, The Great Gatsby, The Color Purple. We'd removed the old pictures and put the prints in their place.

I tried to imagine being in the world outside of the apartment. My chest constricted and my heart revved.

Agoraphobia is an anxiety disorder characterized by fear of being in public spaces or feeling trapped in spaces where there are crowds, lines, etc. It's triggered when we go to those places and have panic attacks.

Originally, they said I had panic disorder, but eventually the right therapist, Dr. Fry, recognized what it was—PTSD resulting in agoraphobia. Panic disorders were triggered by the fear of having a panic attack. The panic attack was the big scary monster. For PTSD, the big scary monster was literally a big scary monster. Maybe not literally, depending on one's definition of 'monster,' but for me, yeah, that was what he was.

He'd been over six feet tall, with massive hands and feet. A dark mask had covered his face. His eyes had been black, the whites a puzzle of red veins. He'd stunk of cigarettes and cheap cologne and sour breath. He'd worn dark jeans and steel-toed boots. He'd kicked me in the face with those boots. If I hadn't turned my head so my nose could take the shot, resulting in the most excruciating pain of my life, he might have gotten me in the temple and I wouldn't be sitting in this chair right now, writing about my so-called perfect day. I'd be somewhere out there with Wren.

In my former life, I'd been attending Northern Michigan University with a major in fisheries and wildlife, intent on becoming a park ranger—my dream job. After the dark night, I'd dropped out of school and now the mere thought of my formerly desired profession sickened me.

I stared at the blank page, thought again of stepping into the world outside of my apartment. My hand grew clammy on the pen.

"Shh… just breathe. You're not going out there." And that was the challenge. How could I imagine that other life when just the thought of it caused my body to prickle with anxiety?

I opened my eyes and returned to the page. I wouldn't visualize it, simple as that. I'd write a few lines about what I'd like to be able to do again even if I'd never actually do it.

On the first blank line, I wrote: *Hiking, ice cream, a swim in Lake Superior, a movie at the cinema. Bed.*

There, done. I closed the notebook and set it on my desk next to my laptop so I'd have it ready when Fry asked about my perfect day on our next call.

I waffled between denial and a desperate, at times irrational, search for my healing, for an escape from the mental prison I lived in. With Dr. Fry talk therapy was the focus, but every month or so I tried less conventional options to heal. I'd screamed into pillows for hours when my downstairs neighbor was gone. I'd drawn pictures of the man who'd attacked us and burned them. None of it worked, and it often triggered a backlash. In the days or weeks after one of my attempts, I'd become especially paranoid about the world outside my little apartment. I'd fear he was out there watching me, waiting for the one night I went to bed with an unlocked window.

A copy of *Blue-Eyed Dropouts*, an indie magazine I'd bought a year's subscription to for Wren years earlier, sat on my desk. I continued to renew the subscription each year despite Wren's absence from my life.

The magazine had a lot of indie music stuff, which Wren was into, but also poetry and a few interesting articles. The idea I'd gotten regarding scream therapy had come from the magazine. I'd also read about and wanted to try smash therapy, which involved wearing protective gear in a room full of fragile objects and proceeding to smash the shit out of everything in sight. The challenge of course was that I didn't leave my apartment.

I flipped through *Blue-Eyed Dropouts* and paused at an article titled 'The Subtle Magic of Poppets' next to a crudely made doll with a black stitched mouth and an uneven red heart in a patch on its chest. I scanned the article, reading about the popularity of poppets, known in some circles as voodoo dolls.

"Poppets are useful in all types of healing," says magical practitioner and tarot reader Maura Lynn. "I've worked with clients who sealed love matches, came into great wealth and even banished very toxic, dark people from their lives."

"Why not?" I asked, leaving the magazine open.

I pulled my knitting box from the closet. With black yarn, I knitted the man from the dark night. Long, thick legs and arms. When I finished, I stared at the figure, unsure what to add. Eyes? His eyes had been as black as the night.

"No eyes," I murmured.

I added a single red slash of yarn for his mouth.

Finished, I stared at the doll. I hated it. Just looking at it made the hairs on the back of my neck prickle and I suddenly wondered what had compelled me to create such a hideous thing.

The article had said poppets could be used to banish people, but it hadn't exactly given a tutorial. I went to my laptop and sat down, typed in 'how to banish evil people with voodoo dolls.'

I clicked on a website called *Voodoo Magic* and scrolled to the banishing spells.

After you've created your doll in the likeness of the person you wish to banish, place it in a container and seal the lid tight. Carry this container outside, dig a hole and bury it in the ground. Then repeat this spell three times:

'You are gone from my life

Your energy does not affect me

You cannot see me

You cannot speak to me

You do not exist

I banish you

I banish you

I banish you.'

I frowned. I couldn't bury it outside. I hadn't walked outside in… months. Maybe it had been a year.

"So, what then?" I murmured, glancing across the room at the doll and shuddering. I wanted it out of my apartment. Gone. I wished I hadn't made it.

On my laptop I searched for 'voodoo banishing spell—no burial.' A stream of sites came back, most of which seemed to focus on love spells rather than banishing spells.

I clicked one named *The Devil's at the Door*. The backdrop of the web page was black, the letters red and drippy. It was hard to read, and I suspected if I spent long on the site I'd have a raging headache.

Halfway down the page, I found a paragraph about how to banish the entity connected to a voodoo doll.

There are conflicting theories about the best way to use a voodoo doll to eliminate the negative entity who has invaded your life—burning, burial, drowning, to name a few. I personally keep my dolls. I secure them in metal boxes, add duct tape, chains when available, and add them to a shelf in my cellar. That way I have access to those entities anytime I might wish to do them further harm, or, rarely, remove the banishment.

A cellar filled with voodoo dolls? No.

He'd mentioned burning and drowning. I couldn't very well burn the thing without setting off my fire alarm. I could drown it, but... then what? Toss it in the trash and wait until Dorian picked it up?

I read further down the page.

A warning. Do not rid yourself of the doll by throwing it away or giving it away, for in doing so, you've lost possession of a powerful magical object and with the loss of possession comes the loss of power. It is bound to you and you are bound to it. Dispose of it by any other means than those listed above at your own peril.

"Well, that answers that," I muttered.

I didn't believe his warning. The guy clearly had veered off the rails. Who in their right mind filled their basement with voodoo dolls in the likeness of their enemies?

"Who'd make one in the first place?" I whispered, again eyeing the dark poppet. "Drowning it is," I decided. I stood and grabbed the doll, but didn't look into its blank face.

In the bathroom, I sat the poppet on the rug and filled the tub with icy water.

I held the doll in both hands and repeated the banishing spell I'd read in the first article.

"You are gone from my life.

"Your energy does not affect me.

"You cannot see me.

"You cannot speak to me.

"You do not exist.

"I banish you.

"I banish you.

"I banish you."

Two more times I repeated the spell as I held the doll beneath the water. My hands grew numb from the cold.

After the third incantation, I continued holding the doll under. I looked at it now and brought up an image of the monster with his dark mask and dark eyes.

"Die," I muttered.

I released the doll and stood, wiping my cold hands on a towel. After I drained the bathtub, I left the doll and shut the bathroom door behind me. It would have to dry out before I could dispose of it.

I didn't expect it to work. Dr. Fry had said more than once that my own inability to believe in my healing kept me trapped.

I wondered what he'd have to say about my creation of a voodoo doll. I didn't intend to find out.

In my bedroom, I opened the curtains on the single large window that gazed out from the back of the house. In the backyard, my down-stairs neighbor Earl sat in a lawn chair with a newspaper open in his lap.

On the shelf beneath the window sat a pair of binoculars. I picked them up and, standing far enough back that Earl below couldn't see me, I scanned the houses whose backyards were separated from my own by a little alleyway. Three houses down stood the brick building Wren and I had lived in before the dark night.

We'd shared an upper apartment in a four-unit building of red brick with ivy crawling up the exterior. It had been the perfect apartment. Two bedrooms, two bathrooms. A big square kitchen big enough for a table and four chairs, forever strewn with Wren's music, my knitting and our schoolbooks. Sun had filtered through the windows and washed the scratched floor in shades of bronze.

Our living room had been outfitted with retro furniture Wren and I had bought at an estate sale the summer after our freshman year in college: beaded curtains, orange shag rugs, a velvet lime-green couch and a purple bean bag so big we'd barely gotten it through the front door.

Wren had filled her room with music equipment, purchasing antique and even broken instruments (many of which she didn't play) from garage sales and thrift stores. She'd crammed the space with guitars, banjos, a non-working keyboard, bongo drums, and wind instruments. Often the room was so packed she could barely open her closet door.

The instruments were transitory visitors to our space. They came and went. She gave them to friends, to people at the retirement home, to anyone who posted online that they were in search of an affordable instrument.

My own room had been significantly less cluttered, but packed just the same. I'd bought an enormous shelf of cubbies that occupied an entire wall and I'd stuffed it with everything from hiking equipment to books. We'd had a vintage record player that worked about half the time and so many records they trickled from under the coffee table and lay stacked beneath our beds.

After the dark night, I'd returned to the apartment one time. I'd walked in and the gravity of Wren's death had rolled over me like a bulldozer. Dorian, Wren's older brother, had been there, and he'd caught me when I fell. I'd passed out. One moment I'd been standing there feeling the pressure bearing down, the realization that here was Wren's and my world and half of it had ceased to exist, and the next moment I'd disappeared into the void.

I hadn't been out for long, a few seconds maybe, but when I'd come to, I'd started screaming and crying and clawing at the bandage on my neck. I remember it vaguely. Looking back at that moment is a bit like peering through a pair of smudged binoculars that are slightly out of focus.

The guy who lived across the hall from us, Wyatt, helped Dorian lift me up and carry me out of the building. I'd been so hysterical Dorian had taken me back to the emergency room and they'd admitted me. I'd never returned to our apartment. I couldn't set foot inside. Dorian and my dad had emptied it.

I'd stayed with my dad and Janice for one month, a horrible month where Janice had either fawned over me like a newborn or given me the silent treatment. The woman had always been mercurial, but she'd been especially angry during that time because her own beloved son, Jeffrey, had had to stay with friends after I'd encountered him outside my bedroom door one night in the dark and tried to hit him with a baseball bat. In my defense, he had no reason to be there. His room was on the other side of the house, and I'd woken, heard the creak of footsteps, and been positive the man who'd murdered Wren had come back to finish me as well.

Now the apartment Wren and I had lived in was occupied by two Northern Michigan University students I'd nicknamed the Twiggy Twins, thanks to their tall, willowy frames and matching long blonde hair. If I angled my binoculars just right, I could see into the large window that peered into their living room. Now, in daylight, the window was only a glare, but at night sometimes I watched them.

Strange, I knew, but I couldn't help it. I studied how they'd arranged their furniture, the way they sometimes both crowded in the bay window, occupying the narrow bench and staring at their cell phones. They had friends over regularly and they'd sit in the living room with their long legs stretched in front of them, drinking cans of beer or seltzers and laughing.

Sometimes they threw little parties in the backyard. I recognized Wyatt, who apparently still occupied the apartment across the hall. He and the Twiggy Twins and their friends would play beer pong and corn-hole. They'd turn the music up loud enough that I could hear it and I'd sit with my window half open, enthralled.

It was such an ordinary thing, a party in the backyard, a thing I'd done a hundred times in my life before, but now it seemed as if that life belonged to someone else. I had to be careful watching them at those parties, listening to their music. A song might trigger me, send me diving to my floor, struggling for breath, images of the dark night stabbing my brain as if a knife-wielding lunatic had been unleashed in my skull.

More than once I'd hyperventilated until I passed out and then I wouldn't open that window for weeks, carefully avoiding any sounds or sights that might take me back.

I returned the binoculars to the ledge and sat on the edge of my bed. Sometimes I missed the old apartment, missed the brick walls and wood floors, but mostly I missed Wren and me inside it, our lives in full bloom.

Now I lived in the upper section of an old house split into two apartments. Earl, a middle-aged man who frequently travelled for work, lived in the apartment below me.

This place was both my sanctuary and prison. One bedroom, one bathroom, and equipped with everything a person needed to become a total recluse—and that was what I was.

Eventually I returned to the bathroom, removed the soggy doll and tossed it in the dryer. Once it was dry, I stuck it in a shoebox, duct-taped the box closed, and buried it in the back of my closet beneath hiking gear I hadn't touched in two years.

After a dinner of frozen chicken tenders, heated in the oven, and a handful of baby carrots dipped in ranch, I changed from my day sweats into my night sweats and got ready for bed.

I eyed the sleeping pills I'd stopped taking weeks before. I didn't want sleeping pills. Instead of making me sleep, they suspended me in a bizarre realm between sleeping and waking where my limbs felt like bags of wet sand and my mind a tumbling mess of thoughts and memories.

Humming the tune to the ABCs, a holdover from my childhood days that Wren's mom had taught us to ensure we brushed for long enough, I scrubbed my teeth. I rinsed my toothbrush and leaned beneath the faucet, filled my mouth with water and swished it around. I spit and stood up.

Behind me, the face of a man loomed in the mirror. I shrieked and dove to the floor, pushed myself into the corner and curled into a ball, my hands covering my face. He didn't attack. No sound except water running into the sink.

I kept my eyes clenched shut, opened them after several moments of silence. I pulled my hands away. The door to the bathroom remained empty. No man stood there. He'd crept back into the apartment, was hiding beneath my bed, in the closet. There were a million possibilities.

I scrambled on hands and knees across the tile floor, slammed the bathroom door and locked it. I stood, snatched my phone from the bathroom counter, and leapt to the toiletries closet. It was packed with stuff. From the floor beneath the lowest shelf, I yanked out a scale, a bucket of cleaning supplies and a stack of ragged washcloths. I crammed myself into the meager space. It was so cramped I had to tuck my head between my knees.

My breath gusted in rapid bursts. I punched Dorian's name on my phone and waited, listening to one, two rings.

"Hey, what's up?"

"There's…" I choked it out, barely a whisper, waiting for the avalanche of sound when the man kicked the door in. "A man… a man in my apartment."

3

———————

"Okay. Try to stay calm—just breathe. I'm putting on my boots, walking out the door. Glo? Are you there?"

"Mm-hm." I tried to make as little sound as possible.

The intruder had seen me, heard me empty the closet, there was no pretending I wasn't there, but maybe… he'd forgotten. Maybe he was high on crystal meth or bath bombs or whatever people snorted these days. Maybe he'd thought I was a figment of his imagination, left the doorway and blacked out on my couch.

"I'm in my car. Three blocks and I'll be there. Two minutes tops. Do you need to call 911?"

I'd called the police before—four times in the two years since the attack. I'd called when I'd woken to a gunshot that turned out to be fireworks, and when I'd heard a weird sound in the hallway—there had been no one there. I'd called twice for strange cars on the street outside. I hated the way they looked at me, the way my skin crawled as they moved through my apartment.

I said nothing. I didn't want to call the police.

"Turning onto Sycamore," Dorian said. "I can see the little old schoolhouse up ahead. Remember that one with the ugly black shutters? Turning left on Coventry Lane, pulling into the driveway."

"Wait," I hissed. "He'll attack you. Where's your gun?"

"I'm armed. I'm taking my gun out of the holster now. I'm going to hang up the phone, okay? I'm entering the house. I'll be upstairs in less than thirty seconds."

"Okay."

He hung up, and I clung to the phone, listening. Did I hear something in the hall outside the bathroom, the squeak of the knob, a muted rattle as someone tried to turn it? I gritted my teeth and reached for the shelf above my pretzeled body. My fingers scrambled over hair clips and scrunchies. Was there nothing sharp? Nothing more sinister? I found an aluminum bottle of hair spray. If he opened the closet, I'd spray him in the eyes.

From inside the apartment, I heard a sound, footsteps, then a knock on the door.

"Glo, it's me, Dorian. I'm inside the apartment. There's nobody out here."

I stiffened, waited for the attack. He hadn't looked hard enough. The man was creeping up behind him as he stood unaware outside my bathroom door. I needed to shout, "Watch out, turn around," but my mouth remained frozen shut, every muscle tensed for the confrontation that was coming.

The knock came again. "Gloria? I need you to open the door."

Slowly I unwound myself and crawled into the bathroom, ears perked, hand poised on the can, ready to blast a streak of acrid chemicals into the eyes of the perpetrator.

I stopped at the bathroom door and listened. "Dorian?"

"I'm here."

"Did you check the bedroom? Under the bed and in the closets?"

"Yes."

"And the kitchen? The pantry?"

"Yes. I checked all the rooms, Glo. There's nobody in your apartment."

"The laundry room? Did you check the big hamper?"

"Hold on."

I heard his footsteps walk away, again braced myself for the terrible scream. It didn't come. Dorian's voice again. "The hamper is empty. I swear to you there is no one in here. Your apartment door was locked. All the windows are closed. There's no one in here."

"Are all the windows locked? They should all be locked."

"Just a sec."

I knew he was irritated, though he kept it mostly from his voice.

"They're all locked."

I leaned heavily against the door, the spray bottle so tight in my fist all the blood had run out of my hand. It was pale and growing numb. I loosened my grip but didn't release the bottle. Shakily, I stood and unlocked the bathroom door, opened it a crack.

One of Dorian's green eyes filled the gap. "It's just me. Everything is okay."

I opened the door further, took a faltering step, and almost collapsed. He caught me around the waist and guided me to the couch. I sat and pulled my knees into my chest as he grabbed the afghan I'd been knitting for the last year and a half from the back of the couch and draped it over me. The blanket was huge, would dwarf a king-size bed, but I could never seem to stop working on it, to decide it was done.

"What happened?" he asked.

"I saw a man in the mirror. He was standing behind me."

Dorian nodded slowly. "But the apartment is empty."

"So you say."

"Does that mean you think it's not empty? You think there's a man hiding in here?"

"I saw him."

"Let's look then, shall we?" He offered me his hand.

I didn't want to look. I wanted to stay pressed beneath the weight of my blanket, pull it over my head, curl into a ball and fall asleep. Tiredness tugged at the corners of my eyes. The exhilaration, the fear, had exhausted me.

"Glo, we have to look together. Otherwise, you won't sleep a wink tonight."

I sank deeper into the couch, but he pulled off my blanket and hoisted me to my feet.

"Hold on," I said, hurrying to the kitchen to grab a can of bear spray from the cupboard.

He took out his gun and let it lead us. He'd done it many times before, but I'd never seen someone in the apartment with my own two eyes until now. I'd heard things—whispers, shuffling feet, the creak of a door closing. Things that seemed to signal someone had broken in. Dorian would come over and, armed, he would search, usually with me in tow because otherwise I'd call again in the middle of the night.

I followed him out of the living room and down the hall. We stopped in my bedroom first. He got on his belly and pointed the gun under the bed. "You too," he said. "Get down here and look."

I knelt and leaned forward on my hands, my arms shaking both from anxiety and from weakness. In my prior life, I'd had strong arms. I'd worked out at a gym, lifted weights. A lot of good it had done me.

Dorian climbed up and pulled open the closet, brushed aside the clothes—empty. We walked to the laundry room—hamper empty. Back to the kitchen. We looked in the pantry, in any cupboards a man might squeeze into. My desk stood along one wall in the living room. We peeked behind it, behind the couch. Dorian threw back curtains, lifted blankets.

No sign of a man.

"Mirrors do that sometimes," he said. "You see things that aren't real, light bouncing off an object behind you, making a shape."

I'd seen the man's eyes, his face, but it wouldn't help to explain that to Dorian. The man no longer occupied the apartment. Somehow, he'd slipped back, locked the door behind him. It defied logic and yet had to be true.

It wasn't only that I'd seen the man. I'd recognized his eyes. They belonged to the man who'd abducted me and Wren.

I thought then of the poppet I'd created and drowned in the bathtub. The doll that now sat in the back of my closet. I wanted to tell Dorian about it, but embarrassment at having created it dissolved the confession on my lips.

After we'd searched, I collapsed on the couch, spent from the burst of adrenaline that had long since faded. I wanted to sleep, but suspected such a reprieve would elude me that night.

Dorian perched on the arm of the couch, watching me. He was poised to leave, had likely been in the middle of something when I'd called.

I drew my blanket from the floor and wrapped it around me, looped it over my head like a hood.

"Do you feel better?" he asked.

"Yeah. Sorry I bothered you."

"You didn't bother me. You scared me."

"I'm sorry I did that, too."

"What are you thinking?"

"That I want to turn on *Gilmore Girls* and zone out."

Dorian glanced at the door and seemed to come to a conclusion. "Turn it on then. I'll make the popcorn."

I half-smiled. "You don't have to do that. I'm sure you have better things to do than sit in my apartment and watch *Gilmore Girls.*"

He stood and walked to the kitchen, opened the pantry door and grabbed a package of movie-theater butter popcorn. "Nothing comes to mind," he told me.

"What about Rylie?"

"She's having a sleepover at my parents' tonight."

"And Val? I'm sure she'll be thrilled you're blowing her off to sit at my apartment."

"She's at some party downtown. I told her I'd probably meet her, but she won't mind if I cancel." He stuck the popcorn in the microwave and hit start.

I laughed. "I bet." His girlfriend would be furious if he canceled, but I didn't remind him of that. He already knew and, frankly, I'd never cared for Val.

"I didn't feel like going out tonight, anyway. I should thank you for saving me from the slight headache I'd be waking up with tomorrow." He grabbed the popcorn and returned to the couch and dropped down beside me. He peeled open the bag and flinched. "Whew! Steam bath."

He held the popcorn out to me and I took a handful, though I wasn't hungry.

"I met one of the Twiggy Twins the other day," Dorian told me.

"You did?"

"Yep. She was rollerblading out front when Rylie and I were leaving. She pointed out Rylie's sloth. Rylie must have dropped it when she was getting in the backseat."

"Sabrina the Sloth? She'd have been heartbroken if she lost that."

"Exactly. Saved by a Twiggy Twin."

"Huh. Was she nice?"

"Very."

I rolled my eyes. "You do have a girlfriend still, right?"

Dorian chuckled. "I can say a woman's nice without wanting to sleep with her."

"Yeah, well, that look in your eye tells another story."

He leaned back and put his hands behind his head. "Nothing wrong with noticing a beautiful woman."

"From nice to beautiful, huh? Which one was it? Giraffe Neck or Bird Legs?"

"Those are *your* nicknames," he said. "It was Bird Legs. Honestly, you'd like her. She's studying criminal justice at NMU."

"And why would that appeal to me?"

"You and Wren used to love those crime documentaries. *Forensic Mysteries* or whatever."

"*Forensic Files*," I corrected him.

Wren and I had regularly watched crime documentaries. We'd grumble about how the woman willingly got into the man's car or allowed him to tie her up. We'd insisted we'd fight back, overpower him.

But when you were in it, in the suddenly infinite moments on a dark trail, a man in a mask holding a gun on your best friend's face, none of your previous proclamations mattered.

That was the problem with watching horror movies and true crime shows. From the safety of the couch, we were all cool and collected. But when actually faced with death, our ancient brain kicked in, that glob of gray matter in the back of the skull that wanted to live. That part of the brain wasn't thinking in complexities. It was simple. *He has a gun. Don't run, don't fight. Take the path of least resistance.*

"Anyway," Dorian continued, "she was pretty interesting—grew up near Detroit, comes from a family of cops."

"Did you also find out her sun sign and her birth order?"

He cocked an eyebrow. "For someone who doesn't like the Twigs, you spend a lot of time spying on them."

"I don't spy on them. I spy on my old apartment. I want to make sure they don't trash it."

"Okay," he said sarcastically. "Keep telling yourself that."

"I will because it's true."

"Come on." He gestured at the remote. "Let's see what Rory and Lorelai are up to."

∼

Dorian left around midnight. I listened to his key turn in the two deadbolts and the knob lock. His footsteps were muted as he walked the carpeted hallway, but I still heard them.

I considered returning to my bedroom, but I'd have to pass the bathroom and the thought made my heart skip a little faster. Instead, I pulled my afghan over me and settled in for another night on the couch.

4
————————

In the morning, I ate breakfast, my usual two pieces of toast and a container of yogurt. My bladder tugged heavily as I drank my coffee. I gazed at the closed bathroom door. I didn't want to open it. I'd not been inside since the night before, but unless I wanted to pee in a bucket and wash it down the kitchen sink, I had to go in there.

I grabbed my can of bear spray, then darted down the hall, past the bathroom door and into my bedroom. I opened the side table and grabbed the taser Dorian had given me the year before. Tasers weren't legal in Michigan. Dorian had bought it during a trip out west he'd taken with Rylie.

I'd never actually used it, never needed to, but the black plastic was worn from the many nights I'd lain clutching it in my hands, straining at a sound I thought I'd heard. It was probably a miracle I hadn't zapped myself with it by accident at some point.

Taser in one hand, bear spray tucked under my arm, I twisted the knob on the bathroom door and shoved it in, stepping back, ready to immobilize anyone who came hurtling out. No one did. The door swung to the wall, knocked gently against the doorstopper and came to rest.

The mirror reflected my face—pale, the skin beneath my eyes puffy and bluish, my short hair a mess of knots. No man hovered in the glass.

I peered into the bathroom. The shower curtain was pulled back to reveal an empty bathtub. Toilet, sink, small closet stuffed with towels and toiletries. There was nowhere for an intruder to hide, for *him* to hide.

Still, I kept the taser in hand until I'd closed and locked the bathroom door behind me. I averted my eyes from the mirror. He wasn't in there, couldn't be in there, but I feared looking up and seeing him towering in the tight space behind me.

I set the taser and bear spray on the vanity counter and I took a tentative look at my face.

In my previous life, I'd been pretty with long chestnut hair. Though a tomboy at heart, I'd occasionally worn eye makeup and flattering clothes. I'd had a daily beauty routine to keep the wrinkles away. The biggest snag in my life before the dark night had been sleeping in and showing up late for class, or wondering if Tom Russell, the guy I'd been harboring a crush on, liked me too.

Now I washed my face with harsh soap and kept it scrubbed clean. My hair was sheared above my ears. I cut it myself and it was lopsided and ugly. I showered at least twice a day, but often three or four times. I never felt clean, though. Ever since that night, I felt coated with grime, a layer of something so vile I could barely stand to be in my own skin.

According to my therapist, this was normal. This was a typical victim response. This was a defense mechanism.

I no longer had a gauge for normal. In my previous life, I must have. I must have somehow made sense of the world and my place within it. No more. Now every moment felt a bit like walking on a high wire— one stumble and it would all be over.

I wanted to take a shower, a long, scalding shower, but I couldn't bear the thought of being naked and trapped in a slippery bathtub.

Teeth brushed, face scrubbed, hair combed, I exited the bathroom and returned to the living room and sat at my desk.

I logged into my work email. I'd been lucky in some ways after the dark night. I'd worked at Black Rock Outfitters, a store that sold outdoor gear—everything from hammocks to rock-climbing equipment. I'd started working there when I was sixteen, primarily for the discount, and by the time the dark night occurred, I'd been the assistant manager for a year.

I'd attempted two shifts at the store after my so-called recovery. Both times, I dissolved into a hyperventilating mess, locked in a dressing room.

Fortunately for me, Arthur, the owner, had grown fond of me over the years. He created a job for me I could do from my apartment. Thus was born the hybrid sales-shopper-copywriter-newsletter creator position I now held. I did a bit of everything from my virtual office. I even attended online video meetings twice a month with the other staff, which I'd found humiliating in the beginning and now looked forward to.

In those meetings, I was the only one working remotely while the rest of them gathered around a plastic folding table in the store room, eating whatever cookies one of them brought in—usually Arthur, who baked like he was a seventy-something retired grandma and not a fifty-something forest enthusiast and bachelor.

I enjoyed my work, and it paid the bills and kept me in insurance. I had therapy appointments by video chat and they'd found a doctor willing to make house calls. It wasn't ideal, but it sufficed.

The agoraphobia hadn't happened instantly the moment the dark night was over. Instead, it had grown on me, as if each time I stepped into the big scary world it cut off another piece of the person I'd been before until nothing remained of her, only this new traumatized, terrified me who sometimes wondered what I'd do if the house ever caught fire. Would the trauma win? Would I simply crawl into a closet and die?

I sifted through Black Rock emails, replied to several, deleted the spam and forwarded one to Arthur from a news station who wanted to interview him. I checked the inventory and ordered products that had fallen below the minimum baseline.

A new pair of women's waterproof hiking boots had just come in at the store. Blue with purple stitching, a low heel to reduce slipping and leather around the ankle for mobility. They were beautiful, and old Gloria would have bought them in an instant. Across the room sat my worn fleece booties, house shoes with a rubber sole in case I ever ventured outside. They'd never stepped on a sidewalk or a blade of grass.

At noon, I took a break and made a tuna sandwich, sitting on my couch, the television playing too low to hear. I often left it on, sometimes for days at a time. The murmuring comforted me, made me feel less alone.

Post-lunch, I returned to my laptop and opened the newsletter I'd started the day before, consulting the Black Rock Outfitters calendar to let patrons know about upcoming deals and events.

Saturday Sugarloaf Hikes, I typed in big bold font. A little knot formed in my stomach as I pasted the picture of a previous hike beneath the headline. Two of my co-workers, Bethany and Nick, stood on the wood viewing platform with panoramic views of sloping forests and sprawling Lake Superior behind them. Five other hikers crowded with them, smiling, the sun glinting off their sunglasses and water bottles.

I used to lead the Saturday morning hike up Sugarloaf Mountain two Saturdays a month. It was a short hike, less than a mile and a half round trip, but beautiful and wooded, rocky in parts, ending at the wood viewing decks that offered a feast for the eyes. Sugarloaf Mountain was a place I'd visited weekly in my life before, often alone. Sometimes I'd take a book and cut away from the path, find a little outcropping of rock to sit on and read until my tailbone ached.

I'd written dozens of newsletters with images from the hikes and still it pained me every time I looked at those photos. The images created an odd conflict within me, a longing for that place, for those gone moments, and a terror too. Terror at who might lurk in the shadows just off the path. A terror at the openness—no walls or doors or deadbolts. Nothing to protect you from the monsters of the world.

The Upper Peninsula of northern Michigan was an especially rich hideaway for those who wished to lurk in the shadows. The Upper Peninsula of Michigan was not the same as the Lower. In the lower part of the state, linked by a massive bridge of steel and concrete, plains and flatlands reigned—cornfields, urban sprawl, strip malls, and parking lots.

Up here it was different. Drive out of the city and you could cover fifty miles without seeing a gas station. If there was one, it was liable to be an old shack with a few pumps on a cracked pavement lot. The bathroom would be tucked around the back, unlocked by a rusted key hanging from a big wooden block. The shelves in such a convenience store were bare save a few cans of baked beans, marshmallows for roasting and a cooler with milk that was likely spoiled.

Marquette, the city I'd called home since birth, was its own little world, a civilization carved from the wild. The streets sloped toward the Lake Superior shoreline, a shoreline dotted with massive ore docks and rugged cliff faces.

Beyond the city limits, the untamed Upper Peninsula reigned.

There were hunters, ATV guys, snowmobilers in the winter, but the masses of unlogged, untouched forest could never be fully explored. In the summer, much of the woods were so dense, so filled with brambles and tall bushes, nettles, blackberry thickets sharp with thorns, you couldn't walk them if you tried. There were seasons for mosquitoes and black flies where the insects were so rampant a cloud of buzzing and biting followed anyone who dared to step into the woods. There was also the cold season, winter, frigid and endless. April arrived not with flowers, but flurries.

It was the toll the land demanded of us, the price we paid for the most glorious nature that existed on Earth. Sandstone cliffs that guarded the clear blue-green waters of Lake Superior. Old-growth trees, sandy and rocky shorelines, waterfalls, rivers, bears, elk, even a few moose.

It had been my paradise and now I touched it in memories alone.

At five, I closed down my work computer and folded laundry. I carried it to my bedroom, balancing the basket on my hip, and pushed the door open.

I stopped abruptly, as if I'd opened my door to find a stranger's bedroom had replaced my own. Everything looked as it had when I'd last been inside hours before, but it felt... occupied.

The smell hit me then. His smell. Cigarette smoke, perspiration and eye-watering cologne. The scent of a murderer.

5
____

The scar on my throat itched, a sensation I hadn't experienced in ages—over a year. A sensation that had driven me crazy during months of healing. There had been times when the itching had felt like insects burrowing into my throat. More than once, I'd ripped my bandages off and scratched until I bled.

I recoiled, backed up, and lurched into the bathroom, dropping my basket on the floor and letting fresh laundry tumble out. I locked the door and fumbled around the room, grabbed the bear spray. I gripped it in my hand, pulled my cell phone out, and punched Dorian's name.

He answered on the first ring. "Hey, I'll be there in ten. Just checking out at the grocery store."

My breath caught, the bear spray canister clutched so tight my fingers threatened to cramp and let go.

"Glo?"

More silence. I couldn't get it out. *Speak!* My brain shrieked. *911. Help, the man is in my apartment.*

"Come quick," I finally squeaked.

"Why? What's going on? Are you okay?" His voice was serious, worried.

What did I say? *I smelled him. He's in my room right now.* How could he be in my room? I'd spent the day in my living room. He couldn't have gotten in without walking right by me. If he'd come in through a window, I'd have heard the breaking glass. The windows were locked. There was no crawl space from an attic, no possible way into that room.

"I just… I heard something and got spooked."

"Okay. I'm ten minutes away. I'll be there in eight." He hung up.

I pulled back the shower curtain and slumped down on the edge of the bathtub. "What's happening?" I murmured. I let the bear spray fall to the rug, and I cupped my face in my hands.

I was afraid. Not of the man in my apartment… but of what was happening in my own mind. Was this what Dr. Fry had talked about? Bits of that night I'd lost coming back? Except I wasn't getting flashbacks or moments of clarity. The night itself had been stripped away and only the man remained. But not only the man. My new, safe life surrounded him. He was invading the fortress I'd built without having to break a single window, smash through a single door.

For seven minutes, I sat there. I gnawed at the skin around my nails, picked lint from the rug, scratched at the grime that had accumulated in the grout of my tiled bathroom floor. When I finally emerged, I stepped toward my bedroom, grabbed the door and yanked it shut, holding my breath to avoid inhaling that dreadfully familiar scent a second time. I backed away, watching the door, hair raised on my neck as I half-waited for the knob to turn slowly. It didn't.

Behind me, a knock sounded on the front door and I jumped.

"Glo, it's Dorian. Open up. My hands are full."

The deadbolts slipped beneath my sweaty fingers as I opened them. I twisted the knob and stepped back as Dorian barreled through with my groceries.

Each week I sent him a list and he grocery-shopped for me. I'd told him a dozen-plus times that I could hire someone to do it, but he'd waved me off like a pesky fly.

He sat two paper bags on my counter. "Milk, bread, three frozen dinners. They were out of the turkey and gravy, so I got you two meat-loaves and a personal pizza."

I fidgeted close to him, eyeing the groceries, but mostly thinking about my bedroom, the smell, the sense of the man having been inside it. "I need a favor."

He added a stack of frozen dinners to the freezer. "What?" His eyes flitted over me, a little crease between his eyebrows.

I pointed down the hall to my bedroom. "I heard… I thought I heard something in my room. Can you check it?"

His eyes followed my finger to the closed bedroom door. "Sure, yeah." He started down the hall.

"Do you have your gun?" I asked.

"No, it's in the car."

I thrust the bear spray toward him. "Here then. Take this."

He sighed and held out his hand. Near my bedroom door, he paused and gestured at my laundry. "What's up with this?"

"I dropped my laundry when I heard the noise."

He nodded and turned the knob on the door. The breath trapped in my lungs whistled out. I took an automatic step back as the sliver of dark room appeared. He flipped on the light. I saw the edge of my bed, the beige carpeted floor, the nightstand that held my lamp, some paperbacks, a glob of yarn, and two knitting needles.

Dorian disappeared from sight as he moved around the room.

"Anything?" I called. I walked backwards until my hips met the wall and pushed with my heels as if the plaster might become liquid and allow me to disappear inside.

"Nope, nothing here. I'm checking under the bed."

I rubbed at my neck, scratched at the thin flesh, pushed on the hard contours of my trachea.

"Nobody under the bed." He moved across the open doorway. "I'm looking in the closet."

I heard the closet door slide open, tugged on the hem of my shirt, picked at my lip, imagined the poppet buried in there and felt a scream gurgling in my chest.

Dorian appeared in the doorway. "There's nothing in here, Glo. Windows are shut and locked. Nobody and nothing anywhere."

A bit of the tension flowed from my legs, and I slumped against the wall.

"Okay..." I said, finding a deeper breath.

"Maybe it was a squirrel jumping on the roof? That happens now and then. Why don't you come in and look? It's better if you see for yourself that it's empty."

I didn't want to, but knew he wouldn't take no for an answer. In the hall, I scooped my laundry back into the basket and carried it into my bedroom, grimacing at my first inhale, expecting the scent of the man to permeate the room. It didn't. It smelled like my room again.

I set the basket on my bed and swept the room with my eyes. No man in a dark mask reeking of cigarettes and cologne.

Dorian picked up a t-shirt off the top of my laundry basket. The collar was ripped and a brown coffee stain marred the white fabric. "Why do you still have this? Didn't you tell me two months ago you were throwing it out?"

The t-shirt said 'Yooper Flipflops' in green block lettering above an image of two old-fashioned snow-shoes. I yanked the t-shirt from his hand and clutched it to my chest. "It's so soft, I can't bear to part with it."

He chuckled and walked from the room. I rubbed the shirt against my cheek and dropped it back into the basket. It was very soft, but my reasons for clinging to the old shirt were deeper than the fabric.

Wren had given it to me, along with a box filled with other funny Yooper gag gifts, for the last Christmas we'd spent together. We'd had our own little fake tree that had come pre-decorated with strobing purple lights that Wren said made our apartment walls look like a strip club at night.

In the kitchen, Dorian and I unpacked the rest of the groceries. At the bottom of one bag, I discovered a bag of red licorice. "I love these. Gosh, I can't remember the last time I had them," I said, holding it up.

"I figured," Dorian said. "I remember how you and Wren used to each keep a bag in your cars."

"Thanks." I ripped the bag open with my teeth and pulled one out, offering it to Dorian.

He took it, walked to my couch, and sank onto it. "So, what was the sound you heard?"

I followed him to the couch and sat, propping my socked feet next to his on the coffee table. I glanced toward the open bedroom door and shook my head. "I don't know. I just... probably what you said—a squirrel jumping on the roof."

"Last night you thought you saw someone, and tonight you thought you heard someone. Have you talked to Dr. Fry about this?"

"About what? My growing paranoia?" A brittle laugh escaped my throat.

He tilted his head. "Maybe..." He fidgeted, turning his licorice over in his fingers. "Maybe it's time to dig into that night, start talking about it again, working through it. Didn't Dr. Fry say you guys would need to do that at some point?"

I chewed through a piece of licorice and picked up another, grateful to have something in my hands to keep me from scratching at my neck.

"I'm not ready," I said finally. "Where's Val tonight? Schmoozing some new buyers?"

Dorian gazed at me for a long moment, and I suspected that tonight would be the night he refused to drop it, insisted we talk about those things I'd never shared.

He sighed. "She drove to Sault Ste Marie for dinner with her sister. It's her sister's birthday."

"That's nice of her."

"Yeah. Believe it or not, she's not all bad."

"I never said she was."

He gave me an appraising look, but said nothing more.

"What's up with Rylie?"

"Sleepover at her friend Clara's."

I eyed his t-shirt. It said '#DADICATED' in red letters. "Nice shirt."

He looked down and grinned. "Rylie got it for me. Well, her and my mom."

"Dadicated, huh? Seems appropriate."

He patted his shirt and leaned over, grabbing another licorice. "I guess that's the adjective you take on when you have a baby at seventeen. It's all good though. Once upon a time I dreamed I'd join the air force, be a pilot someday." He laughed. "Now I'm lucky if I can fly coach to Florida once a year to take Rylie on vacation."

I stuck another piece of licorice in my mouth and chomped off the end. I'd never much considered Dorian's plans. As teens, Wren and I had been so absorbed in our own lives her older brother's story only had landed in the periphery—as something crazy to gossip over—especially when Wren learned she'd be an aunt at twelve years old.

We'd thought the typical things teenagers think. *He's in deep shit. Who could care for a baby at seventeen? Hopefully it's a girl.* It had been a girl, and Wren had missed a whole day of school so she could be at the hospital for Rylie's birth.

After that, Rylie had become a staple in our lives—the little girl with Dorian's luminous green eyes. Everything else about her reflected her mother, pale hair and paler skin. Rylie's mom had attended Marquette High with Dorian and they'd only been dating for two months when he discovered teenage fatherhood was on the horizon.

As many teen parents do, they tried to make it work and stayed together for two years before throwing in the towel. They didn't have anything in common and it wasn't 'opposites attract' in the cute way.

She wanted to party, to travel, to be free—hated that she'd given up her teen years to be a mom. She happily let Dorian take over as the primary parent.

Now she flitted in and out of Rylie's world with the lifestyle you'd expect from a woman named Journey. She wasn't a bad person, merely an untethered one, a drifter. She lived the vagabond lifestyle, and she loved it. Couchsurfing, hostels, hopping in a van to trek to Alaska to work on the pipeline, spending a year with a group offering tours by moped in Jamaica.

It was an enviable lifestyle in some ways and, more than once, when Journey had blown into town with her cracked leather overnight bag and her crazy stories of meeting a half-naked man in the desert and sharing a dinner of protein bars and ayahuasca, I'd longed to experience that level of freedom.

I'd always had wanderlust, but it had tended to live within certain parameters—woods, water, Michigan. I'd traveled out west twice for hikes and I'd solo-hiked part of the Appalachian Trail, but most of my outdoor adventures had occurred in my home state.

But that had all been before. Now Journey's life filled me with dread. I hadn't seen her since months before the dark night.

Dorian had mentioned her visiting the previous winter, crashing at his house, much to the irritation of his current girlfriend, Val, and the delight of Rylie. Dorian had told me about a few awkward dinners, an uncomfortable morning when Val had walked in on Journey using the toilet, and how hard Rylie had cried when her mother had gotten in a van for a ride-share to Wisconsin.

My envy of Journey's life was always tempered by my frustration that she continued abandoning Rylie again and again. Each time she visited, Dorian insisted never again—it was too disruptive for Rylie— but then Journey would appear and the smile on Rylie's face, the way her eyes lit up made him take back his earlier proclamations. The hard thing about Journey was that she had a good heart. She was kind and funny, and showered Rylie with attention and praise when she came into town. Journey brought her daughter quirky gifts from around the world: a coconut carved into a flower, a bracelet made from ocean plastic.

It was impossible to hate Journey—equally impossible to pin her down, to make her stay in Marquette and be a full-time mother.

"You can still be a pilot," I said. "There's a flying club that offers lessons right here in Marquette."

He pulled off his Black Rock Outfitters ball cap—a gift I'd given him on his last birthday—and mussed his flattened dark curls. "I will if you will."

"If I will what?"

"Go back to school, finish your degree."

I gaped at him. "I was studying to be a park ranger."

He shrugged. "Change your major then. But you should finish."

We lapsed into several minutes of silence, both of us perhaps considering our once-big and now seemingly unattainable dreams.

Dorian pulled out his wallet and slipped a piece of turquoise cardboard from one pocket. "What do you think of this color? I'm going to paint Rylie's room and surprise her. I thought this or maybe this." He presented another slightly darker shade of blue-green.

I read the names—tantalizing teal and peacock feather. "They're both pretty. I'd say tantalizing teal. What color is her room now?"

"White. The entire house is, which I'm good with, but Rylie's been talking about having a brighter room. She's obsessed with mermaids lately. My mom's been telling her about Wren's love of mermaids."

I smiled. Wren had gone through a full mermaid stage in our childhood that had followed her well into early adulthood. She'd painted her walls in shades of pale purple and turquoise and covered every surface in mermaid-themed décor. Mermaid posters, a lamp, pillowcases. Her robe had ended in a mermaid's tail. Birthday cakes and parties had been in mermaid themes.

"It's so weird I've never even seen your house," I said, holding up each of the color swatches again. "Definitely tantalizing teal." I handed them back to him.

"One of these days, we'll get you over there."

I sighed and grabbed another licorice. "Think so?"

"There's not a doubt in my mind."

I wanted to agree with him. 'Absolutely!' I'd announce, without a doubt in my mind that someday I'd travel in the world like a normal human being, but I clamped my teeth together and said nothing.

"Tantalizing teal it is," he said, sliding the color back into his wallet. "I'm throwing this other one out or I'll get to the paint store and forget which we picked." He stood and walked to the kitchen and dropped the cardboard in the trash beneath my sink. "I bought a big mermaid decal too and some little lamp that makes rainbow colors on the ceiling."

"She'll love it," I said.

We watched reruns of *The Big Bang Theory* until after 11pm and then Dorian stood and stretched. "I thought I'd bring Rylie by tomorrow?"

"That'd be great. Yeah."

"Call if any more squirrels try to break in."

"Very funny," I told him.

"Oh, wait, I almost forgot." He pulled his backpack from his shoulder and unzipped it. "My mom sent these. Lavender bath salts and candles." He handed me a paper bag.

I peeled it open and looked inside. "That's nice. Tell her thank you."

"I will. She's been getting into all kinds of crafty stuff with Rylie. Candles, bath salts. Apparently they're tackling soap soon, so you can expect some of that as well."

"Ooh, put in a request for coconut lime, will you? I had the strangest craving for a piña colada the other day."

He grinned. "I could just bring over my blender and make you a piña colada."

I shook my head. "Nah. I just… I can't do alcohol anymore."

"I'll make a virgin one," he said.

"Virgin it is. Thanks."

He opened the door and slipped into the hall, turned back to give me a serious look. "Try to get some sleep, okay?"

"It's the only thing on my to-do list tonight," I assured him.

"Take a bath first." He nodded toward the paper bag. "My mom said it'll help you relax."

"Are you trying to say I stink?"

"Hardly. You shower so much I'm amazed you have skin. It might help you… feel calm."

"Well, I'm open to suggestions in that department."

I locked the deadbolts behind him.

In the bathroom, I turned the faucet hot and ran my fingers beneath the water. I hadn't showered at all that day and my skin prickled with the day's sweat.

I added a cup of the lavender bath salts and lit three candles along the lip of the tub. Stripped of my clothes, I stepped into the hot water and sank low, relaxing my head back. A contented sigh slipped from my chest and I pooled water in my hands and pressed it to my face.

I dozed, letting my eyes slip shut.

Arms wrapped around my ribcage as if someone were below me, hugging me roughly, yanking me down until my face slipped beneath the water.

I screamed and water rushed into my mouth, burning my throat. I thrashed and squirmed against the slippery arms, clawing at them, but they held tight, dragging me deeper, impossibly deeper. The tub wasn't that deep, couldn't be.

With a terrified jerk, I sat up. Scrambling, nearly ripping my shower curtain from its hooks, I lurched from the tub and onto the tile, sputtering, crawled away as I looked behind me and expected the man to follow—to tower over me as he stepped from the bath.

No man emerged. The bath was empty, the shower curtain askew, my bath mat soaked from the water I'd splashed out.

6

———————

Still dripping, I shut myself in my bedroom and locked the door. I found a towel in my stack of clean laundry and dried off, slid into sweatpants and an oversized t-shirt.

For a long time, I sat on my bed and stared at the door, knees pulled to my chest, heart thumping madly. I wanted to call Dorian or Dr. Fry, but I didn't. I'd left my cell phone in the living room and couldn't bring myself to leave the bedroom. I wouldn't have called, anyway. No one had been in the bathtub, no man. I'd fallen asleep and been gripped by a nightmare. That was all.

Eventually, I switched off the lamp and shuffled to my window, picked up the binoculars and searched for my old apartment.

Lights blazed in the big window. One of the Twiggy Twins sat on the couch, a textbook open on her lap, papers scattered on the gray fabric beside her. She must have been taking summer classes.

I thought of her as Bird Legs—the same one Dorian had met. He said she was studying criminal justice. She looked like an unlikely cop with her flowing blonde hair and long, thin body.

She stood suddenly and walked to the window, paused and stared through the glass straight at me.

I pulled back, binoculars still pressed against the sockets of my eyes. She couldn't actually see me. My room was dark, and she didn't have binoculars, but the gaze brought a flush into my chest.

As I watched, someone moved into the apartment behind her. For an

40

instant, I saw the silhouette of a person and then the light in the apartment extinguished and the window went black.

Seconds ticked by and then minutes. I waited for the light to come back on. I scanned the rest of the building, but only one window of their apartment faced me, so I could not detect light in any other room. Had it been the other twin turning off the light as they readied for bed?

No. Surely she wouldn't cast her roommate into the darkness in the middle of studying.

For fifteen minutes, I scanned the alleyway and nearby houses, searched for any sign the girl had gone out—maybe with a boyfriend. I spotted an older man walking a dog down the narrow street, but no sign of the girl.

Nothing else. No light reappeared in the apartment. All was dark.

I set the binoculars on the windowsill and climbed into bed, thinking of the girl at the window, how I'd felt her staring back at me and then… nothing. I picked at my eyebrows and lips, worried at the hem of my comforter.

Finally, fitfully, I drifted into sleep.

Something tugged at the blankets near the foot of the bed. Half asleep, I pulled them higher and tucked them tight beneath me. The pull came again, and this time my eyes popped open. I came fully awake, aware that something was dragging my blanket down.

I lay perfectly still and listened.

The tug didn't happen again, but the sense of something, some*one* hovering at the end of my bed remained. I didn't want to look.

Pull the blanket up, turn over, and clench my eyes shut. That was the best option, but I couldn't do it. My body stiffened. Seconds and then minutes ticked by.

Finally, I lifted my head and looked toward the end of the bed.

He stood there, crouched, face half illuminated in moonlight, eyes as black as the surrounding shadows. Though I'd closed the curtains before bed, they were open now.

I opened my mouth to scream, but could not muster a sound.

As I stared, immobilized, he vanished, fading into the inky shadows around him so completely he might not have been there at all, might merely have been an odd assembly of my chair, laundry stacked on it, and a trick of moonlight.

Shivering, teeth chattering, I stood, snatched my comforter and ran from the room. I closed the bedroom door behind me, wanted to slam it, but didn't, afraid I might wake up my neighbor downstairs.

My hand shook as I lifted the remote and turned on the television, clicked to play an episode of *Gilmore Girls*. I sat heavily on the couch, wrapping my comforter around me, unable to see the screen.

I saw only him: the monster hovering at the end of my bed, watching me sleep. The masked man had been unmasked and for those suspended seconds, I'd seen, truly seen, the face of Wren's killer.

Unlike his appearance in my bathroom mirror, this time he had vanished before my eyes. Proof of what? That he wasn't real? That I'd hallucinated him?

"He's a ghost," I whispered, and the words spoken aloud sounded ominous, like a spell or a curse.

I tasted blood on my lip and realized I'd been picking. I stood and walked to the kitchen, not looking down the hall to my bedroom.

In a kitchen closet, I pulled out a cardboard box of infant hats. I'd already knitted two boxes of them since Christmas. Dorian delivered them to the local hospital to keep the heads of newborn infants warm after delivery. I was sure the hospital had more than enough to last them the rest of the year, but I returned to the couch, pulled out a partially knit hat in pink and yellow and set about finishing it. If nothing else, the knitting kept my hands away from my face.

My fingers trembled as I stuck the needle into the yarn. I was terrified, as terrified as I'd been that night when he'd been a real solid human being.

That night, I hadn't been brave, hadn't fought back, escaped, run for help. I'd just lived, that was all, against the odds, but it hadn't been any feat of my own. My body had somehow survived. Probably the elements really, the icy river water slowing the rush of blood after he'd slit my throat. Or maybe it was him, his bad luck, his inattention, not cutting deep enough.

You're so brave, you're so strong. How many times had I heard those words in the days and weeks after it happened?

These days I rarely heard those proclamations, unless of course it was in a letter from some unknown, some stranger who'd read my story and found it inspiring. That was the thing with looking at people from afar—they were distorted. Through the lens of those who reported on the case, I was a hero, a survivor.

They called me 'the girl who got away,' as if I actually had gotten away. I hadn't. For all intents and purposes, he'd killed me, he'd left me for dead, and I'd died. Gloria Cline, nineteen years old, avid hiker and outdoor enthusiast, had perished that night in the woods alongside her best friend, Wren.

That girl had died and this girl... well, she was barely alive at all. That was what I'd once heard Dorian's girlfriend Val say—that I was squandering my second chance, taking it all for granted. I'd been furious when I overheard those words. I'd wanted to take my full cup of hot tea and toss it out the window onto her head, but I knew where my rage really stemmed from—the fear that she was right.

Before that night, I had thought myself brave, independent, strong. I knew how to build a shelter, light a fire without a box of matches, forage for food in the woods. If I encountered strange men during my solo hikes, I smiled, but coolly, kept it clear I wasn't looking for a companion. I wasn't afraid, not of them, not of the wildlife or of getting lost or bad weather. The unknown was the appeal.

The world I lived in now was a polar opposite. I wanted nothing unknown, zero uncertainty. I watched the same shows, ate the same food, lived the same routine.

I'd built a fortress of familiarity around myself, but somehow, the monster had gotten in.

7

Dorian and Rylie showed up at my apartment the next day mid-morning. I'd slept a few hours and gulped a pot of coffee, which had left me alive, if not refreshed.

"Glo!" Rylie ran across the room and clutched me around the waist. She pulled away and squinted. "Your hip bone poked me in the eye. I brought a cupcake for each of us, but you better have both."

She shoved a plastic container into my hands. I could see two cupcakes, frosted in purple, adorned with sugar mermaids. "They're mermaid-themed," she told me.

"I see that," I said. "They look really tasty." I carried the cupcakes to the counter.

"Want to eat one? They're super-good. The inside is strawberry-flavored cake."

"I just had breakfast. Let's save them for later?"

Rylie shrugged and returned to the door, where Dorian stood with a paper bag.

"She brought crafts," he said, gazing into the bag. "I hate to say it's mermaid-themed."

My stomach did a little flip. I knew why they'd made the cupcakes, bought the mermaid crafts. Wren's birthday was days away, gradually getting closer. Mine would follow just two days later.

In less than a week, Wren would have turned twenty-one years old, a birthday we'd been planning since we were twelve. We'd never nailed it down. At twelve, we'd agreed on a hot-air balloon ride. By fifteen, it was a White Stripes concert. As of the final summer, we'd been waffling between a road trip to New Orleans or whitewater rafting in West Virginia.

We'd go to the bar, sure. After all, we'd legally be allowed to buy a drink, but by nineteen we'd been drinking illegally long enough that the sparkly fizz on the surface of a glass of beer now looked like foam—the shimmer had disappeared. We'd intended to mark the occasion with something far more memorable than getting inebriated.

I closed my eyes, clutched the edge of the counter, pushed until the edge bit into my palm and forced me back into the here and now.

Rylie was still talking. "Jolene said mermaids are real, and Mrs. Palmer, my science teacher, said they're certainly not real, which I know is the truth. But you know what I wonder?" She took the bag from Dorian and carried it to the table. "Maybe they were once real, like the dinosaurs and stuff, and we just haven't found their bones. I mean, they're in the ocean. How would we?"

I looked at Dorian. He was watching me with his concerned face, his 'should we go?' face.

"I'm good," I told him, and joined Rylie at the table where she'd unloaded colored paper and bags of sequins. "They might have been real once," I agreed. "Who are we to say what was swimming in the ocean a million years ago?"

"I think so too. I think most of the stuff I read about in like Harry Potter and stuff was probably real. Dragons and trolls and witches and wizards and maybe even those plants that screamed and cried like babies."

Dorian started across the room and his cell phone rang. He looked at it and scowled. "New tenants just checked into Martin's place and there's no hot water. Do you mind if I run and get that figured out? Two hours, tops."

"Not at all. Go for it."

Rylie and I sat at the table. She explained we were making paper mermaids with yarn hair. As we worked, we lapsed into a contented silence. It was one of the things I loved most about Rylie. We could just be together. Eight-year-olds didn't do small talk. There was no need to fill the awkward silence because the silence wasn't awkward, it was peaceful.

Sometimes sitting with Rylie was the closest I came to the feelings I once had on my long hikes. I hadn't been alone in the woods, anything but. Life surrounded me, but none of it needed to comment on the weather or complain about co-workers. Rylie and I didn't even have music or television playing. The only sound was the occasional puff when she squeezed the glue bottle or the sound of me stretching a length of tape and snapping it off.

"Grandma Lee said it's your birthday soon," Rylie said after a while. "She said you and Wren had birthdays that were only a few days apart."

"Yep. Wren was June twenty-first and I was June twenty-third."

I'd learned when Wren and I became friends and our mothers met for the first time that our due dates had been the same day. We'd both been expected to arrive in the world on June twenty-second, but Wren had been born a day early and I'd been born a day late. Wren's mother said we were fated to be best friends—we were star sisters.

"My dad's birthday is in March and my birthday is in October," Rylie said.

"I know," I said. "I still remember your first birthday. Grandma Lee made you a red velvet cake and you smeared it all over your face. You looked like a toothless vampire."

Rylie giggled. "A toothless vampire! That's funny."

"What do you want to do for your birthday this year?" I asked.

Rylie pursed her lips and leaned close to the page, carefully gluing iridescent sequins onto her mermaid tail. "I want to go to a water park. Jolene went to a water park for her birthday last year and it was so cool. There was a waterslide that was just like a big black tube. You couldn't see the bottom. I was so scared, but I did it and then when I came out at the bottom everybody gave me a high-five."

"Waterparks are fun."

"Yeah, I think so too. What do you want to do for your birthday?"

I slowed my breath, focused on the glitter glue, and tried to ignore the memory of Wren's face, voice, laughter in the back of my mind. I had this weird sense that I was supposed to make it count, celebrate for both of us, and yet I knew it was impossible.

What I most wanted was to pretend the day wasn't happening at all —to wake up and eat my toast and watch *Gilmore Girls* for the umpteenth time, microwave a meal or two, and go to bed none the wiser that a supposedly momentous day had come and gone.

Even if I could get everyone in my life on board with the idea, which

I couldn't—Janice would text me some passive-aggressive birthday wish—my brain would remind me every ten minutes all day long what day it was.

Today's the day, twenty-one, the big birthday. Wren and I should be flying above Lake Superior in a hot-air balloon, or stomping our feet to the White Stripes, or road-tripping somewhere fantastic. We should be holding glasses of dollar beer and cheersing our friendship that had withstood the tests of time. We should have been talking about how fun last weekend was and how much more fun next weekend would be and how we both vaguely dreaded graduating from college because then we'd have to get real-world jobs and start considering our future as something more than a series of fun weekends.

"I'm not planning on anything," I admitted. "Maybe I'll make something special for dinner."

Rylie made a face. "That's it? That doesn't sound very fun."

"Fun is overrated."

"What is 'overrated?'"

I sighed. My colored yarn—aka mermaid hair—refused to stick to the glue. "It just means… that some things are not as big a deal as we make them out to be. After a certain age, birthdays don't matter as much as when you're a kid."

"Really? My dad is older than you and he still does stuff on his birthday. On his last birthday, we played laser tag and watched like three Marvel movies. My mom made him a double chocolate cake with chocolate frosting, which is his favorite. He went out with Val that night." Rylie scowled. "And I had a sleepover with Grandma Lee and Grandpa George."

"That sounds like fun." I knew what Dorian had done on his birthday the previous March because he'd told me all about it. He'd also stopped by to drop off a slice of his mom's chocolate cake, which had been delicious.

"Is it because of Aunt Wren? Is that why you don't like your birthday?" Rylie asked.

I glanced at her sidelong, feeling as if it were too big a question for an eight-year-old, and realizing for the hundredth time that our tragedy had cut a chasm through her life as well. She probably pondered all kinds of things normal eight-year-olds wouldn't have given a second thought.

"My dad said you and Aunt Wren celebrated your birthdays

together. My friends Sicily and Paris do their birthdays together because they're twins. Their last birthday was a *Phantom of the Opera* theme and it was so cool. Their uncle played the piano in this spooky mask and cape and the punch had smoke coming off of it."

"That's a pretty fancy party."

"Yeah." Rylie colored her mermaid's face pink. "They travel all over the world. This summer they're going to Japan. Last year they spent the summer in Europe. Grandpa George says their dad is a bigwig."

"It sounds like they go to a lot of interesting places. I always wanted to go to Europe." I felt a twinge in my stomach at all the places I'd never see.

Someday, I reminded myself, much as Dr. Fry did whenever I got fatalistic about my future and started talking in nevers.

"Maybe we could have a party here for your birthday this year. Me and you and Dad," Rylie said. "My mom could bake a cake or cupcakes and we could watch movies."

I nodded and added an additional four eyes to my mermaid and then colored huge red puckered lips. "Maybe," I agreed.

Rylie leaned over and laughed. "That's one ugly mermaid."

"They can't all be Ariels. This is a mermaid witch who's hideous, but has more power than all the other mermaids in the sea."

Rylie giggled. "That's fair, I guess." Rylie continued decorating her mermaid and then paused. "What's it like having a stepmom?"

I drew pointy fangs coming from my mermaid's mouth, wondering what had spurred the question. Val? Was Dorian thinking of marrying Val?

"It's okay," I lied. "It really depends on the person, you know?"

"My dad said you call your stepmom Cruella de Ville."

I hid my smile. "Yeah, that's not very nice of me. Janice is not nearly as bad as Cruella de Ville. As far as I know, she's never paid anyone to skin a bunch of puppies."

"But is she kind of mean?"

I leaned my head back and rubbed a kink developing in my neck, considering the woman who'd been a part of my life for nearly a decade. A woman who'd made a career out of pointing out my flaws and spent a good chunk of those years trying to turn me into the type of daughter she could take proudly to lunch and show off to her friends.

"She wasn't mean, exactly. She just never accepted me as I was. I liked to play in the woods, build forts, collect insects. She thought I'd been too long without a mother and it had turned me into a wild child, but even before my mom left, I was a forest kid. My dad has pictures of me in a diaper roaming through the woods with sticks in my hands and mud on my face."

Rylie giggled. "I like the woods too, and jumping on my trampoline and making art stuff. Val mostly likes to talk about work and shopping for shoes."

"Adults can be like that. Now that I count myself among them, I realize I haven't been missing much."

"I hope Val doesn't become my stepmom."

"Well, I'll give you some advice that my therapist has given me. He says when we worry, we live the thing we don't want to happen over and over again even though it might never happen at all."

"What does that mean?"

"Well, say every time you got on your bike, you thought about crashing. You felt it in your whole body and you got scared and imagined what it would feel like. You've pretty much felt what it will be like to crash your bike and you haven't even ridden out of the garage yet. Not only that, but by thinking about it and scaring yourself, you're making it more likely that you'll crash your bike."

"So, if I worry too much that Val will be my stepmom, then she probably will be?"

I frowned. "I don't know, Rylie. Maybe. But either way, worrying about it won't change what happens. You can't decide if Val becomes your stepmom, but if it's really bugging you, talk to your dad about it."

"But I don't want my dad to be alone. I just don't want him to be with Val."

"I get it, believe me." And I did because I too had wanted my dad to find someone.

For a time, I'd been fixated on my middle-school art teacher, Mrs. Percy, as his potential future wife. Turned out she was married, but she was still the face I'd pictured each night when I prayed for him to fall in love and be happy again. Instead, he'd met Janice. Janice with her red manicured nails and cloying perfume and a glare that could wilt flowers.

The time with Rylie had softened my nerves, calmed the part of me that had been working into a tighter and tighter ball over the last several days. Together, we opened the windows and let the summer breeze flow through the apartment. We stripped my bedding and washed it. When we put it back on, Rylie stretched across my bed and I fanned it over her. She said it felt like wings fluttering against her face.

I paused at the window. "Oh, good, the mailman. I should have a book in the mail."

"What's it about?"

"Women's empowerment." And it was—sort of.

The book was *Eat, Pray, Love*. I'd read it years earlier, long before I needed it, but several days before it had popped into my head. I remembered reading about Elizabeth Gilbert's dark night when she lay sobbing on her bathroom floor and then somehow picked herself up and went on a great adventure. The thought of such an adventure filled me with cold terror and yet I wanted to live vicariously through her story, which I was sure Dr. Fry would say was progress.

My former reading habits had been all about adventure, solo hikes like Cheryl Strayed's *Wild*, or Aron Ralston's *127 Hours*, a harrowing book about severing his own arm in a canyon when a boulder fell on him during a hike. I'd never had a second thought about such stories in my life before, but in this new life, I focused on reading material that triggered nothing. When I searched online for books to purchase, my search terms included 'feelgood,' 'happy,' and 'easy reads.'

"I'll go get it."

"No, that's okay. Your dad will be back soon and he can bring the mail in when he comes."

"I don't mind."

Before I could argue, she skipped across the room, pulled open the door, and disappeared into the hall. I stood frozen, staring at the now-closed door. I dashed to the window and peered out, counted the seconds, waiting for her to emerge. It was taking too long. What if she'd fallen down the steps?

Beneath me I heard the front door of the house open and then Rylie appeared on the sidewalk, skipping again, her pale hair swinging long down her back. She reached the mailbox, opened it, and took out the stack of mail, including a brown parcel, my book.

As she turned, a car appeared at the end of the street. It slowed and coasted to the curb in front of my house. It was a stranger. The window rolled down. I couldn't see inside. They were trying to lure Rylie to their car. If she got close enough, they'd reach out and grab her, yank her inside.

8

———————

I gaped at the car as Rylie paused on the sidewalk and turned back toward the car.

"No!" I screamed and pounded my fists against the glass and then, with hardly a thought, I turned and sprinted from the apartment. I raced down the hall, took the stairs two at a time, and ran out the front door. I missed the second step that led off of the porch and plunged face-first toward the sidewalk. The heels of my hands vibrated as they struck the cement walkway, pebbles biting into the flesh. My knees throbbed when they smacked the cement.

"Rylie," I croaked, the awareness of what I'd done slowly dawning as Rylie raced to my side.

"Glo, you're outside! Oh, my gosh, you came outside. Ouch, are you okay? That must have hurt."

Black spots danced behind my eyes. The pain in my hands and knees was the only thing keeping me conscious. I could feel the terror seizing my lungs, squeezing, stopping the flow of air. My vision blurred as I blinked at the car at the curb. The passenger door opened and someone climbed out. Long tan legs ended in beige ankle boots. Not a man at all, but Val.

I wheezed and cupped my hands in front of my face. *Breathe, breathe.* But I couldn't breathe. The air made my skin prickle. Far off I heard a siren and closer other sounds, a thousand sounds, traffic and birds and

51

doors slamming and a man's voice calling, "Moose… Moose!" A dog perhaps. The closer sounds of Rylie and now Val.

"I think she's having a panic attack," Rylie said. Her little hands were on my back.

"Of course she is," Val snapped. "Jesus, why did you come out here in the first place?" she grumbled, grabbing my arms.

She tried to pull me to my feet. I curled deeper into myself, formed a little ball, shut my eyes and struggled for breath.

"Rylie, where's your dad? Jesus Christ. I can't pick her up. We're going to have to call an ambulance."

No, please, no. I hated the hospital, hated ambulances and paramedics and the probing hands of doctors and the bright fluorescent lights.

My memories of the hospital after the dark night remained burned in my memory, those first excruciating moments when I'd woken for the first time. Bedsheets had been bunched in my fists, dim sunlight cutting through the slanted shades. There were beeping noises and breathing noises. They had stuffed something huge and alien into my throat and I couldn't breathe.

I had tried to scream, pulse pounding, nausea rising, hysteria taking hold. "Get it out, get it out," I wanted to shriek, but I couldn't speak around the massive something in my throat. I had thrashed and clawed and bucked.

First my father's face had appeared above me, then a string of unfamiliar faces—doctors and nurses, based on their white coats and green scrubs. They'd been talking and gesturing and touching me.

Then I'd gone into a freefall, cool and dizzying, back into unconsciousness.

The next time I'd woken, the object—a long plastic tube—had been removed. I'd been intubated, my dad told me, but I was breathing on my own and they had taken it out.

That moment marked the beginning of the terrible weeks that followed. Shaking, disoriented, shrunken with guilt, ballooning with rage—all of those sensations and so much more had paraded through in the six weeks I'd remained in the hospital. They'd taken up residence, moved in like house guests who long outstayed their welcome.

I'd lain in that sterile white room watching the ordinary world carry on. Sitcoms and reality shows on the television. Nurses in the hallway complaining about husbands and boyfriends. Other patients walking the halls in white gowns and slippered feet. All the comings and goings that painted a picture of a life unchanged, but all the while Wren lay rotting in the woods.

I'd never doubted that Wren was dead. I'd watched it. I'd experienced the absolute horror of witnessing my very best friend, my soulmate, if such a thing existed, die in front of me. That moment of all moments was there with such sharp, horrific clarity that when I thought about it, and I tried not to, I couldn't breathe.

In those first days, everyone was there and they needed to know what happened. Where was Wren?

My throat had been cut. I couldn't speak, couldn't tell them what happened, so I'd written it. I'd been crying so hard it had been difficult to write. My letters were big and sloppy. My hand had trembled so viciously, I'd had to use the other to steady it, which pulled on my IV cords and made the needle site throb painfully.

Wren's mother Lee had fallen to her knees when she'd read the paper. Wren's father, George, had stood stiff and scary-looking, blinking at the sheet of paper as if a severed hand had materialized on my table. Dorian... Dorian had said nothing at all. His face had paled and tears had streamed down his cheeks.

Afterward I'd begun to shake, uncontrollable shakes, and they'd sedated me. When I'd woken again, the Ashbys were gone.

After the revelation of Wren's death, my dad had faded from the hospital. He'd never been good with bad news, with uncomfortable shows of emotion.

Dorian had taken up vigil at my bedside, copies of *Popular Mechanics* opened on his lap. Sometimes he talked. I still couldn't. Other times, he napped or showed me photos on his phone.

On the table sat vases of flowers, a stack of cards, Styrofoam cups with straws, a paper bag with a grease spot that must have been takeout.

Days had followed, then weeks. Sometimes I'd been lucid, sometimes I'd been hysterical.

Now Dorian's voice pulled me from the memories of those bleak hospital days. I was still on the sidewalk, pebbles biting into my side.

"What's happening?" Dorian shouted. "Is that Gloria? Here, get out of the way. Back up."

Val hissed out an angry breath. Dorian's hands pushed beneath me. He lifted me and held me against him. "Rylie, open the door."

I felt the shift as we moved from the outside into the stairwell, where it was darker and cooler. Another door opened, and we were in my apartment, though I hadn't opened my eyes. I held them clenched shut. My breath whistled in as if someone had forced a straw into my lungs and blown in a tiny puff of air. I struggled for more, for a deeper breath.

He laid me down on the familiar softness of my bed. I didn't unfurl. I stayed, head tucked in, eyes closed, knees pulled tight against me.

"Is she okay?" Rylie asked in a small voice.

I wanted to reassure her I was okay, but I couldn't speak, still could barely breathe.

A weight settled on the edge of the bed—Dorian. His fingers brushed my forehead. "Should I call Dr. Fry? Just nod if you want me to."

I didn't nod. There was nothing Dr. Fry could do.

The weight lifted, and I heard Dorian move out of my bedroom. "Why was she outside?" he demanded.

"I went to get the mail," Rylie answered.

I heard Val's voice, clipped, irritated. "Who knows why she came out? She probably thought Rylie was going to get attacked by the old woman across the street."

"Why were *you* out there, Val?" Dorian asked, an edge in his voice.

"Because I saw Rylie all by herself near the road," Val snapped. "I can't believe you'd leave her here alone with Gloria. I don't want to tell you how to parent, but—"

"Val, stop." Dorian's voice was sharp.

"I'm sorry, Daddy." Rylie sounded on the verge of tears.

I wanted to call out, tell her it was fine, I was fine, but I said nothing. I didn't trust myself to speak. My heart had slowed but still bounced furiously behind my ribs. The terror that had sent me bursting from my apartment, from the house, hadn't fully dissolved. It had felt so real, as if I were witnessing Rylie's abduction.

"*You're* the reason Gloria left the house."

"Excuse me?" Val snapped.

"You're in Lucy's car. It's a strange car. She probably watched Rylie get the mail and saw a strange car pulling up beside her. She panicked."

"And somehow that's my fault?"

The door to my bedroom creaked open.

"Glo?" Rylie whispered.

I forced my eyes open, lifted my head away from my knees. I was trembling, and sitting up was difficult, but I managed it.

"Hey…" I forced a deep breath in, held it, let it out slow. "It's okay," I said. "Come sit with me."

Rylie smiled and hurried across the room, jumped onto the bed and burrowed into the pillows. "I'm sorry," Rylie said. "I'm sorry you got scared."

She twined her fingers with mine. Her hand was so small. I squeezed it. "It's not your fault, Rylie."

I heard Dorian's and Val's voice fade. After several minutes, the bedroom door opened and Dorian peeked in. He looked at Rylie and then at me. "Is she okay in here?"

I nodded. "She's great."

"Are you okay?" he asked.

"Yeah," I breathed.

My lungs opened back up and my muscles relaxed. The adrenaline drained away.

Dorian sat on the bed, kicked off his shoes and swung up his feet. He settled back onto the pillows and pulled out his phone. "Who wants to watch funny videos of animals?" he asked.

"I do!" Rylie exclaimed.

We stayed that way, the three of us, watching animal bloopers and not talking about my terrifying tumble into the world outside.

9

———————

It was almost nine pm when they left. I followed them into the living room, watching as Rylie pulled on her jelly sandals, which had apparently come back into style.

"Are you good?" Dorian asked me as he slid open the first deadbolt.

"Yeah. I'm fine. Thanks."

"You should probably call Dr. Fry tomorrow."

"Sure thing, Dad."

Rylie grinned. "If he were your dad, we'd be sisters. I would kind of like a sister." She turned pleading eyes toward Dorian.

"Thanks a lot," he told me, handing Rylie her bag of leftover crafts.

"Don't bend my mermaid," she whined, grabbing it from the bag and flattening it out.

"How about instead of a sister, you can get a new fish," he suggested.

"The fish I have now won't even look at me if I press my face against the tank. What's the point?"

"Maybe if you'd stop pressing your face against the tank like some kind of fish-eating monster, it would come out from behind its plastic bush now and then."

She made a face at him and he nudged her toward the door.

"Hey, before you go, you didn't see the Twiggy Twins out and about today, did you? Rollerblading or whatever?" I asked.

He looked at me curiously. "No... why?"

56

I shrugged. "No reason."

He narrowed his eyes at me. "Come off it. No reason? That's a load of crap."

I sighed and tugged at my hair that had grown just past my ears—too long. It tickled the back of my neck and I swatted it away. "Last night I saw… nothing, probably." I laughed dryly.

"You were watching them?"

"One of them, the one you met, Bird Legs."

"Kelly," he corrected.

"Sure, that one. And then all of a sudden the lights went out in the apartment and then nothing."

"Okay, so she turned off the light and went to bed."

"Someone else turned off the light."

"How do you know?"

"Because she was standing by the window."

Rylie shifted her gaze back and forth between us.

"Then the other Twig turned off the light, and they went to bed," Dorian said.

"Maybe."

"Or…?"

"I don't know. It creeped me out."

"But you didn't see who turned off the light and the logical explanation is usually the right one, so it makes sense—"

"Yeah, yeah." I waved him towards the door. "Never mind."

"Don't get carried away with this," he said. "Okay? Call me if you need anything."

"Will do." I sat on the couch and picked up the remote.

Dorian stood in the doorway, watching me for another moment. "Not ready for bed yet?"

I shook my head, not willing to admit that I was afraid to sleep in my room. I'd wanted to ask him to go look out my window, see if he could see into the Twiggies' apartment, but then he'd demand to know why I didn't want to go in there.

After they left, I watched the growing dark with dread. The light faded—going, going, gone. I didn't move from the couch, not toward the bathroom to brush my teeth nor the bedroom to rest my unnaturally weary bones. Tired from doing nothing—from fleeing, marathon-style, from the monster that lived in my head.

As *Gilmore Girls* played, I scrolled through the selfies Rylie had taken of us earlier that day. Photos of us each holding up our mermaids. Photos where we stuck out our tongues.

I paused as I reached the last photo she'd taken. We were sitting, the camera tilted down to catch our faces. Just behind Rylie another face loomed, distorted, so blurry that if I didn't know what I was looking for, I'd have written it off. It was him, angled behind us as if he were standing on all fours, as if he'd crawled across the carpet on hands and knees as we'd sat obliviously pasting yarn hair onto our mermaids. My fingers trembled as I turned the phone off and shoved it onto the coffee table.

I went to my laptop and looked up mermaid tail blanket patterns. I couldn't knit one for Wren as a birthday gift, but I could knit one for Rylie and it would give me something to focus on.

I printed the design and rifled through the hall closet. I didn't have teal yarn, but I did have purple and dark blue. Back on the couch, I took out my knitting needles and set to work on the mermaid's tail.

I woke with a start, the edge of a dream dissolving as the room came into focus.

It was a pee dream, a nudge from the subconscious that I needed to get off my couch and into the bathroom before I wet my pants. I pushed open the bathroom door, flipped on the light and froze.

He stood there, reflected in the mirror, the monster, the man from the dark night. His mask was gone, his dark eyes and pockmarked face as clear to me as if I were gazing at my own reflection. His nose was slightly crooked. A tattoo glared from the side of his thick neck—a red and black scorpion.

My bladder let go and pee ran down my legs, but I didn't budge, didn't breathe.

He stared into my eyes and I into his. A smile crawled slowly up his face, revealing his teeth, an incisor missing.

His arm suddenly swept in front of me. The box-knife swooshed up and drew fast across my throat. Blood spurted from my neck and down the front of my t-shirt. I shrieked and grabbed for my throat to staunch the flow of blood, catching my reflection, expecting to see blood rushing from the wound.

There was no blood at all. No man. I was alone, my face the color of bone, my eyes bulging, my hands clutching my narrow throat. I struggled to breathe, sank to my knees, aware of the wetness beneath me, but barely registering the sensation.

I stripped off my pee-soaked pants and wiped myself down with a wet rag in the kitchen. I returned to the bathroom for only a moment, long enough to drape a blanket over the mirror and run back out again.

～

I did not sleep again that night, but sat on my couch trembling. I knitted Rylie's mermaid tail, dropped the stitch half a dozen times, but refused to quit, intent on focusing my attention away from the man in the mirror. *Gilmore Girls* played on the television and I looked up now and then, soothed by the mundane dramas of the women's lives in their idyllic small town of Stars Hollow, Connecticut.

When daylight finally trickled through the window, I made coffee and scalded my tongue slurping it down.

As I sat at my desk, my cell phone rang, my dad's name on the screen.

"Hi, Dad," I answered.

"Gloria, hello. How are you? Did you get my email?"

My eyes were crusty, and I rubbed them with one hand while holding the phone with the other. "Yeah, I got it. I've just been busy…" It was a stupid thing to say. I didn't leave my apartment. How busy could I be?

"That's okay, no big deal, but… what do you think about a visit?"

"I don't know, Dad. I'm really tired right now and—"

"I miss you, Gloria. I've been thinking… What if you moved home with me and Janice?"

My mouth fell open. Was my dad completely out of touch? Did he not realize not only could I not step into the hall outside my apartment, his wife hated me? She'd sooner burn their house to the ground than move me back into it. "I can't do that, Dad."

"You're not getting better there, honey. If anything…" He trailed off, but I knew the words he hadn't said. *If anything you're getting worse.*

"When you watch your best friend get murdered in the woods and then have your throat slit, you can tell me what's best for me. Until then, I'd prefer if you kept your opinions to yourself."

I'd never said anything so harsh to my dad and it had been spurred by a kind gesture on his part, an attempt to help me. Guilt flared at my reaction, but I didn't apologize.

"I'm sorry, Gloria. You're right, I absolutely cannot imagine what it was like for you, but... I am your father. I have a right to my opinion and my opinion is that living alone, holed up in that apartment, is not a way to heal. You're so alone there."

"No, I'm not actually. Dorian comes over every day."

"Dorian."

"Yes."

"That's great, but Dorian isn't family. Dorian is the brother of—"

"Stop," I barked. "I don't want to hear this."

"You might not want to, but I think you need to."

"You know what I need, Dad? For you not to bring your wife to my apartment so she can walk around with that smug, judgmental look on her face."

"It's not judgment, honey. It's concern. Janice is worried about you, just like I am."

"Ha, that'd be the day."

"Jeff will go back to school in the fall. If you'd prefer, we could wait until then, but honestly, even with Jeff in the house, there's plenty of room for you."

Jeff—Jeffrey to his mother because Janice treated him like he was forever four years old—was my much-detested stepbrother. I'd never liked him. Not merely because he was Janice's son. It had more to do with his underlying arrogance, which he glossed over by being fake-friendly, a trait I was sure he got from his mother.

On the outside, Jeffrey was perfect. Handsome, tall and blond, with one of those straight white smiles that reminded me of a wolf readying for the kill. People described him as charismatic, a life-of-the-party type, but I always found him to be off. He laughed too loud at his own jokes and constantly passed around significant looks as if everything was an inside secret.

I'd been twelve when my dad married Janice. Jeff had been fourteen. Fortunately for me, during the school year he stayed in Escanaba with his dad.

Jeff and I never had a warm relationship despite my dad's assurances it would get better with time. When he came home, Jeff intentionally ate the snacks I preferred, even ones he didn't like. He borrowed the brand-new mountain bike I'd gotten for my sixteenth birthday and bent the frame. In front of my dad, he put on his polite persona, but the instant my dad stepped from the room, mean Jeff reappeared.

I coped with Janice and Jeff by making myself scarce, which wasn't hard because I'd always preferred the woods. When I wasn't wandering the forests, I stayed with Wren, who lived only two blocks away.

Janice never complained about my disappearing act when her precious Jeffrey showed up because, frankly, she wanted her beloved Jeff to get her and my father's undivided attention.

After Jeff graduated from high school, he'd gotten into Michigan Tech, but he still came home each summer and stayed in his old bedroom at my dad's house.

I rubbed my eyes and chased away the unpleasant memories of Jeff.

"Can I come visit this afternoon?" my dad asked. "Janice and I? I'll bring Hercules."

I closed my eyes, wondering if he'd heard anything I just said, if he listened to me at all. "I'd prefer if you only brought Hercules."

He sighed. "Okay. Just me and Hercules. How's two o'clock?"

"That's fine. I need to get some work done, so…"

"See you then, honey. If you need me to bring anything, send me a text, okay?"

"Yeah. Thanks."

We ended the call, and I made a second pot of coffee. It tasted bitter and grainy. The filter had partially collapsed and allowed a quarter-cup of grounds into the pot. After forcing down a cup, I poured the rest into the sink and sat down to work.

I couldn't concentrate, couldn't stop thinking about my dad's unspoken words: *You're getting worse.*

10

When the dark night was over and the so-called healing and recovery began, people rallied around me. *Take as much time as you need,* they said. *This may be a lifetime of healing and recovery.*

But even as people said those words, something within them was praying they weren't true. With the passage of time, I'd return to the original Gloria I'd always been. The grotesque scars would fade and the vivid memories would slip further into the recesses of my mind and perhaps take the nightmares with them.

At the one-year mark, people fell away, as if I had wallowed too long in my grief—taken the trauma of that night and wrapped it around myself like a cloak. They feared at every visit I'd whip that cloak open and reveal all the dark things hidden inside it and they'd have to sit there pretending not to see, gazing out the window, making small talk about the weather.

We were truly not a society built to handle grief, despair, evil. The news displayed stories of children mutilated, of women beheaded, of evil people shooting, stabbing, strangling other human beings, and we munched on our morning cereal, slid into suits and cars and went about our day. I myself had become practiced in this type of bypassing, stepping around the horror as if it were a puddle of water on the floor that would evaporate if I ignored it long enough.

It didn't evaporate, not when you'd lived it. It grew as if fed by a hidden spring until one morning you stepped into that once-shallow puddle and you were swallowed whole.

In the first days after the dark night, I'd experienced absolute and overwhelming relief and gratitude that I was out of the woods. When I was warm again and dry and they had wiped away the blood, when my throat had been sewn shut and my broken bones had been set.

But that relief was an animal instinct, like a dog who had been beaten and left to die. When he was brought inside and laid by the fire, somewhere in those bleak hours he would be filled with whatever version of gratitude a dog might feel, for he was alive, the pain was gone. But inevitably he would remember the person who put him in that sorry state—the hitting, the whipping, the chaining to the post. He was not healed from all that pain by a single sliver of kindness. His life was saved, death was thwarted, but the bulk of his trauma sat untended, weeping sores that no one could see. That he himself could not see, that I myself could not see.

I could not see where my psyche had been slashed and stabbed. I could not stop the loss of blood; the river did not slow it. So my body had its own way of dealing with these internal wounds. *Lock yourself in a room, know every inch of that space, triple locks on the door, windows locked and shaded, bear spray in the closet, taser in the bedside drawer, cell phone always an arm's length away.*

I'd barricaded myself so completely in this place that if I had an accident and Dorian was unavailable, someone would have to break in. They'd have to get a ladder, climb up to the second story and smash out my window. Not an easy feat with triple-paned glass.

There really was no guidebook on healing from trauma, on which trail covered one mile instead of fifty-two miles, which path had sheer cliffs at the edge, which had roots for you to trip on. My recovery was ugly and cumbersome and more often than not I questioned whether I was recovering at all.

∼

Dressed in green jogging pants and a long-sleeved Black Rock Outfitters shirt, I sat in the chair by my open window and watched for my dad. I could have busied myself in other ways, but the anxiety that accompanied a visit from my dad guaranteed that it'd be impossible to concentrate on anything else. It was easier to give in to the compulsion to sit and wait and watch.

I chewed the cuticle on my thumb and when that grew sore, I plucked at my eyelashes and eyebrows.

My dad's cream-colored SUV pulled into my driveway at ten to two. I hadn't made lunch or coffee or set out cookies or done the things people were expected to do when having visitors. My dad stepped from the driver's seat, a bouquet of orange and pink flowers wrapped in tissue paper in his hand.

From the passenger seat climbed Janice. Her white-blonde hair was pinned high. She wore a dark turtleneck despite the heat and long dark pants with heels. I heard her pointed shoes click across the paved driveway and I balled my fists, furious that he'd brought her.

My dad opened the back door and Hercules leapt out. My heart surged, and I clapped my hands, nodding my head and swallowing the rage over Janice.

I'd focus on Hercules, on our happy, loving dog, and I'd do my best to be polite to Janice because my dad deserved that much.

We'd gotten Hercules when I was thirteen from a neighbor whose dog had ended up birthing a litter of six puppies, some mixture of golden retriever—that was the mom's breed—and possibly a Siberian Husky, though the father dog's lineage was a mystery. Hercules raced to the steps of the house. He wagged his tail and turned expectantly toward my dad.

I stood to unlock my door and then paused, looking back at the car as the back door on Janice's side flung open. Jeff stepped out.

My eyes bulged, and I recoiled from the window.

What was he doing here? How could my dad have let him come?

All my joy at seeing Hercules withered and tears pricked the backs of my eyes. My reaction was extreme, the response of an insolent child, and yet the emotion wrapped me in its icy embrace and refused to let go. I stood frozen, listening as they tromped up the stairs and down the hall. The knock sounded on my door.

"Glo, it's Dad. We're here."

I didn't move. My heart thundered in my chest. My palms grew slick and my eyes burned as sweat trickled from my hairline into my eyes.

Open it, I told my body, but my body didn't move. I couldn't open it, couldn't allow them inside, couldn't feel their suffocating presence in my peaceful little place.

"Gloria, honey?" he called.

I let my breath out slowly and forced my feet to step one after the other to the door. My fingers were clumsy as I undid the bolts and I imagined the irritated looks Janice and Jeff exchanged in the hallway.

I opened the door and retreated, forcing a smile that I was sure looked as ungenuine as I felt.

"There she is!" my dad announced, stepping through the doorway.

Hercules ran in and I bent down and scooped him into my arms. "Hi, baby boy. Look at you. You smell like you had a bath."

"He sure did," my dad said. "Thanks to Janice, who found one of those groomers who comes right to your house."

I glanced up at Janice, who quickly erased the look of disgust she'd been directing toward Hercules—or perhaps it was at me. "Hi, Gloria," she said. "How are you?"

I stood and pulled my sleeves down over my hands to keep from fidgeting. "I'm good, thanks. And you?" My voice was stiff, my body stiff.

Janice's thin, tight smile widened. "Just lovely. Summer is here and my Jeffrey is home." She linked her arm through Jeff's and I shifted to look at him.

He stared back at me, his gaze intense. It had always been that way, but for some reason on this day it felt especially piercing. He had blue, oddly pale eyes, which made his pupils darker—like bottomless holes.

"Hi, Jeff. How's it going?"

He grinned. "Can't complain. Busy as usual, but trying to take the summer easy. Mom's orders." He winked at me.

My eyes drifted shut and when I opened them the room tilted. I put out a hand and Jeff caught it. "Whoa there," he said.

His fingers were cold and dry against my own warm, sweaty ones. I jerked my hand away, blinking, my breath suddenly trapped in my lungs, which seemed to be constricting. I lurched away down the hall toward my bedroom.

"Gloria?" my dad asked, his tone unsure.

I braced one hand against the wall to keep from tipping and stumbled to my bedroom.

"What is she doing?" Janice hissed.

In my bedroom, I closed and locked the door, leaned my forehead against the wood. My legs slowly collapsed beneath me. I sank onto the floor and curled into a ball.

11

———

"Glo..." Dorian called my name and knocked gently on my locked bedroom door.

Hours had passed since my dad's visit. I'd heard them leave, been terrified that the apartment door would remain unlocked behind them, but couldn't seem to get out of my bed to deal with it.

"I'm not up for seeing anyone," I told him.

"I'm not anyone. Can you please unlock the door?"

"No."

He said nothing for several moments. "Okay. I picked up a pizza and I'm turning on *The Big Bang Theory*."

I heard him walk down the hall. I pulled the blanket back over my head and tugged at my hair.

Minutes ticked by. I heard the voice of Sheldon from the television, and I slowly peeled back the blanket. I plodded out to the living room, where Dorian sat on the couch, a pizza box open on the coffee table before him. He glanced up and smiled.

"Pizza gets you every time," he said. "Come on, eat."

I slumped onto the sofa and grabbed a slice of bacon and pineapple —my favorite—and took a bite. Cheese and salt and the touch of sweetness from the pineapple. It tasted great and yet my mouth felt dry as I struggled to chew and swallow. I returned the slice to a paper plate and tucked my hands into the opposite sleeves of my shirt.

"What happened today? Your dad called me."

My throat thickened, the emotion from that afternoon roaring back as if it had been waiting patiently in the corner for its chance to break free.

"He…" I paused when my voice caught, felt stupid, childish—hated myself for becoming this person, continuing to be this person.

"Brought Janice and Jeff," Dorian finished, taking an enormous bite and dropping a glob of cheese on his shirt. He tried to lick it off, missed, and it fell into his lap. I smiled.

He glanced up, lifted an eyebrow. "Is that a smile I see?"

I sighed and closed my eyes. "I don't want to be this way anymore. I was so angry at my dad today, so crippled by the sight of Janice and Jeff…" I shook my head. "And it's not his fault. Janice is his wife, Jeff is his stepson, my stepbrother. I have no right to act like this. I'm furious with this"—I gestured at my head—"mental bullshit. This PTSD bullshit. I am sick to death of myself, but my nervous system doesn't seem to be able to tolerate anyone else. It's just me and me and me and some more me."

"And don't forget me," Dorian added.

I laughed and kicked a socked foot at him. He caught it and tickled the bottom of my foot.

"Ahh… no… I don't want to add peeing my pants to the day's litany of humiliations." I thought of the night before and cringed.

"Your dad understands, Glo. He felt terrible about today. He didn't want to bring them, didn't plan on it, but they… they kind of tricked him. Janice asked him to drop her and Jeff at some appointment, but then Jeff got a call on their way and the appointment got cancelled, so Janice insisted they come along so they could say hi."

I frowned. "Typical Janice," I muttered, but even as I said it, I knew Janice wasn't the problem. She was just a person, an unpleasant one, but she was not a threat. There was no logical reason to have a panic attack at the mere sight of her.

"Why such animosity toward Janice? Beyond the usual 'evil stepmother' syndrome."

"I didn't look at her like that in the beginning," I said. "I swear it. I wanted a stepmom. Shit, I wanted a mom-mom. But then…"

"She didn't live up to your expectations?"

"I didn't live up to hers. Nothing in our world lived up to hers. She moved in and stripped the pictures from the walls, hung this hideous wallpaper in every room. She spent three months bossing my dad to haul a piece of furniture to the curb every week when the garbage truck came and then she pressured him into buying all this expensive, ugly, leather furniture, glass tables, abstract art.

"After she purged the house, she started on me, throwing out clothes she thought were too boyish. I had to physically fight her, I kid you not, to keep my Pog collection. She tried to yank it out of my hands and I lay on the ground kicking her until my dad ended it." I shook my head. The memory still stung, the way he'd led Janice down the hall, patting her hair and murmuring, and left me lying in the hallway with tears streaming down my face. I'd gotten up, packed all my prized possessions and run to Wren's house where my Pogs, stone collection and comic books then lived in perpetuity.

Dorian grimaced. "That's terrible. Didn't your dad put an end to it?"

I snorted. "No, he didn't. He hid from her and from me, I guess. He snuck off to the garage or out to the backyard for a smoke. She could do no wrong in his eyes."

"I guess that explains why you practically lived at our house from sixth grade on."

"Yep. Thank God your parents let me. Especially after Jeff moved in." I shuddered.

"He was as bad as Janice?"

"They're cut from the same cloth. He was always sucking up to my dad and messing with me on the sly. He'd set me up to get in trouble. He walked my sneakers in dog poop one time and left them on Janice's favorite rug in the living room."

Dorian shook his head. "No way."

"It happened. I hadn't worn those shoes the day before. I'd borrowed a pair of Wren's, and I knew better than to leave anything on Janice's cherished rug. But sure enough, there they were when I woke to Janice screaming downstairs. She was so mad she picked up this porcelain heart off a shelf—it had belonged to my grandma, who had died—and smashed it on the kitchen tile. I was grounded for a month."

"How did you know Jeff did it?"

"I saw him," I said, remembering. "I didn't realize it at the time, but I'd looked out my bedroom window the night before and saw him kneeling in the backyard long after everyone had gone to bed. I had no clue what he was up to until the next morning."

"Damn... I had no idea it was so bad for you at home. Wren

mentioned a few times how much you detested your stepmom, but... that's just crazy."

I let out a long breath, picturing again Janice and Jeff stepping out of my dad's car earlier that day. "Wren was my lifeline," I murmured. "I don't know how I would have made it through those years without her."

"She thought you were the best thing since ice cream."

I smiled. "She loved her ice cream, didn't she?"

"Obnoxiously so," he said. "I'd be lucky to get a single bowl when my mom brought home a gallon of Neapolitan. And the bowl I got was vanilla because she ate all the strawberry and chocolate."

I laughed. "And she'd get those brain freezes and clutch her head and roll around on the ground. We laughed so much. We could just look at each other and fall down laughing."

"Yeah." Dorian smiled, but sadness dragged the corners of his mouth down. "Man, I wish Rylie could have known her better and vice versa. That Wren could have..." His voice broke, and he angled his face away from me.

"Want some tea?" I murmured, considering my pizza and then standing and heading for the kitchen.

He swiped at his eyes and nodded. "Sure. Caffeine-free, though."

"How about this one? The opposite of caffeine." I held up a canister of tea Dr. Fry had given me called Chill.

"Perfect. I've been stressing about a flood of tourists that are coming in for that country music concert at the casino. I've booked eight rentals in the last forty-eight hours."

"Oh, wow, that many? Who's performing?"

Dorian shrugged and stood. "The Truck Stop Boys or the Pickup Truck Boys. I don't remember, but apparently, they're popular."

I put the tea kettle on the stove and twisted the knob on the burner. "I miss live music," I sighed.

Dorian looked at me, surprised. "You do? I mean, not that... I don't know why I said that. I just haven't heard you say you've missed much in the outside world since..."

I took mugs from the cupboard and popped the lid on the canister of tea. "Yeah, I'm surprised to hear myself say it. I don't miss the big crowd of people. The thought of that..." I shuddered. "But the aliveness, the energy, I miss that."

"I think that's a good thing," Dorian said. "You missing stuff you used to do."

"Yeah—probably."

Dorian plopped his pizza on his plate and stood. "I've got to hit the bathroom." He disappeared down the hall.

I added satchels of tea—a blend of kava root, cinnamon and ginger —to our cups.

Dorian emerged a moment later, wearing a puzzled expression. "Why is your bathroom mirror covered?" he asked.

I poured hot water into our mugs. "Because I'm sick of looking at myself."

He stared at me, skeptical. "Does this have something to do with what you saw the other night? The guy."

I carried the mugs to the couch and set them on coasters I'd knitted on the coffee table. "Pretty much."

"Have you seen him again?"

I sat back and propped my socked feet on the edge of the table. "Not exactly."

I'd seen him. I'd sensed him. He was everywhere and nowhere. He was a waterlogged voodoo doll buried in my closet. He was a figment of my imagination. He was a ghost.

"What does that mean?"

I sighed and scratched at my neck until Dorian's eyes drifted to my hands. I leaned forward and picked up my tea, cupping it tightly in my palms despite the heat of the mug. "I don't know. I haven't been sleeping very well. I've heard things. I'm sure it's a lack of sleep messing with my head."

"Did you tell Dr. Fry about it?"

"No. I will on our next call."

Dorian lifted his tea and sipped it. "I'm not sure covering your mirror is the best plan. Have you looked at your hair lately?" He grinned.

I touched my hair and felt it sticking out at funny angles. I shrugged. "Whatever. I gave up on beauty contests a long time ago. I need to cut it. It's getting too long."

"It's barely past your ears."

"I know. It's tickling them." I fluttered a piece of hair near my right ear.

"Want me to cut it?" he asked.

I frowned. "I've butchered it enough. I don't think your handiwork will improve the job."

"For your information, I have an aunt who does hair. She taught me how to cut hair years ago."

"Aunt Josie? The one who styles her hair in a bouffant?"

"It's a classic," he argued. "Come on, where are your scissors?"

I grimaced and slouched lower on the couch. "I prefer to cut my hair alone."

"Good luck with that when your mirror is covered. Come on, how much damage can I do?"

I frowned. "Fine. They're in the bathroom. The little blue and green striped bag in the closet."

Dorian stood and walked to the bathroom. I moved into the kitchen and dragged a chair to the middle of the floor.

Dorian returned with the bag and a towel. "Have a seat, Glo. Let's see if we can't make you look like a girl again."

"Very funny."

I sat, and he draped the towel around my shoulders. His fingers brushed my neck and a flicker of alarm jolted through me. He felt it and steadied his hands on my shoulders.

"Are you okay?"

"Yeah. I'm good." No one had touched my neck in more than a year. Not since the last of my doctor's visits checking to make sure wounds had healed and stitches had dissolved.

12

———

Dorian ran a comb through my hair, tugging on a snarl.

"Ouch," I muttered. I reached back and grabbed the comb. "I'll do this part," I told him, brushing the tangles free.

He pushed his fingers through my hair, the sensation sending little currents through my body. It wasn't Dorian himself, but touch in general. I no longer experienced regular touch—arms brushing against mine, hands clasping in handshakes, hugs.

Rylie often hugged me, but everyone else kept their physical distance as if the attack had left me not only with physical and emotional wounds, but wrapped in a bubble of fragility that no one dared breach.

"Close your eyes. I'm going to comb your hair in front of your face."

I closed my eyes and wrinkled my nose as hair tickled my nostrils.

The cool of the metal scissors touched my forehead. Snip-snip-snip. I imagined bits of my hair floating feather-light to the linoleum below.

"You have purple dye in here," Dorian said, brushing hair off my forehead.

I opened my eyes and tilted my head to look in the bag he'd set on the table. "Yeah, it was… Wren's idea. I can't believe it's still in there. I never ended up using it, obviously."

"Purple, huh? I could see that being a good look for you."

I laughed, but my eyes stayed glued to the tube. "Okay. Let's do it."

72

"Really? It might be too old." He picked up the tube. "It expired four months ago."

"It's fine."

"Do you have any latex gloves?"

"There are rubber gloves under the sink."

"All right, you sure about this?" Dorian walked to the sink and grabbed the elbow-length yellow gloves. He rinsed them in the sink and then slid them on.

"Sure. Why not? No one will see it but you."

He grinned. "And Rylie, and your dad and Dr. Fry, and everyone at Black Rock Outfitters during your meetings."

"They'll probably be excited. Take it as a sign I'm putting some effort into my appearance again."

Dorian took a glass bowl from the cupboard and mixed the color into it. He clipped my towel around my neck.

"Time to go punk," he said, adding a glob of dye to my hair and combing it in.

He finished adding color, and we waited the customary thirty-five minutes for the dye to set. While we waited, we finished our tea and talked about all the projects he had to coordinate to have the properties ready for the weekend.

The timer buzzed, and he stood, clapping his hands. "It's show-time." He started down the hall.

"Where are you going?" I asked.

"The bathroom. We've got to rinse it out. You can lean back over the tub."

The slippery arms reaching up and pulling me beneath the water slithered into my mind and I hung back. I didn't want to go in there, but I didn't want to tell Dorian that.

I heard the water turn on in the bathroom and, gritting my teeth, I walked down the hall.

He kneeled on the rug near the bath, holding his hand beneath the flow of water. "Perfect," he said. "Here, sit with your back against the side of the tub and tilt your head back."

I sat down and released my head back, exposing my neck.

A terrible flash of the dark night swept through me, the monster yanking my head back by my hair, a burning as he slashed a blade across my throat.

I lurched forward, clutching my neck with both hands.

"Shit… okay. It's okay," Dorian said, pressing his hand on my back. "Just breathe, okay? I'm sorry, that was a stupid idea."

Black spots prickled my vision, but I focused my eyes on the grout between the tiles, the little bits of dirt that had imbedded there. After a minute, I felt the rising panic ebb away.

"I'm all right," I said. "I'll kneel and lean forward into the tub."

"Yeah. That's better. Are you sure?"

I glanced at him. "What's the alternative? Leave this dye in until my hair falls out?"

"Well, I could run home and get my electric razor and buzz it off."

"And reveal my misshapen head? No, thank you." I hunched forward over the side of the bathtub, counting my breaths to keep my brain from rewinding back to my terrifying bath days before.

Dorian poured cupfuls of hot water over my head. I cracked my eyes and watched the purple swirl into the drain. He finished and grabbed the towel and roughly dried my hair.

"You're going to have to take the sheet off your mirror if you want to see how it looks," Dorian told me, securing the towel on my head.

I scowled and wondered suddenly if the whole hair ordeal had been an attempt by Dorian to get me to uncover my mirror. "All right, fine."

He stood and stepped to the mirror. I followed. He tugged the sheet from the glass and stepped aside, allowing me to take his place before the mirror.

"Ta-da!" He yanked the towel free.

I stared at my reflection as Dorian grinned over my shoulder. My hair was damp and shorter than it had ever been, a pixie-style cut. It was also purple. My skin looked especially pale against my purple hair, my cheekbones hollow, my eyes big.

Dorian slowly rotated me to face him. He brushed his fingers through my hair and his eyes lingered on mine for a moment. He turned me back toward the glass. "What do you think?"

"I like it," I admitted. And I did. I felt like I was looking at a stranger. It was a relief in some ways. "I look like a different person."

"Gloria two-point-oh," he said.

"Three-point-oh," I corrected him. "Two-point-oh walked out of the hospital two years ago. This is a new version."

"An upgrade," he said, winking at me in the mirror.

His phone buzzed, and he took it from his pocket, read the message that had come in. "I've got to go. My mom is bringing Rylie home in twenty minutes. I'll call you tomorrow, okay?"

"Yeah. Thanks for the new look." I glanced at the sheet, considered returning it to the mirror, and then ignored it. I might put it back on, but I'd wait until Dorian had left.

As I followed him toward the door, he pointed at the pizza. "Eat some of that, okay? You look like you've lost more weight."

"Doubtful," I said. "It's this new hairstyle. It's slimming."

He chuckled and unlocked the deadbolts on my door. "Don't forget to call your dad tomorrow."

"I won't," I assured him.

I locked the doors behind him, then moved to my bedroom, switched off the light and picked up my binoculars. It took a moment to adjust to the darkness and then to find the brick building. Finally, I did, and I homed in on the Twiggy Twins' window. It was dark. No light, no movement, nothing.

A sound pulled me from sleep and I jerked awake and sat up on the couch. The television was on low, still playing episodes of *Gilmore Girls*.

It came again, a rattling. Someone was shaking my doorknob. I leapt off the couch and stared at the knob twisting back and forth. This was an old house with two apartments, one on the ground floor and mine on the second floor. This wasn't some drunk person confusing my door with their own.

It was intentional.

Suddenly, the bolts slid open as if the person out there had the key. Dorian? But no. I knew it wasn't Dorian. He'd never show up in the middle of the night and let himself in.

My breath stilled as the last bolt slid aside. My heart thudded faster, and all feeling fled from my limbs. I couldn't run for the bear spray or the butcher knife or the taser. I did nothing as the knob turned and the door swung in.

I opened my mouth to scream, found the sound as frozen as my body.

The door creaked on its hinges and stopped. The hall beyond the door stood empty. Nothing moved. No one stood in the hallway, but the smell hit me. His smell. Cigarettes and sweat and cologne.

And then he was there, stepping through my door and slipping past me, his heavy boots not making a sound. He didn't turn to look at me, didn't twitch when I released a startled gasp.

He continued forward, black eyes fixed on something I couldn't see. The black and red scorpion on his neck pulsed in technicolor to my bulging eyes. As he moved down my hallway, I stared, transfixed, at his head.

A massive hole with shards of bone and lumpy gray matter was all that remained of the back of his skull.

13

______

For several minutes I stared down my hallway seeing the man, the monster, with his skull ripped away though he'd already vanished.

Quietly, as if my movements might summon him back from whatever hell he'd returned to, I crept to the closet and crawled inside.

∽

I dreamed of hiking.

In my dream, the uneven ground was firm beneath my hiking boots. I smelled dank earth and decayed leaves, pine forests, mossy bark, the fresh, muddy smell of rushing water. I walked slowly. I leaned down and picked wild flowers. I sat on slabs of warm rock and tilted my face to the sun. I jogged to propel myself up a hill, my quads burning, my eyes longing for the vista over the next ridge.

When I woke from the dream, I was swimming in tranquility and then I blinked into the dark and terror swept over me. Was I in the woods? Fumbling in the shadows, arms bound, blood pouring from a wound in my neck?

The present moment crept in and took hold. I lay in my hallway closet, curled into a fetal position, and as I unwound myself, my legs and arms shrieked in protest.

I was not in the forest, as lovely as it was in the dream. I was safe, surrounded by walls and locks. My cell phone was wedged beneath me.

In the time before that night, nowhere on Earth had felt safer than the woods. The only predators there walked on four legs and were more afraid of me than I of them. They didn't carry knives or twine or rags to shove in someone's mouth. They were often loud, sniffling and bumbling. Only once had I come upon a bear, a black bear, and I'd slid my camera out and taken his photo. He'd paused from his foraging in a bush and looked me dead in the eyes. There had been no malice there, no cruelty, no evil. He'd stared at me and I at him, and then he'd lumbered away and vanished into the forest. I'd never even touched the canister of bear spray strapped to my backpack.

Now the woods were the home where evil lived, where it could hide and watch and creep in.

Fumbling in the dark, I found the handle of the door. The door swung out, and I spilled into my hallway, standing on pins and needles. Hands braced against the wall, I hobbled to my living room.

A glow of pink light streamed beneath my window curtains. My apartment door was closed and locked. I'd done it the night before and then, terrified, I'd run to my closet and scrunched myself inside, eventually falling asleep.

I paid for that choice with cramped legs and knees that popped every time I took a step.

I shuffled to the kitchen and brewed coffee. Sipping from my mug, I went to the large living room windows and opened the curtains. I needed light and fresh air to clear the fog crowding my head. I unlocked one window and opened it halfway, sat in my chair and leaned into the warm morning. I inhaled, smelled fresh-cut grass and the distant lake.

At the end of the block, a car slowed at the stop sign, their windows down. Music blasted from the interior.

The song "Gloria" reverberated up to me. My stomach clenched. I remembered Wren singing that song on our drive to the festival, happy, oblivious to what lay ahead. She used to sing it a lot and complain that no one had ever written a song called "Wren." I'd told her she had a whole bird who shared her name, who needed a song?

I closed the window and backed away. The sun now seemed too bright, too penetrating. I locked the window and closed the curtains, retreating to my computer. I'd only just gotten logged in when I looked back at the window and couldn't remember if I'd locked it. I stood, returned to the window and reached behind the curtain, not looking out. The lock was tight in place.

The coffee kicked in and I managed a half hour of work for Black Rock and then opened a separate window and stared at the blank search bar. I couldn't go on like this, sleepless, terrified, waiting for another appearance from the man.

I considered the right search terms, didn't have a clue what those might be and opted for 'voodoo doll haunting.'

The results included true stories of voodoo dolls, tutorials on making voodoo dolls, and websites that sold the dolls.

I deleted my previous search and typed 'how to destroy a voodoo doll.'

Halfway down the results page, I read the headline 'Paranormal Investigator Tells Harrowing Story of Voodoo Doll Curse.'

I clicked it and read a story about a paranormal investigator named Heidi Ketchum who'd been summoned to Florida by a woman who insisted she'd been gifted a strange doll and feared it was cursed. Three times the doll had moved locations within the house and each time some tragedy had befallen the woman. The first time she'd broken her leg, the second her cat had been hit by a car and the third she'd grown ill with a terrible fever and had to be hospitalized for a week. Ketchum had agreed the doll was cursed and performed a ritual to destroy the curse and the woman had been happily curse-free for more than a year.

I chewed my thumbnail and considered the story, torn between my usual skepticism and a sense that if I didn't do something soon, I'd be dealing with similar tragedies.

I returned to the search bar and typed the name of the paranormal investigator: 'Heidi Ketchum.'

A website that included a location in Alabama and a phone number came back. I dialed the phone number.

"Paranormal inquiries," a woman answered.

"Yes, hi. I'm hoping to speak with Heidi."

"Your wish is granted."

"Oh, wow, great. Umm… I found you online because I have a… a problem, I guess, with a voodoo doll."

"Someone has placed a curse on you?"

"No, actually… I made a voodoo doll and then I drowned it, but now the person I was trying to banish seems to be… umm… haunting me." Color climbed into my face and I wondered at my embarrassment. The woman, after all, was a self-proclaimed paranormal investigator. She probably received bizarre calls daily.

"I see. To be clear, are you saying this person is haunting you in terms of showing up where you are, calling, antagonizing you or—"

"No. I think he's… actually haunting me. Like his spirit."

"He's deceased then?"

"I think so." I remembered the back of his skull and cringed.

"How is it that you're not sure?"

"Well, I didn't know him. I only encountered him one time two years ago. I have no idea who he is."

"Then how did you create and name a doll in his likeness?"

"I thought about him."

"Hmm… this is a conundrum. Perhaps the first place to start is by finding out if he is in fact dead. A simple online search for a death record or grave—"

"I don't know his name."

"You need his name, dear. A curse is a powerful thing and to create and destroy, you must call the individual by name."

"But I never named him and still—"

"And still you drew him to you? It appears you have, and that may be the crux of the issue. The creation of the curse was incomplete. To cast such a curse, or, in your case, a banishing spell, we must invoke the spirit of the entity and then we can cast our spell—banishment. Your spell was fractured because you did not identify him by name. That is your task now. Find his name."

"Any spells to help me do that?" I asked, mostly sarcastically, but not entirely.

The woman didn't speak, and I thought she'd hung up. Then her voice came through loud and clear. "Ask him."

"But how do I—"

"Speak to the entity who reveals himself to you."

"Oh, okay."

I ended the call with the sense that I'd stepped into an alternate reality where magic and ghosts were as common as pine trees and deer. Except no one in my life knew they existed but me.

The closest I'd come to a magical experience was the woman I'd met on the Appalachian Trail who had pulled out a small leather bag and removed a stack of tarot cards bound by a rubber band.

"I read my cards daily," she'd told me. "I like to get a sense of what's ahead on the trail. Shall I read yours?"

"Why not?" I'd said, not having a genuine sense one way or another about the efficacy of tarot—though I doubted they'd reveal anything significant.

She shuffled the deck and pressed three cards face down.

"Past, present, future," she said, tapping the backs of the cards, which were navy blue with the faces of the moon in a circle of waxing and waning white slivers and orbs.

She flipped each card. I could no longer recall what the first two cards had been, but I remembered the third in my future position. The Tower, she'd labeled it. "Many associate it with doom, grief, but ultimately it represents significant change, an unalterable life shift."

And that had been that. We'd switched to talk of the best viewing places in the days ahead and a little store at the end of my hike on the trail that contained all types of unusual and fun gifts, a pleasant way to end my journey and perhaps get a keepsake to remember it.

I shifted back to my computer and tried to imagine how I could possibly track the man who'd attacked us. The one identifying feature I'd noticed on the man in the mirror was a tattoo on his neck—a red and black scorpion. That was something I could work with, something tangible to potentially identify him.

I looked up tattoo parlors in the Upper Peninsula. There were more than I expected, but I narrowed it down by searching for tattoo shops in the cities within an hour of the Porcupine Mountains. I scrolled through their image galleries, but didn't find the red and black scorpion. It was possible that the man had visited one and taken his own artwork, but I was hoping they'd have posted it in their portfolio. The ones that had Facebook pages, I scanned those too. No luck.

An hour later an email came in from Arthur, my boss at Black Rock. 'Hey. Can you do inventory ASAP? Thanks.'

Shit. I'd forgotten about the inventory, which I usually had finished days before he needed it. I logged into the store and started comparing the amounts in stock with the physical inventory submitted by staff.

For the next two hours, I was consumed in numbers, sending the final inventory to Arthur just after noon.

My phone rang. Dorian's name appeared on the screen.

"Hi," I answered.

"Hey. How's it going?"

"Fine. Tired, but finally got the inventory entered for Black Rock and didn't fall asleep halfway through."

Dorian chuckled, but it sounded forced. "Listen, I got a call this morning."

"Okay."

"From a detective."

14

———

I frowned and pressed the phone harder against my ear.

"He wants to meet, to talk to you."

I shifted in my chair, my head growing light. "About... I mean did they find something?"

"No. Actually—" In the background someone yelled Dorian's name. Dorian swore under his breath. "Shit, sorry, Glo. The handyman just got to the rental and needs help finding the electrical panel. I've got to deal with this right now. The detective wants to talk to you this afternoon. I'll come too. Is that okay?"

"Oh, well—"

"I've got to go. Text and let me know."

He hung up before I could answer. I set the phone on my desk and stared at it. My neck itched. My body felt grimy, my hair greasy. My usual two-plus showers a day had been tempered by the man in the mirror, but suddenly the need to shower overwhelmed me. I'd scratch my own skin off if I didn't shower.

I grabbed a blanket from the back of the couch and held it up as I pushed into the bathroom. I secured it over the glass and turned on the faucet. I stood beneath the hot spray, replaying Dorian's words in my head.

The police had never had any leads, never named a suspect. They'd never found Wren's body. The only reason I'd lived was because I'd clawed my way out of that black night. The police hadn't been much help then and now, two years later, I doubted they'd ever find out who attacked us. But maybe they had. Maybe they'd found the man who was haunting my apartment.

I frowned, scrubbing at my hair, and mouthed the word 'haunting.' Was that what was happening? Was he a ghost? Had he died and perhaps left a note, a confession that it had been him, that he'd murdered Wren? No. The man leering at me in the mirror, the man who'd attacked us that night brutally, who'd tried to kill us both without mercy did not have a conscience. He was not a man who'd sit down and pen a confession.

A terrible loneliness overcame me as I thought of my tiny world growing more claustrophobic by the day. I missed Wren so much it hurt. If he was a ghost, the only person I could have confided such a thing to had died at his hand.

I could have told Wren about the ghost. Wren would have believed me. She would have gotten excited, insist we get a Ouija board and make contact. She would not have looked at me as if I were insane—the way I found myself considering my own reflection in the mirror.

Are you going crazy? Was this the next stage of PTSD, of trauma? Was this part of the healing or was this evidence that what had occurred that night had truly destroyed me? Was I destined to live the rest of my life in a slow descent into madness?

With Wren gone, Dorian was my best friend, but he wasn't Wren. He didn't share her intense curiosity, her willingness to believe anything—seen and unseen.

If I told Dorian about the doll and now the ghost, it would trouble him, keep him up nights until he finally sat me down and insisted I tell my therapist. Dr. Fry would talk in circles about the ghost until we came to some reasonable conclusion and the only reasonable conclusion was that it was a figment of my imagination. Except it wasn't.

The ghost was the man who'd abducted us and murdered Wren.

I rinsed the shampoo from my hair and added another dollop to my hand, lathered up a second time, grateful to scrub clean after sitting in my own filth. I hadn't truly been filthy. Normal people went two or three days without showering all the time, but I didn't. Not anymore.

I tilted my face beneath the water and it suddenly turned ice cold. I leapt back, nearly slipped on the slick tub floor, but managed to grab the safety bar attached to the tiled wall. I grimaced and twisted around the icy spray to turn the faucet to full hot. The water didn't grow warmer.

"Shit," I muttered, cranking the faucet off. I'd never run out of hot water in the house. I shared a tank with my downstairs neighbor but he traveled so much it was rarely used.

After the shower, I towel-dried my newly purple hair and ignored the covered mirror, brushing my teeth without gazing at my reflection.

I pushed into my bedroom and, still in my towel, stepped to the window, grabbing the binoculars. I searched for my former apartment and studied the window. The day was overcast and I could see nothing inside. I dropped the focus to the backyard. Wyatt stood on the back deck smoking a cigarette. No one else in sight.

I sighed and replaced the binoculars and walked to my closet. The carpet in front of the closet door was soaked. The carpet squished beneath my bare feet.

"Ugh…" I muttered, moving back and stretching to open the closet door. The logical explanation was a leak, but there weren't exactly water pipes in the closet. I stared at the ceiling. No telltale mark, no sagging drywall.

I checked the hall, but the carpet leading from the bathroom was dry.

Back in the closet, I flipped on the light and searched for the source of the water. Nothing was wet. My shoeboxes sat stacked in the top of the closet, my clothes hanging from the bar beneath.

As I stepped further in, I realized where the water emerged from— beneath the heavy wool blanket I'd thrown over the plastic box containing the voodoo doll. Had water seeped out from the still-wet doll?

Reluctantly, I dug the box out and pried it open. The doll lay inside, dry as a bone.

~

Dorian arrived with the detective just after three in the afternoon. I opened the door to find Dorian standing next to a well-built man in his forties with dark hair.

"Hi, Gloria. I'm Detective Dan Webb." The man extended his hand.

I shook it and stepped aside so they could walk in. "Umm…" I gestured at the couch. "We can sit here."

Webb waited for Dorian and I to settle on the couch, then he pulled an armchair close to the coffee table and sat across from us.

"Have you just taken over the case? Is that why you're here?" I asked.

Webb shook his head. "No. Your case is still with the Ontonagon sheriff's office, since that's the jurisdiction where the crime occurred. I'm a detective here in Marquette and another young woman has disappeared here in town and I believe it may be linked to your and Wren's abduction."

I stiffened, glancing at Dorian, who looked as surprised as me. Apparently, Webb had not told him about the development.

Dan flipped open a notebook and took out a photograph. He set it on the coffee table between us.

My stomach lurched. I turned away from the photo, felt a cold sweat break out beneath my arms.

It was the Twiggy Twin, Kelly.

Dead, she's dead, I wanted to say, though I had no reason to believe that. Maybe she'd taken off, hitched a ride with some hot guy and was speeding down a freeway with the wind blowing back her long hair.

"Holy shit," Dorian breathed. "It's Kelly."

"You know her?" Webb asked.

"I just met her the other day. She was rollerblading outside here. She lives in Gloria and Wren's old apartment."

I clutched the sofa beneath me, allowed my eyes to drift closed. I'd witnessed it. Whatever it was, I'd witnessed it and I hadn't called the police, hadn't done anything.

"Is that… why you think she's connected to what happened to us?" I asked. "Because she lives in our old apartment?"

"That's part of it. It's unusual, that's for sure. We suspect… we think it's possible the same individual is behind it."

Can't be. He's been here with me most nights, lurking in the shadows in the corner of my room, leering at me from the mirror. Would you like to talk to his voodoo doll?

I stifled the bubble of hysterical laughter that ballooned in my chest.

"There hasn't been anything in the paper," Dorian said. "Why not? When did she go missing?"

"The last confirmed sighting of her was three days ago. Her roommate was out of town, returned last night and she wasn't there. The apartment appeared to be intact, but… there were a few oddities."

"Like what?" Dorian asked.

"Nothing I'm at liberty to discuss at this time," Webb told him.

"Something's off here," Dorian said, voice rising. "She just went missing. There's nothing in the paper. For all you know she took off for a week vacation with her boyfriend and yet here you are at Gloria's. Why?"

Dan drew out a clear plastic bag and set it on the table before me. "Do you recognize this?" he asked me.

My breath caught and my pulse quickened. I looked away, tried to unsee it, to resist the memory that accompanied it.

A silver necklace, the chain long and thick, with a silver mermaid perched on an opalesque sphere—a moonstone. Wren had been wearing it that night—she wore it most nights. Rarely had taken it off since I'd given it to her. I'd bought the necklace at the quirky little shop at the end of my hike on the Appalachian Trail. It was filled with oddities, new and old. Antique lamps, paperbacks, goods created by local vendors—candles, soaps and teas. The mermaid necklace had hung from a branch of a lamp carved from driftwood. It had caught the light from the lamp and the moonstone had shimmered. It had been so strange to see the necklace I'd immediately picked it up and bought it for Wren.

The shop owner had told me it had come from an estate sale. It was a unique piece, maybe even one of a kind.

I'd last seen it the dark night. Seen it tangled and resting on Wren's chest, where blood soaked the front of her shirt. Seen it for only a moment in the moon's light that made the stone glow as I'd fled the forest.

15

Dorian moved closer to me, took my hand and held it between his.

"I don't understand," I whispered, my eyes drifting back to the necklace.

"We found it in Kelly's room tucked in a nightstand drawer."

"It's the one you gave Wren, isn't it?" Dorian asked.

I could feel his stare, his eyes searching my expression.

I nodded. "Yes, but... Wren was wearing it. It has to be... a duplicate or something."

"We've sent it to forensics for testing. There was... dark material on the chain and the charm."

"Dark material?" Dorian asked. "You mean... blood?"

"We don't know for certain yet, but we will. You may be right and it has nothing to do with Wren's disappearance, but... In the drawer next to the charm was a newspaper article printed about your and Wren's abduction. She'd circled an excerpt about Wren in the article, which described the mermaid necklace."

"I still don't understand. Do you think the guy planted it in her apartment?"

Dan leaned back in his chair and crossed his thigh on his knee. "That's one possibility. Another is that she knew the man who attacked you and he gave it to her."

My chest felt tight. My lungs had contracted behind my ribs and

88

didn't inflate at full capacity when I took a breath. I closed my eyes and willed the breath in.

"Breathe through your nose," Dorian said, rubbing his thumb across my knuckles. "Slow and steady. Remember what Dr. Fry said. It's not that you're not getting enough air. You're getting too much."

But it didn't feel that way. It felt like I wasn't getting any air—like I was suffocating. I stood quickly, searching for… what? A way out? What an absurd thought. I whirled around, hand pressed against my chest, gulping for air.

The detective stood and moved across my apartment. Dorian too was standing, telling me to slow my breath, to whistle air through my lips. The many tips Fry had given us both for panic attacks. But none of it mattered, not if I couldn't breathe. Dark spots danced behind my eyes. I swayed on my feet.

Suddenly, something frigid and wet was shoved into my hands. I blinked and saw the detective before me. He had one hand on my bicep, the other hand pressed into my palm.

"Ice," he said loudly and, through the wind tunnel that had become my ears, I heard him.

Cold, slick. I felt the heat of our hands melting the ice.

"Just feel it," he said.

I concentrated on the ice. It burned my palm, but slowly the breath whooshed back in. The dizziness slid away. I sank onto the couch next to Dorian. My hand was wet.

"Do you need another ice cube?" Webb asked.

I shook my head, wiped my wet hand on my t-shirt.

"I'm okay. It's getting better." My eyes darted to the table, but the picture of the necklace was gone. Either Dorian or the detective had pushed it out of sight.

"Do you want some water?" Dorian asked.

I shook my head. "I'm good. Really." I brushed both hands back through my hair and then rubbed at the scar on my neck. "Where did you learn that?" I asked the detective. "The ice thing?"

"My mother suffered from panic attacks. Ice nearly always helped. If there was no ice, some other sensation-based object could help draw her out of it."

"She doesn't have them anymore?" I asked.

Webb stayed silent for a moment. He shook his head. "She died a long time ago."

"Oh... I'm sorry."

"Sorry for your loss," Dorian added.

"It's been years, decades, in fact. It gets better."

"Does it?" Dorian asked.

I glanced at him, saw the drawn expression on his face and thought of Wren. I couldn't imagine my memories of her dulling, slipping away, but they had, hadn't they? Already the memories of her laugh, her voice, the notes of her music as she played were less poignant than they'd once been. Did the loss of grief come only if we lost the memories as well?

"Did you know Kelly?" Webb asked.

I glanced at Dorian, went to tug on my hair and found it too short to grab hold of. "Umm... not exactly." My face grew warm. "Sometimes I saw her through binoculars. My bedroom window faces their building, their apartment. Wren and I loved it so much there that... sometimes I just like to look at it again."

"I see. But you'd never met Kelly?"

"No."

"Did you look at her apartment three nights ago?"

I bit my lip, remembered the light going dark.

"Yes," Dorian exclaimed, shifting to gape at me. "Oh, my God. Right? That was the night you said someone was behind her and the apartment went dark."

Webb's eyes widened, and he leaned forward in his chair.

I picked at my lip, pulled out a few eyelashes. "Yeah. I think that was the night. I was, umm... just watching through the window and I could see one of the Twigs on the couch. Kelly, I could see Kelly."

"One of the Twigs?" Webb asked.

I stared down at her picture, frowned, stuffed my hands beneath me on the couch, pulled one free and stuck the edge of my thumbnail in my mouth. "That's what I nicknamed them. The Twiggy Twins. The two girls who lived there."

Dorian stood and walked to my desk, grabbed the two stress ball kitties and returned them to me.

"Thanks," I murmured, taking them and squeezing them in my fists. "So... I was watching through the window and I saw Kelly on the couch. It looked like she was studying."

Webb nodded, took notes on a yellow legal pad.

"And she, umm... got up and walked to the window and looked out and then I saw someone behind her, but they were too far back for me to see clearly, just a dark shape, and then the lights went out."

"You didn't see anything at all distinguishing about the person in the back? If they seemed tall, short? Male, female?"

I shook my head. "It happened so quickly. I just sort of caught the movement and then the apartment went dark."

Webb sighed and tapped his pen a few times. "Okay. Well, that's interesting news. And you didn't see the light come back on?"

"No."

"Approximately what time did you witness this?"

I thought of that night, the scare in the bathtub followed by the scene at the window. "It must have been about midnight. Dorian left around eleven and it was maybe an hour after that."

Webb shifted his gaze to Dorian. "You were here that night?"

Dorian nodded. "I'm here pretty much every night. Since Gloria doesn't leave, I bring her stuff, help her out."

"You don't leave your apartment?" Webb asked.

I shook my head. "Not really, no."

"Okay. Dorian, what did you do after you left here that night?"

"Went home and went to bed."

"And where is home?"

"I own a house on Dune Street."

"Were you alone that night?"

"No. My girlfriend, Val, came over, but it was later after the bars closed, two-thirty probably."

"And she could verify that?"

"Yeah. Of course." Dorian shifted beside me.

"Back to what you witnessed, Gloria. Did it appear that Kelly spoke to anyone while you were watching or knew that someone else was in the apartment?"

"No, but... I'd only watched for maybe a minute when the lights went out. No one saw her after that day?"

Webb shook his head. "She worked at a parking garage until five o'clock that day. Wyatt Meyer, one of the other tenants, saw her return home after work. They chatted briefly outside and then she went in and that was the last confirmed sighting."

I squeezed and released the kitties. "I should have called," I whispered.

Webb said nothing, but Dorian slipped an arm around my back and squeezed. "You couldn't have known, Glo. When you told me, I figured it was nothing."

"Now what?" I asked Webb. "What's the next step in finding Kelly?"

Webb sighed and leaned forward, picking up Kelly's photo as if he intended to return it to his folder, but then he set it back on my table. I wondered what else the folder contained.

"We have a ground search scheduled for this weekend. The apartment search will end today or tomorrow. Her parents are doing a press conference tomorrow morning and the news will release a front-page story. Word has gone out on social media and we're hitting the pavement, talking to everyone who knew her and who might have witnessed something. This is helpful." He gestured at the legal pad. "Plus, if Kelly's case is linked to yours, that gives us a place to start."

"And if it's not?"

Dan stood and picked up his folder. "Then it's not." He took out his wallet and pulled a wrinkled, coffee-stained card from an inner pocket. "That's my direct line," he told me. "The one beneath that is for the Marquette Police Department. If you think of anything, call me. Even if it seems irrelevant. Okay?"

I took the card and set it on the coffee table. "Sure. Thanks for the ice cube."

"Happy it helped." He started toward my door and Dorian followed him.

"I'll walk you out," Dorian said.

I watched them through the window, my stomach knotty, acidic. I'd witnessed her abduction. I'd witnessed it and hadn't helped her.

I imagined what it felt like to stand out there with the sun on my shoulders, the smell of flowers in the air. My chest constricted and a terrible sense of the vast cruel world fell over me. No walls, doors, locks. A void, an endless empty abyss where anything could step in and take hold of you, drag you into the darkness.

I whipped the curtain closed and tried to catch my breath. I was on the edge of a panic attack, seeing the black pinpricks tunneling my vision. I braced my hand against the wall and shuffled to the couch, slumped down and pulled my afghan into a ball at my chest.

Dorian walked in and sat beside me. "What do you think?" he asked.

I pushed the blanket aside, feeling calmer, drew my knees into my chest and rested my chin on them. "I don't know. It's... so unreal. The guy who took Wren and I waited two years to do it again? Then he plants Wren's necklace as if he wants to get caught? Kidnaps someone from our same apartment? We were hours away in the Porcupine Mountains. I just… I don't get it."

I bit back all the other problems with the scenario—primarily that the man who'd murdered Wren had been visiting me nightly, had likely died and I'd summoned him back with a voodoo doll.

"Maybe it's what Detective Webb said. The guy who attacked you guys knew Kelly."

"That feels even more unlikely. These guys don't usually murder women they know. They're crimes of opportunity. That guy saw us walking alone and grabbed us."

"You were walking alone in the middle of a forest and he just happened to have zip ties and a gun? His vehicle parked nearby?"

"Guys like that are prepared if the opportunity presents itself. They carry"—I gestured—"kits. You know? The police call them murder kits or whatever." The word 'murder' hung in the air and I wished I hadn't said it.

Dorian paced into the kitchen, stuffing his hands in the pockets of his jeans. "Still, it can't be a coincidence. She was abducted from your old apartment and she had Wren's necklace. You saw the picture. That was hers."

It was hers, undeniably, but a part of me wanted to deny it just the same. The glaring problem, the problem I couldn't name, was that the man who'd abducted us was haunting my apartment, and I felt sure that he was dead.

So how then had he taken Kelly just three days before?

"I feel like you don't want this to be the guy. Why?" Dorian demanded, leveling me with his eyes.

I pressed my forehead into my knees, tiredness dragging me down. I felt so heavy, so tired of it all.

"Because if it is him," I said, my voice muffled, "then Kelly is dead."

16

———————

That night I slept. I'd camped out on the couch, sure I'd spend the night tossing, images of Kelly Rice playing across the backs of my eyelids, but apparently the previous sleepless nights had finally caught up with me. I slept uninterrupted for nearly nine hours.

When I woke in the morning, I returned to my computer to search for Scorpion. I scoured the websites of every tattoo parlor in Michigan's Upper Peninsula.

I clicked the portfolio page for Savage Ink in Houghton and scanned images of tattoos: hummingbirds, watercolor flowers, initials, Americana. As I neared the bottom of the page, I stopped. A photograph of a man in profile took up one image, showing only the lower part of his face. I could see the curve of his ear and beneath that, tattooed on his neck, a red and black scorpion.

I clicked it. The image grew larger, but there was no description, only the name of the tattoo artist who'd done the tattoo: Levi Foley.

My fingers trembled as I scrolled the mouse back to the homepage. I stared at the phone number for the tattoo parlor. The discovery felt huge, but I knew it could be nothing. Scorpion might have seen the image on this very page and asked some other tattooist to recreate it.

"No… it's him," I murmured. Because it was. This wasn't someone else. I recognized the curve of his jaw, the lobe of his ear. This was the guy.

I dialed the number and listened to it ring three times, four. No one would answer. Would I leave a message?

"Savage Ink," a woman barked into the phone. She sounded out of breath.

"Hi... um... is Levi Foley there?"

"No, he's not in until the weekend."

"Oh... okay, well..."

Click. The woman hung up on me.

I frowned at my cell phone. "Great customer service," I muttered, and set the phone on my desk. I found the bio page for Levi Foley and clicked it. He looked to be in his forties with dark hair buzzed close to his head. Tattoos covered his neck and arms. He even had a tattoo near his temple, a crucifix.

I typed his name and 'Houghton, Michigan,' into the web browser. A page of listings came back. At the top was a news article about Savage Ink. Levi apparently was half-owner. Several listings came up that included phone numbers.

I dialed the number for a Levi Foley located on Honeycomb Lane in Houghton, Michigan, age forty-two.

"Hewo?" a child's voice answered.

"Oh, hi. Is Levi there?"

"Daddy!" the girl screamed.

I held the phone away from my ear.

"Maisy, I told you not to answer my phone," a man said in the background.

I heard rustling and then silence. Had he hung up?

"Hello?" a man asked.

"Hi. Is this Levi?"

"Yeah, who's calling?"

"My name is..." I almost said Gloria, and then I clamped my mouth shut. I didn't know this man. He could be best friends with Scorpion. He could know all about what had happened to Wren and me. "Anne. My name is Anne and I'm trying to track someone down, someone you tattooed. It would have been years ago. I'm hoping you might remember him."

"I can try. What tattoo did he get?"

"Daddy, cup-cup-cup-cup," Maisy boomed in the background.

"Honey, one minute, okay? Go ask Mommy. She's in the backyard.

Sorry about that," he told me. "My three-year-old is not one for waiting when she wants something."

"I can imagine." I tried to remember Rylie at three years old. Wren and I would have been sixteen, just getting our drivers' licenses. I had a vague memory of Rylie riding in the car with us, her car seat so huge in the backseat that Dorian and Wren's dad were squished against the doors on either side of her. She'd been a talker from the moment she could form words. Her first word had been 'no' sometime before she was one year old. I remembered her toddling about Wren's house, releasing a string of 'no-no-no' regardless of the question.

"What was that tattoo?" he asked.

"It was a red and black scorpion on the guy's neck."

The man was quiet, and I tensed, expecting him to start fishing, trying to determine who I was and what I knew. Maybe he'd been in on it. Maybe Levi and Scorpion were co-conspirators.

"Yeah... Let me think. I do remember that tattoo. Man, I must have done that five, maybe six years ago."

"What was his name?"

"Not a clue."

"Did you know him personally? Maybe from around town?"

"Nah. He wasn't local. He came in with a buddy. Hmm... I'll tell you what I can do. I'll be at the shop tomorrow. I can dig through the waivers and see if his name pops up."

"That'd be great. Thank you."

"Sure. Real quick, though. Why are you looking for this guy?"

"Oh, umm... I have a friend who saw the tattoo on your page and thinks she remembers a guy with that tattoo from college. She wanted to reconnect."

"Why didn't she call?"

"She's shy."

It was a ridiculous lie, and I waited for Levi to tell me as much. Instead, I heard his little girl in the background.

"Daddy... ook. A capperpipper."

"A caterpillar," he said. "Wow. A big fuzzy one. I don't think Mommy wants you to bring that in the house, Maisy. Better take it back to the yard." He returned to the phone. "Give me your number. I'll call if I track down a name."

"Great. Thank you." I gave him my phone number and hung up.

I was getting closer, but I knew it was possible he'd forget all about the call or, if he remembered, he might not be able to find the guy's forms.

Still, I felt better having made the call, better than I had in months. As if I were finally doing something that mattered.

I stood and paced to the window and back to my desk. I wanted to do more, keep the momentum going, but I couldn't think of any other way I might track the guy down.

I propped one foot on my window ledge and bent over, reaching for my toe. My legs ached. My whole body ached from a week of sleeping on the couch, plus a night curled in the closet.

In my former life, I'd worked out. I'd biked, hiked and hit the gym at NMU to lift weights. I'd stopped doing all of it after that night. Now my workouts included pacing around my apartment, but as I thought of Kelly Rice, abducted less than a block from my apartment, I felt the weakness in my arms and legs. I hated the way my spindly limbs swam in my baggy pants and long-sleeved t-shirt.

I moved onto all fours on the floor and then into the plank position. My arms shook as I lowered in a push-up. One… two… three.

I collapsed on my belly, turned my head to the side, and struggled for more air. After my pulse returned to normal, I did it again. I managed four push-ups the second time. I repeated the exercise until I'd done twenty push-ups, then I stood and did squats. My knees trembled and the muscles in my legs shrieked if I held the squat for more than three seconds, but I managed twenty-five of those.

I called Dorian.

"Hey, what's up?"

"Do you still have those free weights from our apartment?"

"Huh? Hold on. Todd, the shed is in the back. Yeah, thanks."

"Still hustling to get those properties ready?" I asked him.

"Every single day," he said. "We have a new lawn guy, so I'm trying to get him acquainted with where the equipment is at every house. It's a bit of a cluster with the cleaning crews here, too."

"I won't keep you, but do you remember the free weights? Wren and I had that little metal stand, and it had three sets of weights on it."

"Oh, yeah. I think it's in my parents' garage."

"Can you bring it the next time you come over?"

"Seriously? You want to start lifting weights?"

"Yep."

"Okay, yeah. I'll bring them by tomorrow after work. Val and I are taking Rylie to play miniature golf tonight."

"Perfect, thanks."

"Everything okay? Did something happen last night?"

"No. I just… I'm sick of feeling weak."

"That's good. This whole thing has really creeped me out. My mom thought you should come and stay with me and Rylie. She doesn't seem to grasp that you don't leave your apartment. I have to admit, I wish you could too. I'd feel a lot better if you were there with us."

I sighed and pulled on my eyelashes. "I know, me too. Someday soon, I hope."

"All right. In the meantime, keep your taser close by, don't answer the door for anyone. I know you're more careful than me, but… still."

"Thanks, and I appreciate you bringing those weights by."

17

———

After I completed my work for Black Rock, I started my search into Kelly Rice.

I opened up Facebook, wracking my brain for a username and password I hadn't typed in over two years.

Except for work, I mostly avoided the internet. Even before the dark night, I hadn't stayed up late surfing the web. I'd never been drawn to it the way so many of my generation were. On the rare occasions in my previous life that I spent an afternoon scrolling through social media profiles or reading eye-catching headlines, I tended to feel... empty. Afterward, when I'd walk out of our apartment into the sun or snow or rain, the sensation would feel jarring—as if I'd spent the previous hours living as a single-celled organism and I'd suddenly exploded into a billion cells in an instant.

Wren had spent more time on the web than me. She had a Facebook group of musicians who chatted daily. She helped host a weekly alternative music podcast with a couple of other friends from NMU. She'd heckled me about how I hadn't updated my Facebook profile picture since I was fifteen.

Now, as I typed in the correct username and password, a flood of notifications appeared on my long-neglected page. I ignored them and typed in 'Kelly Rice.'

A slew of results appeared, many with the words #BringHome-KellyRice.

I clicked on them, reading the pleas of Kelly's friends and family as they spoke of the kind, outgoing nineteen-year-old who loved horses and hoped to become a police officer.

'She lights up a room.'

'Kelly is an animal whisperer.'

'Kelly would give you her last dollar if you needed it.'

The words rang all too familiar, the kind of sentiments people shared about Wren, and they'd been true. Wren too had been uncommonly kind, giving of herself with little expectation of anything in return. She simply operated that way, always volunteering, offering, helping. Kelly Rice seemed to be woven of a similar cloth—a future police officer, a young woman who'd organized a horse therapy program in her home-town of Manistique.

The other Twiggy also had a Facebook page. Her name was Nicki Shrum. She'd recently changed her profile picture to one of her and Kelly sitting on a large gray outcropping of rock in Lake Superior, their long, tan bodies twisted in a sloppy hug.

I scrolled her posts, which were many, twenty a day and filled with crying emojis and pleas for anyone with information about Kelly to call or message.

The most recent one stated: *Please bring my best friend home!*

I shouldn't message her. Webb hadn't mentioned not to tell anyone about the necklace, but I suspected the police preferred it not get leaked. Once our two cases were linked a media shitstorm would begin. I shuddered at the thought.

After the dark night, the media had hounded my dad and step-mom. They'd camped out at Wren's parents' house. One of them had even cornered Rylie at school and yelled questions about her murdered aunt. Many of them had come from out of town and within a week or two they'd drifted away toward newer, more sensational stories.

The local paper had reached out to me on the one-year anniversary, but I'd refused the interview. I suspected another call would come soon.

Still, I wanted to know how Kelly had had Wren's necklace and the person most likely to have that information was her roommate and best friend.

I opened the messenger window.

'Hi, Nicki. My name is Gloria Cline, and I hoped to ask you some questions about Kelly. I used to live in your apartment. Thank you.'

I hit send, then opened a new browser window and typed 'Kelly Rice, Marquette, Michigan' into the search bar.

The Mining Journal offered the first result with a headline that stated: "NMU Student Missing."

Authorities say that nineteen-year-old Kelly Rice is missing and they're concerned for her safety.

Kelly Rice was last seen at her apartment on Franklin Avenue just after 5pm. She was reported missing after her roommate returned from an out-of-town trip to find Kelly absent and could not track her roommate down.

Kelly's mother last spoke to her five days ago.

Police are asking anyone who has seen or spoken to Kelly to please call the Marquette Police Department.

Kelly is five feet eight inches tall with blonde hair and blue eyes. She's studying criminal justice at Northern Michigan University.

Her black 2007 Chevy Silverado Pickup truck was parked in its usual spot on the street and witnesses have reported that it has not moved since the day she returned home from work.

The news articles about Kelly's case were bare bones, offering less than Dan Webb had told us.

Despite our seeming isolation here on the shores of Lake Superior, students at NMU are not shielded from the perils of the modern world. Just two years ago next week, two young NMU students were viciously attacked while attending a music festival in the Porcupine Mountains. Only one of the young women, Gloria Cline, made it out alive. Her roommate and best friend, Wren Ashby, is still missing to this day.

The words 'viciously attacked' were a hyperlink. I'd never read about what had happened to Wren and me. Dr. Fry had advised against it during the first months and, in truth, I never wanted to. I lived it daily. In the rare moments I temporarily forgot the horrors of that night, I had no interest in diving into them.

But now… I clicked the link.

A photograph of Wren and me filled the screen. I'd never seen it and my stomach plunged as I recognized the teepee behind us. Leslie Garth had taken the picture at the music festival, the very day of the attack. We'd known Leslie from Northern. She'd taken photos for the college newspaper.

"Say 'hugs, not drugs,'" she'd told us, holding up the camera and snapping our picture.

Wren had hugged me tight around the waist. We were both grinning. Our wrists were speckled black from the henna tattoos we'd gotten hours before. Wren's pink hair hung across her forehead. She wore the shirt she'd cut so it hung off her shoulder—bright yellow and speckled with black cats. Her jeans were ripped at the knees. I'd been in my usual garb, lightweight green hiking shorts and a dry-fit gray t-shirt.

My heart thumped as I stared at myself and Wren. So much of the previous two years had been a practice in blotting out that weekend, but really just that night. So intent on forgetting, I'd given little thought to the day and a half before. The good parts.

The twangy folk music we'd danced barefoot to, the mist on the grass when we'd woken early that Saturday morning to walk to the food trucks and stand in line with other festivalgoers for a cup of coffee and paper-wrapped egg burrito. We'd sipped moonshine a guy named Rex had made in his garage. We'd swum in the river, jumped from the cliff edge as ten other festivalgoers shouted encouragement from the water below. Wren had bought a tie-dye t-shirt from the booth of a lady who'd been a midwife for fifty-three years.

We'd laughed and danced and sung. I'd imagined a thousand times how the rest of that night and weekend should have gone-a walk to an outcropping of rock in the hopes of catching a meteor shower, returning to the main stage to catch the Crow Maidens perform a final time, another late night of dancing to music, maybe smoking a joint, listening to stories. Yoga on Sunday morning by the big teepee, more coffees and egg burritos, a final day of music and then we'd have packed up our tents and gear and driven back to Marquette gushing about how much fun it had been and how the only sucky part had been the porta-potties and my tryst with Tom that had ended in disappointment.

"Oh, Wren." My fingers trembled as I touched her cheek on the computer screen.

I wanted to scream at those two smiling, oblivious girls to *stay there, stay in the mass of people, don't go for that walk.* But that walk was two years gone and no matter how badly I wanted to, I'd never rewrite that night.

I studied the image, the big teepee where they'd had various events throughout the day—herbal tea tasting, a sound bowl meditation, a group of musicians who'd sat on the ground and played songs using sticks and wooden bowls as instruments.

People milled about behind us and as my gaze flitted over their out-of-focus faces, I stopped. In the far-right corner of the photo, blurry, a man stood near the back corner of the teepee. He was tall with dark hair and clothing, and he appeared to be gazing at us. I couldn't see his eyes, but he faced our direction, staring either at us or at Leslie as she snapped the photo.

A shudder swept down my spine, and I felt an impulse to press the power button on my laptop, to watch the screen turn black and take the memories of that night with it.

Instead, I clicked to enlarge the picture. He only grew blurrier, but my heart, already beating quickly, skipped a little faster.

"It's him," I murmured. "Scorpion."

18

———————

I didn't actually know it was him. There were no distinguishing features about this blurred man in the photo and yet… I couldn't shake the feeling that it was in fact him and that he was not looking at Leslie. He was looking at Wren and me.

If it was him, what did that mean? He'd been stalking us that day? Waiting for us to wander off on our own? Why? Why us? There were hundreds of young women at that festival. Why had he fixated on us?

I returned to the search bar and typed in 'Dancing with the Dead Music Festival 2012.' The name of the festival had not struck me as odd at the time, but now it had an ominous ring to it. In truth, it was merely the name of the band who'd originally started the festival. Dancing with the Dead were a trio of brothers who'd moved to the Upper Peninsula from New Orleans. They'd started putting the festival on for friends a decade before and it had slowly grown into one of the largest in the region.

News articles about Wren and I populated the screen. Our story dominated the headlines for the 2012 festival. I scrolled past the news of our attack and found articles about the festival itself.

I clicked on a blog called *Festival Fiend*. There was a brief write-up on the festival: the author's favorite bands, how We're the Cheese Knees Food Truck had the best grilled-cheese sandwich he'd ever tasted. The latter half of the blog was a stream of photos from the event. I went through and clicked them one by one, searching in the background for

Scorpion or for a glimpse of myself or Wren. No luck. I saw a few other people we'd met that weekend as well as two girls we knew from NMU.

I returned to the search bar and found more articles and scanned the photos attached to each one. None included glimpses of Scorpion.

I went back to the search bar and typed in 'Gloria Cline and Wren Ashby.' News articles flooded the feed and I scrolled past them, discovering a Reddit thread devoted to our case.

Username CatsAreLife had posted an overview of the case complete with links to articles and a photo of Wren and I. It was a selfie Wren had taken of us on the shores of Lake Superior when the beach had finally thawed enough to walk on without breaking a leg.

CatsAreLife offered a theory about our assault that included a predator who stalked music festivals. She then described murders at other music festivals around the country.

Rosie923: *It sounds like a typical opportunistic attack. Two girls walking alone in the woods. Bad man sees them. End of story.*

NoGutsNoGlory321: *We had a similar case in my hometown. Turned out to be this guy everyone thought had vanished like ten years before. He was living in a cave about a mile from the music festival.*

NakedandDreaming001: *I bet it was someone they knew—ex-boyfriend, secret stalker. Guy probably followed them to the festival and waited for his chance.*

Nothing of interest on Reddit. I opened an article that included a news video.

I scanned the rehashing of our abduction, and then returned to the top and clicked the video. A woman stood on that chillingly familiar trail, though it appeared different in daylight. Wind whipped the yellow caution tape strung from the trees behind her.

"This is the trail where nineteen-year-olds Gloria Cline and Wren Ashby were abducted two weeks ago. Searchers have combed the woods, but have been unable to locate the remains of Ashby. Cline, who still hasn't given a formal interview to the press, is recovering in the hospital in Marquette with round-the-clock police security in case the madman returns."

I closed the article and thought again of the photo of Wren and I, the dark man lingering at the periphery. Leslie had probably taken hundreds of photos that weekend.

On the NMU website, I searched the directory of students for Leslie

Garth. Her name appeared attached to a myriad of photos, including a graduating class image.

I returned to the search bar and typed her name along with 'Marquette, Michigan.' Pages of results came back connected to photo essays she'd done, photos for local newspapers. She even had a photography website. I clicked it. She was working for the *Mining Journal* newspaper and taking freelance photos.

I found an email and a phone number and copied the email, navigated to my own email account.

Even my email reflected my former self: HikerGirl333@yahoo.com. I was no longer a hiker girl. My beloved pair of hiking boots were gone. One had been ripped from my foot on the dark night. Police had kept the other.

I pasted Leslie's email into the recipient's bar and sent a quick message.

Hi, Leslie, this is Gloria Cline from NMU. I have a few questions about some pictures you took. Please email me back here or call me. I added my phone number and hit 'send.'

I returned to her info page and almost closed the screen. She had a phone number listed, and I stared at it reluctantly. It had been so long since I'd talked to any of my peers at NMU, I felt like I was making a cold call to ask if she needed to extend her car warranty. It was a stupid thought, but it followed me as I punched her number into my cell phone.

"Photos with Leslie," she answered.

I recognized her slightly high-pitched voice. "Hi, Leslie?"

"Speaking."

"This is Gloria Cline."

Pause on the line, little intake of breath. "Oh, my God, Gloria. How are you?"

"I'm… okay. I mean, fine. I'm good." An answer that revealed how not fine I was.

"Great. I'm so happy to hear that. I sent you a card at the hospital. I don't know if you ever got it. You probably had so many it got lost in the shuffle."

"I did get it. Thank you."

I had, and though I'd gotten hundreds of letters in the weeks after that night, Leslie's had been one of the first and one of the few opened by my dad in an attempt to cheer me up. My dad had propped it on my bedside table in the hospital. It had depicted a rainbow over the Lake Superior Ore Docks. I realized now Leslie had probably taken the photo herself, gone to the trouble of having it made into a card.

"I'm so sorry, Gloria. I just… I can't even imagine."

"Yeah, it was… bad. But, umm… I'm calling because I saw one of those photos you took from the festival the day it happened in the newspaper. I wondered if you still had those pictures. The ones you took that weekend."

"Oh, sure, yeah. I took hundreds of them, but I put them on a zip drive, which I gave a copy of to the police. A bunch of people turned over their photos, but… I don't think it helped much. At least not that they told me."

"Could I see them? Could you drop them off at my apartment? Or I could have Dorian stop by your place and get them."

"Dorian Ashby? Wren's brother?"

"Yeah, I see him a lot."

"Oh, that's great you guys have stayed in touch. Sure, yeah. I can bring them myself if you'd like. Or we could meet for coffee."

I cringed, having known it would go there. Some people were aware of what I'd become, but most people weren't. After our story had faded from the limelight, people didn't wonder too much about what had become of the girl who'd survived.

"I probably can't do coffee, but if you could just drop the zip drive in my mailbox, that'd be great."

Leslie said nothing for a moment and when she spoke, she had her usual polite tone. "Oh, sure, yeah. I can do that. What's your address?"

I gave it to her and thanked her, preparing to hang up.

"Gloria, before you go…"

"Yeah?"

"Well… are you looking for something in the pictures? Like the guy who attacked you and Wren?"

I sighed and chewed on the cuticle on my thumb. It was red and raw, and I needed to stop. "I don't know. I saw that picture of Wren and me online and I just wanted to see the others. Maybe to remember the good stuff from that weekend, too."

"Okay, sure. I totally get that. I'm going out to take pictures tomorrow at Presque Isle Park and I'll drop the zip drive after."

"Alone?" I asked. "Are you taking someone with you?"

"No, I go alone all the time. It's totally sa—" She stopped mid-sentence. "Jeez, sorry. I understand why that probably freaks you out."

"You should take someone, or a weapon at least. Some bear spray or—"

"Oh, yeah, of course. I've got some mace on my keychain."

I frowned, imagining the cheap little bottles of mace that wouldn't stop a toddler if they were intent on biting your ankles.

"Okay…" I sighed, swallowing the stream of warnings I wanted to offer. "Be safe."

"I will. It was nice to talk to you, Gloria."

"You too." I hung up the phone and looked at the clock.

Dorian texted me just after seven that evening.

Dorian: *I'm pulling into your driveway. Get ready to open the door because these weights are heavy and I'm not taking two trips.*

I stood at the door and watched through the peephole until I saw him appear. I quickly undid the locks and opened it.

He shuffled in, carrying the metal stand along with six individual weights stacked within it. Wincing, he squatted and set the weights on the floor. "Damn, those things are heavy. I almost dropped the entire set on my toe coming up the stairs."

I bent and lifted one of the five-pound weights. I did a few bicep curls. The weights were in sets of five, eight, and twelve pounds. I used to lift the twelve-pound weights, Wren the eights, but I suspected ten reps of the five-pounders and I'd be sore. "Thanks."

"I can move them somewhere else," he suggested. "I just have to be quick. Rylie's in the car."

"She could have come up."

"We're meeting Val for dinner in ten minutes. It's hard to get Rylie out of here after she's spent the whole day with you, let alone if she only gets three minutes."

I smiled. "I'll move them later."

"What's this?" Dorian paused near my desk.

I added the weight in my hand to the rack and then looked at the paper he held. It was a printout of an article about Wren's and my attack. "It's an article."

"Have you been looking into it? Into what was printed about the case?" He watched me.

I rubbed at my throat, nodding. "Yeah. I realized I never... I've never read anything that was reported."

"And now you want to?"

I brushed both hands through my hair, so short I couldn't easily tug and twist it anymore. "I guess with the detective coming here and now Kelly... I feel obligated, maybe, to see if I can't connect some dots."

"So you do think it's connected?"

"I don't know."

"Well, I do and so does that detective. I'm sure of it." Dorian turned back to my computer, shuffled through more articles on my desk. "Have you found anything that seems important?"

There was excitement in his voice, hope. He was trying not to reveal it.

"Maybe... nothing major, but..."

"I have everything, Glo. Every single article the newspapers printed. I have a binder filled with news and other stuff... rumors happening around town, similar crimes in Michigan, conversations on social media."

"Really?"

"Yeah. The first six months especially, I really dove deep, trying to figure out who did it. I used to talk to the detective on the case every week, but then he got transferred and a new one came on. That one hardly ever called me back, acted annoyed when I left messages."

"You never told me."

"You didn't want to talk about it. If anything came on the news, it... triggered you or whatever. I didn't want my looking into what happened to become a hindrance to you getting better."

I sighed and walked to the couch, collapsed onto it. "I'm sorry you couldn't talk about it with me."

"Don't be. You needed time. I get it. If you're serious about wanting to read all this stuff, I'll bring the binder over. We can go through it."

I tugged on my earlobe. "Okay, yeah. I think it's time."

After I watched Dorian back out of the driveway, I sifted through the freezer for a frozen dinner. I opted for meatloaf, peeled off the plastic cover and popped it in the oven.

My phone buzzed, and I picked it up when I saw Dorian's name.

"What's up?" I asked.

"Are you okay?" His voice held a tremor.

"Yeah, sure. Just heating a meatloaf. Why? What's wrong?"

"I'm on my way back. I'll be right there. I think… get your taser and lock yourself in the bathroom."

A trickle of fear slithered down my spine. "Why? What happened?"

"Just do it. Okay?"

<h1 style="text-align:center">19</h1>

On jelly legs I ran to my bedroom, opened the bedside drawer, grabbed the taser and rushed into the bathroom, slammed the door and locked it. I opened the closet, ready to cram myself into the space at the bottom. The sheet suddenly slid from the mirror and pooled on the floor in front of the sink.

I don't know what compelled me, where the sudden surge of fury came from, but I didn't cower from the glass. Bracing my hands on the cool porcelain of the sink, I stared straight ahead.

"Come on, you sick fuck," I hissed at the mirror. I searched the spaces behind me, the closed door, the white walls that ended at sharp angles. No man lingered there. Nothing moved.

He wouldn't come. As if such a monster was beholden to anyone, let alone to me.

Desperate to busy my hands, I opened the medicine cabinet and took out my dental floss, thrust it so hard beneath my teeth my gums bled—a disturbing sight when I peeled my lips back. The blood jolted me and then he was there, as if the sight of my bleeding had drawn him to me.

He stood behind me as he'd done before, his eyes trained on mine. No smile this time. His mouth was set in a grim line, his eyebrows pulled slightly forward. I couldn't see the back of his head, but I imagined the bloody mess I'd witnessed previously.

I didn't freak out, didn't lose my mind at the sight of him. I committed his face to my memory. Every detail. The slightly crooked nose, the scorpion on his neck, the square chin. His ears stuck from his head, not large, but pronounced. His hair was receding, dark and thinning, though I pegged his age under thirty years old.

"Who are you?" I hissed.

He didn't smile this time, but when I leaned forward to catch more of his reflection, he faded and disappeared.

Someone pounded on the door behind me and I jumped.

"Gloria, it's me, open up."

I opened the bathroom door to see Dorian in the hall, wide-eyed and pale. I peered past him toward the living room, my heart still pumping from my staredown with Scorpion.

"There's no one out here. It's okay. You can come out."

I frowned and followed Dorian. He glanced back at me, studying my face. "You're okay?" he asked.

"Yeah, I'm fine. Why did you tell me to get the taser and hide?"

He sighed and rubbed his jaw. "Rylie... We were practically to the restaurant, and she wondered who was visiting you. I asked what she meant, and she said... she looked up and saw someone in your bedroom window when we were pulling out of the driveway. A man."

I said nothing, but my skin crawled. I knew who Rylie had seen.

"I freaked out and whipped a U-turn and came back."

"Where's Rylie?"

"In the car. I'm really sorry. She must have... imagined it or whatever. Maybe the scare the other day had her seeing things."

"Maybe..."

"I mean, it has to be that. Right? There isn't anyone in here."

I wanted to tell him. I suddenly wanted to spill the whole thing, lead him to the closet and reveal the horrible stupid doll, but I didn't.

He cocked his head, studying me.

"What?" I asked.

"You're... calm. I expected... Well, never mind. I'm sorry if I spooked you."

"It's all right. Tell Rylie not to be upset about it, okay?"

"Yeah. Okay."

I peered out the window and waved to Rylie, who sat in the passenger seat looking back at me with big, scared eyes. She waved back.

I returned to my computer and opened my Facebook page. I had a new message from Nicki Shrum. I opened it.

Gloria Cline!!? The one who was attacked? OMG. Yes, we need to talk ASAP. Where can we meet?

She'd sent the message fifteen minutes before. I stared at her words, at the urgency in her message.

I wrote back.

I live less than a block from your old apartment. I'm home-bound right now, so I can't meet you anywhere but here. You can come over, though.

Without hitting send, I clasped my hands and pressed the sides of my knuckles against my lips. I never invited strangers into my apartment, had only recently had a complete meltdown when my stepmother and stepbrother showed up.

Sucking in my cheeks, I slammed my finger on 'send' before I lost my nerve.

Immediately, her response popped up in my inbox.

I can be there in twenty minutes. Send me your address.

"Oh, shit," I muttered, wishing I could take it back.

Fingers shaking, I typed my address into the messenger and sent it to her.

Afterwards, I stood, hands on the back of my chair, and tried to mentally prepare for this girl I'd never met stepping into my apartment. I'd watched her often enough. Giraffe Neck, I'd referred to her. She danced a lot in their apartment, twirling around, often dressed in floaty dresses that spun with her.

She studied far less than her counterpart, Kelly, and out of the two, she was the one who brought home the most boys. Tall, muscular, jock types who'd drape themselves around the apartment as if they owned the place.

Now she'd be in my apartment. I shuffled to the bathroom, my legs shaky. In front of the bathroom mirror, I yanked a brush quickly through my hair. I stripped off my sweats and rustled through the closet, the carpet no longer wet, in search of jeans. I found a pair, too big, and cinched a belt around my waist. I couldn't remember the last time I'd worn a bra. Flat-chested, I didn't really need one, but shrugged one on anyway, covering it with a long-sleeved purple Black Rock Outfitters t-shirt.

Dressed and halfway presentable, I sat on my couch and fumbled my phone to the relaxation hypnosis. I turned it on, leaned back and closed my eyes.

When she knocked on my door, my eyes popped open. I'd drifted deeply during the hypnosis and I took a deep breath and steeled myself against the rising panic. I stood and peered through the peephole, confirming it was her, then slid the deadbolts aside and opened my door.

Her eyes widened as she took me in. She glanced back toward the stairway as if questioning her choice to come over, then forced a hesitant smile. "Gloria?"

"Yeah, that's me. You must be Nicki."

"I am," she said, her voice breaking. She rushed forward, wrapping her arms around me, and burst into tears.

"It's okay," I murmured, patting her back. Her hair was long and silky and my fingers got tangled in it. "Sorry," I said, pulling them free.

She stepped back, wiping her eyes, and held up a bag. "I brought"— she hiccupped—"some chocolate for you."

I took the bag and drew out a box of hazelnut chocolates. "Thanks. That was really nice. Why don't we sit?"

She followed me to the couch and sat beside me, folding her long legs beneath her. Dark makeup leaked with her tears, causing shadows beneath her eyes.

"I'm so afraid," she said, watching me through her big brown eyes, still tear-filled. "I'm so afraid Kelly is dead."

My neck itched and to avoid scratching it, I stuffed my hands beneath my thighs. "Nicki, a detective visited me yesterday. They seem to think Kelly's disappearance could be linked to what happened to Wren and me."

Nicki tensed. "I didn't want to think that, but… I did. She'd become sort of obsessed with what happened to you guys. It started before we came to Marquette. We were still in Manistique when you were attacked. It was all over the papers and her uncles and grandpa are cops and they were all discussing it a lot. She started digging, looking up similar crimes and stuff.

"We even took a trip to the Porcupine Mountains just to poke around. We didn't find anything and… honestly, it terrified me. After we came to Northern, she dropped it for a while. At least, I thought she had. We got into a massive fight when I found out."

"That she was still looking into what happened to us?"

"No, not that. I was mad because she intentionally moved us into your old apartment."

"She did?" I asked, startled.

"Yeah." Nicki stood and paced away from me. "She has that kind of personality, tenacious. But I couldn't believe she didn't tell me."

"How did you find out?"

"Wyatt, another guy in the building, told me one night when we were all drinking in the backyard. I totally flipped. In my defense, I'd had about three too many cups of beer. I lit into Kelly that night. She apologized for not telling me, but then got all excited to show me everything she'd found out. Except I was drunk and mad, so I refused to look at it. I took a shower and went to bed."

"Is that the last time you saw her?"

"No. That was a few weeks ago. She didn't bring it up again, and neither did I. Now… now I wish I had. I'm such an idiot."

The magnitude of what she'd revealed perched at the forefront of my mind, this enormous, unfathomable thing. Kelly Rice had been investigating Wren's and my abduction. She'd moved into our apartment and now she had vanished. I struggled to put it into its rightful place, but none of it had ever had a place. It existed in chaos, shattered glass, impossible to return to the original image.

"Did she have research in the apartment? Notes?"

"Yeah, definitely." Nicki paced to my window and peeled open the curtain. She stood gazing through the glass, the light in my apartment illuminating her for all the world to see. A cold sweat broke out beneath my arms. I wanted to tell her to close the curtain, to back up, but I gritted my teeth.

"It's all gone though," Nicki said, turning suddenly and watching me through glassy, horrified eyes.

20

———

"Kelly had a red folder and matching red notebook she brought out the night she wanted to tell me what she'd found about your case. I told the detectives, but they didn't find them."

"What about a computer?"

"Her laptop is gone too."

"Damn…" I muttered. I pulled my hands from beneath me and picked at the skin around my fingernails.

Nicki returned to where I sat and picked up the box of chocolates. "Do you mind?" she asked. "Chocolate has been the only thing I've been able to stomach the last few days."

"Go ahead."

She peeled off the cellophane and popped off the box top, setting it aside. She handed me a chocolate.

"Eat one," she said, nodding toward my fidgety hands. "It will give your fingers something to do. And cocoa releases endorphins in the brain. We need all of those we can get right now."

I took the chocolate and set it on my tongue, closing my eyes. It was an exercise I'd done frequently with Dr. Fry during the first months after my release from the hospital. The act of savoring something—the taste of a chocolate, the smell of a bag of freshly ground coffee, the texture of a cashmere scarf—all these things brought me into the present moment and out of the scary past.

The chocolate was rich and sweet and pooled on my tongue, then slipped back down my throat. I opened my eyes to see Nicki too had closed her eyes, though a tiny crease remained between her pale eyebrows.

When she opened her eyes, they were again filled with tears.

"Kelly and I bought these every month," she murmured, slumping into a chair and drawing her knees up to her chest. She wrapped arms around her legs. "Chocolate week—aka PMS week. We were always synced; you know, when your period happens at the same time?"

I nodded. Wren and I had been as well, though instead of chocolate we'd usually spent those PMS days eating pizza and watching true crime documentaries.

"How long have you and Kelly been friends?" I asked.

"For a long time," Nicki murmured, winding her fingers through her long hair and blinking back her tears. "We met in third grade. My family moved to Manistique from Wisconsin. On my very first day, Kelly asked if I wanted to be her reading partner in class and from that point on, we were inseparable.

"People thought we were twins." Nicki laughed and pulled her hair over her opposite shoulder. "It is weird in a way how alike we've always looked, except my eyes are brown and Kelly's are blue."

"You both wanted to attend Northern?"

"Oh, yeah, we both love the Upper Peninsula and hiking, kayaking. Manistique is on the shore of Lake Michigan, so we thought we'd try life on the shore of Lake Superior and it worked out because NMU has a bachelor in criminal justice, which Kelly is studying, and also a bachelor in dance, which is my focus."

"Kelly wants to be a cop?"

"Yeah, a detective. It all started in middle school when she heard about the unsolved disappearance of a babysitter in Manistique. The girl had vanished in like 1990 and some kid in our class did a report and presentation on her. It's still unsolved. Kelly got pretty into it, but..." Nicki shrugged. "There wasn't much to find. The police believed the babysitter ran away. Her parents were convinced someone kidnapped her. Nobody knows and it's kind of an urban legend around there now. Like if you visit the house where it happened at night, you'll hear the babysitter calling out for help."

"That's creepy," I said.

"Yeah. My thoughts exactly. I never really understood Kelly's interest in becoming a detective. There's never anything happy in a job like that. It's just one terrible thing after another."

"And you want to be a dancer?"

She smiled and tucked her hair behind her ear as if a bit self-conscious about her major of choice. "Yeah. I know it doesn't sound very serious. Most people think I'm throwing money into a black hole, but..." She shrugged. "I love to dance. I've always loved it. I get this one life and I'm going to spend it doing something I love."

I swallowed thickly, remembering my own similar pledges. Someday I was going to be a park ranger, I was going to spend my life in the place I loved most—the woods.

For a moment, the smell of forest drifted in as if someone had thrown open a window. Sharp pine and the sticky-sweet scent of sap and the merging of wildflowers and crisp lake air. I rubbed my eyes and pushed down the tears threatening.

"I think you should go after what you love. To hell with everyone else," I told her.

She smiled, but her expression was sad. "I don't know how I'll go on," she said faintly. "If... if Kelly doesn't come back."

My eyes welled, and Nicki softened and blurred. I pressed my fingertips against my eyelids, Wren's face clouding my mind. I wanted to assure Nicki that she'd go on, that she'd survive even without her best friend, but I had no such guarantees.

"Nicki," I said, clearing the thickness from my throat. "The detectives found a necklace in Kelly's bedside drawer, a mermaid. Do you know anything about that?"

Nicki frowned. "A mermaid? Hmmm... I don't remember ever seeing that and I've seen everything Kelly owns. We share closets. Plus, Kelly doesn't wear jewelry except a little silver ring with her birthstone on it, an emerald. Her little brother gave it to her."

"You never saw it then?"

"No, that's really odd. I don't know why she'd buy something like that."

I scratched at my throat and then pulled my sleeves over my hands to block my fingers. "I don't think she did. Please don't tell anyone this. I'm sure the detectives don't want it to get out. The necklace was identical to one I gave Wren, one she was wearing the night we were attacked."

Nicki stared at me, unblinking, her body very still. "But how...?"

"I don't know. It's never been found. Wren was wearing it."

Nicki stood again and walked into my kitchen, circling the room and then pausing. "Does that mean—? She couldn't have found Wren, right? I mean…" Her face was pinched, scared.

Still, she was beautiful, all angles and high cheekbones and luminous brown eyes.

"No. I don't think so. The detective implied she might have known the man who attacked us. Maybe he kept Wren's necklace as a souvenir and gave it to Kelly. Was she dating anyone? Had she made any new male friends?"

I thought of Scorpion with his black eyes and pockmarked face. This was not a man I could imagine being involved with Kelly Rice.

Nicki shook her head slowly, but then she stilled. "There was someone…" Nicki bit her lip. "I don't know his name. Just… one day she got home kind of late from work and she mentioned having coffee with some guy. I asked if she was into him, but she said no, it wasn't like that. I figured… maybe it was somebody from class. I don't know. Normally we would have talked all about it, but I was cramming for an exam that night."

Nicki's phone buzzed and she looked at it. "It's my mom," she told me. "She and my dad along with Kelly's parents are all staying at the Landmark Inn. Me too right now." She typed a return message.

"How are Kelly's parents holding up?" I asked.

"They're okay. Kelly's mom is really positive and focused. Flyers and organizing press conferences and getting things done. That's where Kelly gets it from. Her dad seems… lost. He just sort of has this dazed expression. Kelly's brother is still in Manistique."

Nicki's phone buzzed again and she frowned. "My mom wants me to come back right now," she said. "They're regrouping and making a plan for tomorrow. Can I call you, Gloria? Can we stay in touch?"

"Yeah, absolutely."

I gave her my phone number and closed and locked the door behind her, then I hurried to my window and peered out, ensuring she made it safely to her car. After she backed out of the driveway, I stood in the center of my apartment, feeling frustrated and helpless.

Kelly Rice had vanished looking into our case. Did that mean she'd found something? Scorpion? But he was dead. He had to be.

I suddenly wished I could follow Nicki out, jump in the car and go with her to the meeting as they assembled to figure out the next steps in finding Kelly. Trapped in this apartment, I could help no one.

My apartment didn't have a porch or balcony. That had been part of the appeal. I wanted the second floor with a single entrance. No way for an intruder to slip in through a sliding glass door. But now I wanted an easy way to transition, to take baby steps towards that outside world.

I stood at my door and slipped open the two deadbolts. I unlocked the doorknob, but I didn't turn the knob. It seemed to pulse. When I closed my hand around it, I was surprised it wasn't hot to the touch, vibrating, something.

"I'm not going out, just… I'm just going to open it. Okay?"

I stared at the door, lifted my hands and began tapping on the side of my hand—the karate chop point.

"Even though I am scared to open my door, I deeply and completely accept myself." I repeated the words and moved through the tapping sequence Dr. Fry had taught me the previous year. I tapped from the top of my head to the space beneath my arms.

The scared voice in my head still wanted to argue, but I silenced her and turned the knob. My stomach lurched as I pulled the door open a crack. It whined as I drew it in further, further, stepping back to reveal the hallway, the opposite wall. It was the same color as the walls in my apartment, identical really except it was out there, out in the dangerous world.

The carpet in the hallway was old. The landlord had installed new carpet in my apartment before I moved in. Soft and beige. Threadbare blue carpet ran down the hall, pilled and faded.

My heart pounded and sweat trickled between my shoulder blades. I clutched the knob in my hand, tight enough to make my fingers ache. I wanted to slam the door shut, frantically secure the locks, but I imagined my feet encased in cement boots. I would stand there for one solid minute.

"Sixty, fifty-nine, fifty-eight, fifty-seven, fifty-six…" I murmured.

Nothing stirred in the hall. The hammering in my heart grew softer.

"Ten, nine, eight…"

A door slammed in the apartment downstairs. I lurched back and shoved my door closed, slid the bolts into place, my fingers slippery on the metal. Turned the lock on the knob and stepped away, wide-eyed, heart battering against my ribs.

For a long time, I stood and stared at the door, waited for my pulse to calm. Despite the sudden terror at the sound beneath me, I smiled and rested a hand against my chest. I'd done it. I'd stood in the open doorway for an entire minute.

"Yes!" I blurted, clapping my hands together.

~

I woke in the morning with an optimism I hadn't felt since the days before the dark night.

I'd stood in front of the open doorway two more times the night before. The second time I'd lasted three minutes.

Now, without even making coffee, I strode to the door, unlatched the bolts and opened it. I stood and gazed at the morning light, which dramatically changed the color of the blue carpeting, revealing the faded checked pattern. By most accounts, it was ugly, but I found it oddly beautiful. My chest ached as I stared at it, at this hall I'd rarely seen.

I braced my hands on either side of the door frame and took a tentative step onto the thin carpet. It was prickly beneath my bare feet. I took another step and another until I could turn and press my back against the opposite wall, not staring back into my apartment, but rather out from it. My pulse thrummed; my knees felt wobbly. Terror and elation gripped me and I clung to the elation. Dr. Fry explained such emotions on a spectrum, all essentially versions of the same thing—excitement, the brain sending signals to the body for the nervous system to light up, take notice.

I pressed my palms into the wall behind me, flattened myself and focused on the carpet.

"Just breathe. That's all you have to do."

After a while, I inched sideways, one step, pause for five breaths, another step. At the top of the stairs, I faltered. A dark veil fell over my eyes and the ground beneath me tilted. I flung out my arms, grasped for the wall or the hand rail. Nothing. I pitched forward and suddenly my hands landed on something firm.

I blinked the dark spots away, my breath stuck, unable to squeeze into the pinhole of my throat. The thing beneath my hands shifted. I stared and a head materialized. A man with short dark hair, a blue hooded sweatshirt. My hands were on his head and I realized his hands were on me then, on my waist, keeping me from tipping forward and plunging headfirst down the stairs.

"Gloria." His mouth made the shape of my name, but the world had gone silent. I couldn't hear anything, not even my breath, my heartbeat.

I still couldn't breathe.

His voice broke through then, the sound deafening. "Gloria. It's okay…" He wasn't shouting but somehow it registered that way, loud, booming.

I reeled away from him, fell onto my hands and knees and crawled back to my apartment. He followed me. I heard his footfalls, felt the movement of the floor. He was in my apartment, getting closer.

21

———

Before me lay the couch with my blanket and I wanted to dive beneath it, cower there and disappear. My eyes skittered over the rack of hand weights. I half-stood, lunged toward them and swiped one up, swung around.

The man's eyes went wide. He was standing in my open doorway, familiar, vaguely. He took a step back, held up his hands. "Gloria, it's me, Arlo Goff. I mow the lawn."

The free weight was heavy in my hand, raised above my head as if I intended to throw it at him or smack him with it, which, honestly, I had. Slowly, I lowered it and let it fall to the floor. The beat of my heart had built to a crescendo, felt as if my heart might leap from my chest and go bouncing across the floor.

I pressed a hand against my chest and wheezed, bent over, struggling to calm the torrent of fear crashing through me. I swallowed and blinked and breathed.

"I'm sorry," I said, finding my voice. It was raspy. I hadn't even had a drink of water since waking.

The fear on his face fell away. He gazed at me sympathetically, a look that bothered me more than the terror. "It's okay. I startled you. I thought you were about to fall down the stairs."

I said nothing, watched him. I *had* been about to fall down the stairs. The proper thing to do was to thank him profusely. Who knew how long I might have lain there if I'd gotten badly injured? Hours at least until Dorian came by in the afternoon.

"Umm… all right. I'll get going." He backed through my door.

"Wait!" I called after him and he paused, turned to look at me. "I'd like to… follow you out, down to the front door."

He frowned. "Are you sure? I thought… that you didn't go out."

"I do," I announced, and I shut down the tiny angry voice in my head shouting her disagreement. "I do now."

"Okay. Sure."

He waited for me, and I followed him to the door, my legs quaking. In the hallway, I counted my steps and my breaths and focused on the bob of his head as he walked.

Arlo paused at the top of the stairs. "You're comfortable walking down?"

I nodded, didn't trust myself to speak. I pressed a hand against the wall, took the first step down, the second, slid my palm along the smooth plaster. Fifth step, sixth, seventh and then the landing. The carpet was even more bristly here, so thin I could feel the hard floor in patches beneath.

Arlo opened the front door. The burst of sunlight blinded me and I shielded my eyes, stared at the ground until the black spots subsided. When I looked up, he stood in the open doorway, waiting, an encouraging smile on his face.

I refused the inner voice its fearful sermon and pushed on, stepping through the doorway into the warm fragrant morning. Sun drenched the grass and the faded wood of the porch and the cracked walkway that led to our mailbox. Arlo's truck and trailer were parked on the road, his lawnmower not yet unloaded.

He closed the door behind us and tilted his face to the sun. "It's a good morning to sit on the porch," he said, nodding toward the canvas folding chairs my downstairs neighbor had propped outside.

"It is," I said, amazed to hear my voice not quivering, not breaking. I walked to the chair and slowly sank into it.

"Are you good?" he asked. "I was going to start mowing, but I'd hate the noise to disrupt you."

"I'm good," I assured him. "I like the sound and the smell."

I don't know how long I sat there. Time was as immaterial as the clouds drifting in the agonizingly blue sky. Every sound and smell and image stole my breath. Nothing rattled me, not the whir of the mower or the cars that drove by or the slamming of doors on nearby houses.

The appearance of Leslie in my driveway finally broke the spell. She hopped out, envelope in hand, and started toward my mailbox. I stood and winced—my right foot, which I'd tucked beneath me, had gone numb.

"Leslie," I called, flexing and releasing my toes.

She turned at my voice and a big smile spread across her face.

"Hey!" She waved and jogged over. "Wow, look at you. I love the purple hair."

She opened her arms to hug me and I stepped awkwardly into the embrace. "You look so different," she told me, taking a step back. "Gosh, I doubt I'd have recognized you if you hadn't called my name."

"Yeah." I brushed a hand through my hair. "No more long hair."

"To say the least," Leslie continued, lifting one of my arms. "You're as skinny as a toothpick. You actually look a lot like…"

She trailed off, but I knew she'd been about to say Wren. Wren, who was always waif-thin with short hair in varying shades of pastel.

"I'm sure my therapist would agree and offer some deep insight into why I'm morphing into my dead best friend." I'd meant to make a joke, break the ice, but my words lingered morbidly.

Leslie winced and handed me the envelope. "I'm so sorry, Gloria. I truly am. If you ever need to talk—"

The sound of a siren cut her off, slicing through the quiet. I dropped to the ground and covered my head, heart hammering against my chest, my body instantly shaking with terror. As if I hadn't been comfortably outside for hours, the magnitude of my situation fell upon me.

Exposed, exposed. Nowhere to hide, no walls, doors with locks, no blankets, nothing to crawl beneath.

"Oh, my God, Gloria. What's happening? Do you need medicine or something?"

I squirmed toward the door, half crawling, half rolling. The siren grew closer, deafening, and I was back in the woods on the edge of the river with hands on my body and voices shouting.

"Her throat's been cut," someone said.

"We thought she was dead."

"Back up, back up."

There was something firm beneath me, an oxygen mask clamped over my mouth, needles in my arm. "Too dehydrated, can't get a vein."

"Gloria, Gloria..."

I don't know how long Leslie had been saying my name. She knelt in front of me, eyes searching the lawn behind us as if a savior would step from between the shrubs.

I blinked at the scarred wood planks of the porch and drew in more breath until I could speak.

"It's okay..." I whispered. "Can you please help me inside? Just... walk with me up to my apartment."

I didn't want company, didn't want to invite Leslie in, but I feared ascending the stairs alone, falling, breaking something, lying there for hours.

"Yes, yes. Here." She extended her hand, and I took it.

Mine was slick and nearly slipped out, but she gripped my forearm with her other hand and pulled me to my feet. I pushed through the front door and into the dark hall of the house, took one trembling step after another until I reached the second floor. Leslie moved close behind me as if ready to reach out should I careen over backwards.

I touched the knob of my door, thought of all the locks on the other side I'd left carelessly open as I'd stepped into the outside world that morning.

I turned the knob and pushed in, a rush of gratitude at my familiar space. I took a few faltering steps toward the couch and sank onto it, pulling my oversize afghan across my legs and up to my neck. It was warm in the apartment, but the blanket was heavy and comforting.

"Can I get you a glass of water?" Leslie asked, moving toward the kitchen, the door standing ajar.

"Please, can you, umm... close and lock the door first."

"Oh, yeah, definitely." She closed the door, turned only the lock on the knob, and I resisted asking her to lock them all.

She filled a glass of water and brought it to me. I slurped it down. I'd had nothing to drink that morning and I realized for the first time how thirsty I was.

"Thank you," I said, after finishing the glass. I set it on the table and leaned my head back, tiredness creeping in.

"You look exhausted," Leslie said. "I'm just going to leave the zip drive here on your table."

Eyes still closed, I nodded. "Thanks, Leslie. Thanks for bringing it by."

"My pleasure. It was really good to see you, Gloria. Please call anytime."

"Sure," I murmured, though we both knew I wouldn't call again.

I heard the door open and close as Leslie left, and I was so tired I could have drifted off to sleep, but I was painfully aware of the unlocked door. I pushed the afghan off and stood on leaden legs. I locked the knob, slid the deadbolts into place and returned to the couch.

After I woke, I scrolled through photos for hours. Leslie's zip drive revealed she'd taken three thousand photos the weekend of the music festival.

At first looking through them had filled me with dread, as if the very first photo I clicked would reveal the leering face of Scorpion. Obviously, it hadn't.

My eyes were grainy with exhaustion from staring at the pictures, searching for a face I'd only seen as it appeared shadow-like around my apartment.

A photo slid across the screen and I paused. Tom Russell smiled at the camera. He held up a red plastic cup, as did the four guys who stood around him, including his best friend Rob and two other guys I'd known from NMU. It was strange to see him.

Before the dark night I'd thought about him constantly. I'd developed a crush of epic proportions on the guy and now… nothing. He was still handsome, but no butterflies exploded in my stomach at the sight of him. His image conjured nothing at all within me except a vague amusement at my own prior desperation. What had it been about Tom Russell that had so enchanted me?

That weekend I'd slept with Tom, been all in, only to see him twelve hours later making out with another girl. In the matter of a single weekend, the dream that had consumed me for months had died. But so much had died that weekend that the experience with Tom had simply ceased to exist.

Before Tom I'd never felt so drawn towards a guy. In my current life, the thought of any kind of romantic love simply didn't exist. There was a void there and not the kind of void that longed to be filled. A mere emptiness, an unoccupied corner of the closet where nothing needed to go.

I wondered what had happened to Tom Russell. Was he still at Northern? Maybe graduating soon? He'd been a year above us. The question brought little more than a vague curiosity. In truth, I didn't much care what had become of Tom.

Click, click, click… images zoomed by and then I paused, finger on the mouse. The teepee stood in the background. Leslie had caught a side angle of Wren, who was bent over laughing, pink hair falling in her face. She looked so happy, so carefree. I was out of the screen. I searched for Scorpion but didn't see him in the other festivalgoers.

I clicked to the next picture. Another shot of Wren. This time I too was in the frame. She was still laughing but had stood up straight. My mouth was stretched wide in a smile and my eyes focused on something beyond the image. I tried to rewind back to that moment. What had we been looking at or talking about that had Wren laughing so hard? I couldn't remember.

The next photo was the one from the paper. Wren and I grinning, arms around each other. There, in the background, hovered the blurred image of Scorpion. I moved to the next photo. Leslie had captured Wren and I walking away. We were headed in the direction of the main stage, away from the teepee. I searched for Scorpion and found him, more in focus now. He'd moved from the shadow beside the teepee and into the light of day. He was only one of a dozen people milling in the back of the image, but again his eyes trailed us. His head was tilted down slightly, but his eyes followed us.

22

———

I picked up the kitty stress balls, squeezed them tight in my palms as I studied him, searched for a memory of the man. Did I know him from somewhere? Had we met him that weekend? Nothing arose. I could not place him anywhere beyond that night, and even that night he'd been masked, hidden.

I swallowed the saliva building in the back of my throat. Seeing him, truly seeing him with such clarity made my breath quicken, my gut twist into a little knot.

I looked at my closed bedroom door and imagined him in there, right behind the door, breathing his sour breath against the wood, wanting to reach through and grab me on the other side.

Had he come back for me? Was that it? I'd survived that night, so he'd come back to finish me. Was he dead? Was he alive and somehow projecting his spirit into my apartment? Or, worst of all, was he a hallucination? A figment of my splintered psyche?

A text came in on my phone.

Dorian: *Hey, I'm almost at your place. I'm going to run up this binder of stuff from the case. I can't go over it tonight. Val's with me.*

I moved to the window and pushed it open, leaning toward the screen and breathing the lingering scent of the freshly mowed grass.

Dorian's car pulled in. Val sat in the passenger seat, her window rolled down.

"I just don't understand why you have to come here every single day," Val said.

"To check on her. She's alone up there, Val."

I leaned my ear close to the screen, straining to catch their conversation.

"Because she chooses to be, Dorian."

"She was almost murdered. She saw my sister get murdered. You can't possibly fathom what that was like for her."

"I'm not trying to be insensitive here, but you're crippling her. Encouraging her to be a victim forever."

"Another girl has gone missing. This guy is still out there. She's right to be afraid."

"Dorian, your mom told me how obsessed you became after they were attacked. You lost your job, your girlfriend. Do you want that to happen again?"

"I'll be right back."

I watched through the slit in the curtain as he jumped from the driver's seat and started up the walkway. Dropping the curtain back into place, I hurried and unlocked the door, thinking about what Val had said. He'd lost his job, his girlfriend.

I tried to remember those early months. He'd started his property management business around that time and there had been a girlfriend before the music festival, Carly or Carrie—I no longer remembered her name. By the time I'd thought to ask about her, they'd been broken up for months.

I opened the door and poked my head in the hallway as Dorian appeared at the top of the stairs.

He paused, surprised. "Whoa, hey. You good?"

"Yeah." I smiled and took a tentative step into the hallway, pushed my hands into my pockets to still their shaking.

"Holy crap. You're in the hall." He grinned and walked to me, giving me a one-armed hug. "That's amazing, Glo. I'm so proud of you. When did you—"

"I went on the porch today," I told him when he released me.

His eyes widened. "You did?"

"Yeah. I lost it a bit, but I was out there for a couple of hours. I did it."

He followed me into the apartment. "Alone?"

"Well, not entirely alone. I walked out with Arlo."

"Arlo, the lawn guy?"

"That's the one."

"Huh." Dorian set the binder on my coffee table; his forehead creased.

"What? I thought you'd be happy to hear that I did it. I left the apartment."

"I am happy. Truly. But Kelly disappeared half a block from here. I'm not sure this is the best time to be going out."

I swallowed, knowing he was right and unable to explain why I still felt compelled for the first time in nearly two years to surge ahead regardless of the risks.

"What are these?" Dorian asked, pausing beside my desk. He studied the grainy pictures I'd printed from the festival. Two of the photos captured Scorpion in the background.

"They're photos a girl from NMU took at the festival that weekend. I forgot they existed until I read an article about that night. I asked her to give me all of her pictures from the weekend."

Dorian nodded slowly. "And these were the ones with you and Wren."

"Yeah…" I considered the man in the pictures, the man who'd later abducted us.

How could I tell Dorian I recognized him when I'd never seen his face that night? That his image had only become clear to me when he started appearing in my apartment?

Photo still in hand, Dorian's shoulders tensed. He stared at Wren, at his dead sister, for more than a minute.

I leaned over and pointed at Scorpion in the background. "I get a weird feeling about this guy."

Dorian glanced at me, blinking. He returned to stare at the picture, looking closer. "Really? You mean… like, he might be the guy?"

"Maybe."

Dorian sat in my computer chair and wiggled the mouse until the screen lit up. "Where are the pictures at? I want to see the originals."

"Are you sure? Isn't Val in the car?"

He frowned and picked up his phone.

I heard Val's voice.

"Hey, I've got to do something quick. Five minutes, tops."

"Are you serious? We have dinner reservations in fifteen minutes." Her tone was high and shrill.

"Take my car," he said. "I'll meet you there in Gloria's car."

"You're kidding, right?" Venom filled her voice.

"No, I'll be right behind you."

"You know what, Dorian? I'm going to sit here for one more minute and if you don't come down, I'm going to take your car and drive home and then I'm going to get in my car and whether you'll see me again is hard to say."

Dorian pulled the phone from his ear and looked at the screen. "She hung up," he said.

"You better go," I told him. "This isn't worth breaking up over. Okay? I don't want your relationship to end because of me."

He stood, nodding, and took a step toward the door, then glanced back at the printed picture. Turmoil twisted his features.

"I'm not going," he said. He returned to my chair and sat down. "Show me the pictures."

I dragged a chair from the kitchen and sat, maneuvering the mouse to the file titled 'Leslie Pics.' Three thumbnail images appeared in the folder I'd moved the pictures of Wren and me too.

"Here they are," I told him.

He opened one and it filled the screen. It revealed Wren bent over and laughing.

Fresh pain ballooned at the sight of her and I turned away and picked up the binder. On the first page, protected by clear plastic, was a newspaper article titled 'Terror at Dancing with the Dead Music Festival in the Porcupine Mountains.'

I read the words about the discovery a local couple made on the banks of the Big Carp River. The body of a young woman.

'We thought she was dead,' said Gene Balmer, part of the husband-and-wife duo who were walking their dog Mustard when he suddenly took off, broke away from the path and ran to the river. 'Mustard led us straight to her. Had he not taken us there, we never would have found her.'

Through the window I heard the blare of a horn followed by tires squealing on the pavement. Val had left. Dorian glanced toward the street, his jaw set, but said nothing.

Investigators have not released a statement, though one should be forthcoming, according to the Ontonagon Sheriff's Office.

A press conference is scheduled for tomorrow.

More newspaper articles followed with black and white images of forest searches, a picture of myself and Wren, images from the festival, photos of police, a picture of Dorian, Rylie and Wren's parents huddled together, candles in hand for a candlelight vigil that had been held two weeks after the attack when I'd still been in the hospital.

My head swam as I scanned the pictures and the headlines.

"Do you recognize him from anywhere?" Dorian asked, interrupting my thoughts as he tapped on the computer screen. "Do you remember seeing him that weekend at the festival?"

I looked at the man's face. "No. I've wracked my brain trying to place him, but... nothing."

"But you still think it might have been him?"

"Yeah."

"He is watching you guys. That's pretty clear. In both of these photos, he's looking at you."

"I thought so too."

"The question is, how do we find him?" Dorian wondered aloud. "I could post this online, hit the social sites and just say 'does anybody recognize this guy?' I could make up something. Maybe we're trying to talk to everyone who saw you both that weekend."

"Two years later, though?"

"If he's a Yooper, someone will probably recognize him." Dorian leaned closer. "There's something on his neck here... See that? It almost looks like a tattoo."

A scorpion. I didn't say it because again, how could I explain it? How could I explain the scorpion or that the man had acne scars and a crooked nose? That he was a smoker, wore too much cologne—the cheap kind that gave you an instant headache.

"No..." Dorian murmured, still staring at the photo. "We don't want him to find out we're looking into him. He's liable to see the post himself and take off."

No, he's not...

"We should show this to Detective Webb. He's got to have some way to track people down, right?"

"Yeah, I've wondered about that."

"Call him. I can be here if you want when he comes over."

I shook my head. "No, that's okay. You've got enough going on. Even more now."

Dorian pursed his lips, but didn't respond, shifting instead back to the photos.

I continued through the binder, pausing at a clipping that seemed unrelated to our attack.

The headline stated, "Local Man Arrested for Home Invasions."

"What's this?" I asked.

"Remember that bouncer Wren thought was following her?"

I nodded and skimmed the article. The bouncer, Bryce Dobbs, had been arrested for a string of home invasions, which had ended when he'd broken into a vacation home in Marquette only to be met by the owner's Doberman Pinscher, who'd cornered Dobbs while the homeowner called the police.

"Wow," I murmured. "I forgot all about the guy. He was a total sleaze."

"Yeah. I encountered him at a few bars when he was working the door. He always had this way of looking at the women that made me want to punch him in the face."

"He was there that weekend, at the festival. He got in Wren's face."

Dorian shifted his attention back to me. "Yeah, I remember you said that. The police supposedly looked into him and couldn't find a link, but I've always wondered."

"Is he still in jail?"

"Nope. Released four months ago. He served less than a year for those home invasions."

"And living in Marquette?"

"As far as I know, but I'm sure he's not working security jobs anymore. The last I heard of him was a little write-up in the paper about his getting released. Someone who'd been robbed wrote an angry editorial about it, but…" He shrugged. "I doubt anything came of it."

23

Two Years Ago
June 21, 2012

"Gloria, I swear to God if you don't get your ass out here in ten seconds, I'm leaving without you."

I leaned out the window and waved. "Five seconds, tops," I called, then ran back into my closet, yanked off the blue skirt and pulled on the red one. It was shorter, sexier, and if I ran into Tom, I wanted him to see me in it.

I slipped on my heels, slung my bag over my shoulder and gathered the rest of my stuff before hurrying down the stairs and half falling out the front door. I'd never mastered heels, and I'd be an accident waiting to happen after a few drinks, but I ignored the near-ankle roll and continued down the steps to where Wren stood beside her white Civic.

She raised both eyebrows. "Trying to make a statement, are we?"

I smoothed the skirt down. "Whatever do you mean?"

She laughed. "You realize the Dancing with the Dead Music Festival is in the woods, as in your stomping ground. You literally have fifty outfits more appropriate for this occasion."

"I just want to make an appearance in this and then I'll put on my shorts and t-shirt," I told her.

"You know you can't walk in those, right? You're going to have to go barefoot if you want to dance."

"Who doesn't go barefoot at music festivals? That was my grand plan, anyway. Once Tom gets an eyeful of me in this skirt."

"You dressed in that is like me donning a colonial prairie dress replete with apron," Wren said, squinting in the side-view mirror and adjusting her nose ring.

"Hardly. This is merely a slightly dressier version of my usual canvas shorts and t-shirt."

Wren smirked. "Where did you even get that skirt?"

I pulled a face. "Janice. She forced me into a"—I made air quotes—"'bonding' shopping trip and refused to go to the sporting goods store. Skirts, high heels and even a pair of earrings. Apparently she didn't notice my ears weren't pierced."

Wren grinned. "I can change that." She leaned through the passenger window and popped open the glove box to reveal a piercing gun crammed between a pile of receipts and bags of M&Ms.

"Explain to me why you carry a piercing gun in your car?"

"Because inevitably someone at a party wants a piercing. It's a smart business decision."

"Really? Are you charging for this service now?"

"Sure, why not? Ten bucks, twenty if they drive a nice car, and boom, they've got pierced ears."

Wren narrowed her eyes at me as I loaded my duffel bag, my hiking boots and my walking stick. "You know hiking is not my jam, right? I mean walks, yes, but five- or ten-mile tromps through the great outdoors are not on the agenda for me this weekend."

"But music is your jam." I pointed at the line-up of artists on the flyer lying on her dashboard. "This is a marriage of our two interests. Falling perfectly between our two birthdays as if by some cosmic design."

"And because it's my birthday today, I'm officially declaring I will not be doing any ten-mile hikes. Leisurely trips to the porta-potty, maybe a trek to a waterfall so long as it's less than a mile away."

"Yes! This is going to be awesome. And it gets me out of that damn anniversary dinner with Janice and my dad."

"Whoa, what are the Peculiar Pals up to this weekend?" Wyatt—our across-the-hall neighbor—asked as he came around the side of our four-plex.

"Dance with the Dead Music Festival in the Porcupine Mountains," I called, dropping into the passenger seat and sliding out of my heels.

Wyatt had labelled Wren and me the Peculiar Pals due to our differing looks, interests and all-around personalities.

Wren called herself 'punk light.' She dyed her hair in varying shades of pastel, wore faded black jeans and a stone-washed jean jacket, played the guitar, had a nose ring and loved punk rock and country music equally. She volunteered at the senior center reading to the elderly, playing board games with them, and twice a month, she borrowed shelter pets from the humane society to let the old people pet them.

I'd gone with her a time or two and usually stood around awkwardly. I'd never had close grandparents and had little experience with the eighties and older sub-culture that existed in assisted living homes—walkers, hip and knee replacements, grocery day, that new girl Marnie who brought the mint cookies, that old guy Vince who made the floor extra-wet when he mopped in the hopes of sending one of them to an early grave. And death in general was a huge part of their daily discussion. Who'd died, how they'd died, when they'd died, where they were getting buried, what kind of service they'd be having, who was eulogizing them.

Wren fell into these conversations as if she were an eighty-year-old herself, cracking corny jokes and happily whiling away an afternoon in some old man's room, stinking of medicine and Old Spice, hearing about the guy's experience in the war, how his wife had died a decade earlier, and how much he missed television that wasn't full of profanity.

I wanted to be like Wren and perhaps that desire was the glue that held us together during so many years when our divergent interests might have sent us down different hallways in school. Likewise, Wren said she envied my independence, my strength.

Unlike my best friend, I was a selfish person. I mostly thought about me. I wanted to be more giving, more generous, more 'out there.' But I'd always found solace in the woods. That was my happy place, alone amid the trees and forest animals. A quiet so full of the best sounds— running water, chirping birds, the whir of a dragonfly's wings. Seriously, if you're quiet enough, you can hear their wings.

Camping, hiking, sitting in thigh-high weeds, watching fox kits play along a river bank. I'd set my sights on working as a park ranger and started school at NMU to get a degree in fish and wildlife management. Wren had started alongside me, pursuing a degree in social work.

Where Wren had style, I veered toward functionality. Dry-fit t-shirts, canvas shorts with pockets for supplies, hiking boots, wool socks. I wore my hair long but nearly always braided or drawn into a ponytail.

"Happy birthday," I told Wren, dropping a small box wrapped in tissue paper in her lap.

She glanced down and scowled. "We agreed to save gifts for when we got back."

"This is a bonus gift."

She glared at me then smiled. "Fine, but I'm buying you something extra at the festival this weekend."

"You better open it before you start throwing out generous offers."

She grinned and, keeping one hand on the wheel, tugged the paper off. She lifted the lid on the box.

A keychain lay inside with an image of a mermaid drinking from an enormous cup of coffee. The words *Sea Witch Before Coffee—Mermaid After* were painted in glittery red letters.

"Ha! I love it. And it's true," she said, fumbling to get the keychain on her keys in the ignition.

"This cord is going to light on fire," I told Wren, holding up the black cord that connected her cell phone to her car, where a playlist of indie and punk music would accompany us on our drive.

"No way," she said. "Sparky? He'd never do me like that."

"I'm afraid to guess why his name is Sparky."

She laughed and fumbled around on the dashboard, littered with sheet music, lip gloss, and several plush stuffed animals. She found a stick of chewing gum and unwrapped it. "There's another one up there somewhere," she told me. "Maybe an entire pack."

I frowned at the mess, fighting the desire to wad it all up in my hands and toss it in the backseat. "How can you drive with all that chaos?"

She glanced my way. "What? It's basically a shelf in my car. What am I supposed to do with it?"

"Leave it empty so you're not pulling gum out of the heat vents every year."

She shrugged. "That's Dorian's job. He's the car guy in the family."

I laughed. "That'll be the day. He told me he changed the oil on your dad's truck last month and it leaked out all over the driveway."

Wren smirked. "Well, I didn't say he was a *good* car guy."

"Bummer that Rylie is sick. Is his girlfriend pissed they're not going?"

"Doubtful. Callie is not exactly a folk music festival kind of gal. The last time I had dinner with them, she spent like an hour lecturing me on how jazz is a much more sophisticated music. 'True musicians play jazz,' I believe was her exact phrase."

"Jazz?" I grimaced. "I'd rather listen to the top forty hits."

"I second that. Anyway, I'm sure Dorian would prefer to spend the weekend feeding Rylie saltine crackers and Popsicles than listen to Callie bitch about the music, the mosquitoes and how her hair is frizzing like a dandelion gone to seed."

"Yeah, what a drag."

"I'm pretty sure that goes for relationships in general," Wren said.

"Not if the relationship is with Tom Russell." I gazed dreamily out the window.

"Why are you so into him, anyway? What is it about Tom that has you all hot and bothered?"

I picked lint off my skirt and rolled it into a little ball. "He's… I don't know, like my dream guy."

"Just make a wish on Nixie then." Wren wiggled the little silver mermaid with iridescent scales hanging from fish line on her rearview mirror. "Or on Esmerelda." She lifted the mermaid charm that hung around her neck.

"I don't think wishing on your lucky mermaids will suddenly pique Tom's interest." I leaned back and watched the trees whoosh by.

"If Tom's not interested, then he's a moron."

I rolled my window down and leaned into the warm wind, pleasant until the smell of roadkill invaded my nostrils.

I recoiled, and Wren shouted, "Ew, roll the window up."

On the side of the road, we passed something bloody and rotting in the summer sun. I couldn't even make out what kind of animal it had been.

"I feel like I could gag," I said, waving at the air in front of me as if that might dissipate the stench.

"That might have been a sign." Wren looked at me with mock alarm.

"A sign of what, exactly?"

"That Tom is bad news, that getting with him is synonymous with… dun-dun-dun death." She cackled maniacally.

24

I was dreaming.

The forest pitched black and steep as I ran, feet pounding the earth, grass crunching beneath my shoes, twigs cracking. All of it loud, deafening, practically a beacon to my location. Still, my noise didn't drown out the other noise, the heavy breath and grunting. The noise of a man committing the most vile act.

"Stop…" I shoved my hands over my ears and tried to drown it out, but it was closer now and I was no longer running. I was pinned to the earth, to the ground, cool and wet with night, and he was over me, on top of me. Sour breath in my face and his grunting was louder and I couldn't shove him off because my hands were bound behind me.

I woke and sat up so quickly I fell off my couch and missed cracking my knee on the coffee table by an inch.

The dream withered, but the sounds did not. They were coming from my room. The man, Scorpion, groaning, breath rasping. It grew louder.

"Noooo…" I whimpered. I crawled onto the couch, curled into a ball, yanked my blanket over me, and stuffed my head so deep into the corner of the couch I could barely breathe.

When I dared to emerge, the sound had died, but the scent of him remained. Cigarette smoke, cologne and a new tinge to his sweat, the sex smell. My stomach rolled, and I ran to my bathroom and jerked up the toilet seat, vomited a thin line of the microwave dinner I'd eaten that night.

The memories of those moments, those excruciating minutes for first Wren and then me made my body spasm as if by vomiting I might rid myself of the memory. I threw up until I was empty, until dry-heaving brought nothing but a croaking rasp up from my stomach.

Spent, I tucked my knees beneath me and pressed my forehead into the linoleum. It cooled my sweaty face.

Late morning, I dialed the number for Detective Webb. He answered on the second ring.

"Detective Webb," he said.

"Hi, Detective, this is Gloria Cline."

"I hoped you'd call," he said.

"I had a few things I wanted to talk about… and I'd like to see the file from my and Wren's case. Is that possible?"

"Yes. Some of it is confidential, but I can bring it by this afternoon?"

"That'd be great. Thanks."

Even though I was expecting him, the knock on my door startled me. I peered through a peephole to see the detective in the hallway.

I unlocked the double deadbolts and opened the door. I'd traded in my usual sweatpants and long-sleeved shirt for a pair of jeans and a slightly nicer long-sleeved shirt.

"Thanks for calling, Gloria. I was happy to hear from you."

I nodded and backed into my apartment. "You can come in."

He did and walked to my kitchen table, dropped a folder on the surface.

"Is that my file?"

"It's a copy of your file, yes."

I sat in a chair opposite him and then realized I should offer him a coffee or something. "Are you thirsty or—"

He shook his head. "Nope, I'm good." He flipped open the folder.

"There are photographs of you in here that I've turned upside down. You don't have to look at them if you don't want to."

I nodded. I knew the photos he referred to, the ones they'd taken of me at the hospital. I vaguely remembered the officer, a woman, camera to her eye, light flashing every few seconds as she circled my bed and captured the damage.

He slid the top sheet of paper out. "This is a transcript of the 911 call made the morning you were found."

He slid the paper toward me and I drew it closer, reading.

Dispatcher: *911. What's the address of your emergency?*

Caller: *I'm on Big Carp River. I found a girl here in awful shape, big gash on her throat. She's about dead.*

Dispatcher: *You found a girl there?*

Caller: *Yeah, a teenager, I think. My wife's with her now, but you better send somebody quick.*

Dispatcher: *Can you give me the coordinates of your location?*

I read the words slowly. I'd met Gene and Harriet Ballmer at the hospital in the weeks after the attack. They'd brought me a 'Get Well Soon' balloon illustrated with a lion holding a handful of daisies. Their sympathy card was in a box with countless others. I'd never opened it. Everything from the hospital had gone into a box that still sat at my dad's house.

Webb took out another sheet of paper and handed it to me. "These are the typed notes of the first officers at the scene."

White female, approximate age 17-25. Wound on throat, abrasions on face, neck, wrists and arms. Possibly a broken arm. Extensive bruising on face, including black eyes and a broken nose. Clothing includes a t-shirt ripped at the neckline. No pants or underwear. One hiking boot on her left foot. No identification.

No initial statement as the victim was in and out of consciousness when we arrived.

"Should we keep going?" he asked me.

I nodded. He slid another sheet of paper across the table.

I read the words typed at the top.

Initial statement by victim. Transcribed from voice recording. Taken on June 27th, 2012—five days after the victim was found.

I tried to remember the interview, but I couldn't, not a moment of it. Had it happened in the hospital? In a police station? I didn't have a clue.

In the report, I described our walk into the woods, the sudden blinding light in our eyes, the man's cold voice. The details were sparse and even then, I was using words to distance myself from the night, words like 'he assaulted us,' which didn't describe what he'd actually done, the horror of it, the physical pain, but something much deeper than the splitting of skin, it was like the splitting of our souls.

I frowned and leaned closer to the page where the interview had written the words 'possibly two perpetrators.' "Two perpetrators?" I murmured.

Dan studied me. "Yes, you mentioned that a few times during your interview."

I scratched at my neck. I tried to remember a second man. Had there been one? Or had Scorpion merely been insane, muttering to himself, or even talking to make it appear more than one man had grabbed us?

I read the last of the interview.

Interviewer asked the victim what happened after her own throat was cut.

Victim: I was lying in the grass and heard the man. I wasn't sure if he was talking to himself or if there was a second man there. I tried not to breathe loudly. I lay totally still. When the sound of the moving in the grass got further away, I stood up and started running. My arms were bound behind me. I remember branches whipping me in the face and this… sensation in my neck… like fire.

I heard the river, and the ground fell out beneath me and I plunged over the bank and I knew it was the only hope. I'd heard something. I was sure he was after me. I curled up and let the water take me. I don't remember anything after that.

I sighed and looked away from the page. My throat itched, but I didn't lift my fingers to the line of raised flesh that would forever mark that dark night.

We sat in silence for a long time, me looking at the page, but seeing another place and time, remembering when the world grew dark.

"Are you okay?" Dan asked. "We can stop if you don't feel capable of talking about this."

"No." I blotted the memories, pushed them away. "I need to talk about it. It's time."

Webb nodded. "You said you didn't recognize the man who attacked you. Not his voice, not his face or build? Is that still true?"

I picked at the cuticle of my left thumb, inserted it into my mouth and chewed the edge. The man in the mirror rose up. I could give this detective a description of the man—much more than I'd given before. One particular piece—the scorpion tattoo.

But how would I explain this fresh memory, this specific description that didn't jibe with my original story? The man had worn a mask. How could I have seen his neck?

I didn't watch the shows anymore, but my forays into true crime before the dark night had been enough to confirm that changing your story was a big no-no in the world of criminal justice. Once a witness changed their story, they were no longer credible. Sometimes their changing stories even led investigators to question their involvement in the crime.

25

Dan studied me with the stare I'd come to associate with detectives. It was unique, piercing. It felt like more than a stare—something akin to the way I felt in childhood if I told my father a lie and it was so blatant, I was practically wearing the truth in red marker on my face. I squirmed and looked away.

"No. I didn't recognize him," I said.

"Okay." Dan swept the transcript back into the folder. "Usually in a violent crime, the first place we look is close to the victim. Boyfriends, friends, family members. In reading through your file, I noticed the original detectives focused more on strangers, which makes sense. The crime occurred at a music festival with over two thousand people and many aspects of the crime pointed to a stranger abduction.

"Still, when I embark on a case, I begin at the center and the center is you and Wren. The names on this list"—he slid a piece of paper from my folder—"include friends, family and acquaintances of the two of you. Most of them had cursory interviews, but I want to dig deeper, if that's okay?"

"Sure."

"Let's start with Dorian Ashby."

I looked at him, surprised. "He had absolutely nothing to do with it."

"I believe you, but in the service of being thorough, I want to ask the questions."

"Okay."

"Dorian is Wren's older brother, correct?"

"Yes, he's five years older than us."

"What can you tell me about him?"

I reached a hand up and touched my short hair, smiled at the memory of Dorian dyeing it days before. "He's a really good person. A lot like Wren. He always puts other people first. That's mostly been his daughter, Rylie. He became a dad at seventeen. I grew up with Wren and Dorian like they were my own siblings. We lived two blocks apart. After that night... Dorian became my... savior, I guess. That's a weird word to use, but that's how I think of him. My very own, very human superhero."

A small smile appeared on Webb's face. "And his relationship with Wren. Did they get along?"

"Great. They confided in each other. Wren spent a lot of time with Dorian's daughter, Rylie. Dorian has a very grown-up way of viewing the world. Wren is... was... a lot more unconventional. They balanced each other."

"Dorian didn't attend the festival that weekend?"

I shook my head. "He had planned to go, him and his then girl-friend, but Rylie got the flu, so he stayed home. He could have left her with his parents, but he'd never do that. He knew Rylie would want to be home with him since she didn't feel good."

"That's a very decent thing to do."

"That's Dorian."

"And what did Dorian tell you about Kelly after he met her?"

"Just that she was nice, studying criminal justice. Umm... Rylie had dropped her stuffed sloth, and Kelly picked it up for her."

"Did he say they exchanged phone numbers?"

"No."

"Would you be surprised if I told you we found Dorian's phone number posted to a corkboard in Kelly's room?"

I shrugged. "Not really. He's a friendly person. I could see him giving her his number."

"Not in a romantic capacity, then?"

"I doubt it. He has a girlfriend. He and Val have been dating for like a year."

"Happily?"

I remembered him blowing Val off to look at the festival photos with me. "We don't have a lot of deep talks about his relationships."

"What do you have deep talks about?"

"Me, mostly." I released a dry laugh. "Lately I've been… having a hard time. He comes over and looks to make sure no one is here. We talk about Rylie, we watch TV together."

"Do you ever talk about Wren?"

I swallowed. "Yeah, sometimes."

"Do you ever talk about that night?"

I shook my head. "He wanted to, more in the beginning, but… I just couldn't. Eventually he dropped it."

"And he didn't make it to the music festival because Rylie was ill?"

"Right."

"It appears only he and Rylie were home that evening. No other adult could corroborate his story."

"Because no other adult lives with him. His then girlfriend was…" I shook my head. "I'm not sure where she was."

"She was in town, but he asked her not to stop by because Rylie was sick."

"There you go."

"But according to his story, Rylie slept all night and couldn't confirm if Dorian was, in fact, home the entire night."

I snorted. "The music festival was two and a half hours away. You think he snuck off to the music festival and somehow made a five-hour round trip plus time at the festival and slipped back in without Rylie noticing?"

Webb tilted his head. "What do you think?"

"I think that's the most ludicrous thing I've ever heard."

"Okay. Let's move on from Dorian. I have a name for Wren's last boyfriend: Seth Waterman. Tell me about him."

"Seth was a musician. He flitted into town once a month or so. It wasn't serious."

"Who ended the relationship?"

"Wren."

"An amicable breakup?"

"Yeah. He hadn't been in town in a couple of months and it mostly fizzled out, but Wren called him to do the official 'let's call it quits' thing."

"And you previously dated a man named Marty Burks?"

"Yes. We broke up my senior year in high school."

"Any leftover feelings there? A passionate break-up?"

I snorted. "No, definitely not. Marty's gay. Our relationship was more like friends with… well, not even with benefits. I don't know what our relationship was. Friends who kissed sometimes." I blushed, feeling foolish at how clueless I'd been with Marty.

"In one of your earlier interviews, you mentioned a man named Tom Russell."

"Did I? Wow, yeah, I guess that makes sense."

"Were you and Tom dating?"

"No. I had a crush on him."

"How did you know Tom?"

"We had classes together at NMU."

"And did he know Wren?"

"From afar. I'm sure they'd talked a time or two at a party or the bar. Marquette's a pretty small place, especially if you go to Northern. Eventually, you get to know everyone."

"He was at the festival that weekend?"

"Yes."

"And how did that go?"

"Fine." I shrugged, remembering the night in the tent and not willing to spill my secret.

"How about Jeffrey Calder?"

I scowled, and Dan cocked an eyebrow.

"Not someone you're fond of? I have a note here that he's your stepbrother."

"Yeah, he is. I'm not fond of him or his mother."

"Why is that?"

I rubbed at the scar on my neck. "They're birds of a feather—Jeff and Janice. They have these 'better than everyone' personalities." I heard my complaints—sounded like a typical bratty kid spouting off about a stepmother and stepbrother.

"And he attended the festival?"

"Yes."

"Any altercations with Jeff?"

"No. I saw him at the start of the weekend and in passing once or twice. We never even said hello."

"Okay." Dan made a note on his list. "Your mom is not in the picture?"

"Not really, no."

My mother had hated Marquette, which was why she'd left for the dazzling mayhem of Las Vegas when I was seven. I'd been there once, flown alone, clutching my backpack to my chest, terrified when men slapped little cards at me depicting half-naked women.

My mom lived in a condo she shared with another blackjack dealer. She was not attuned to the needs of a child. During my visit, we'd walked the Strip at night. We'd eaten at the old hotels in downtown Vegas, the Golden Nugget and the El Cortez, with five-dollar buffets and shrimp cocktail as big as your head.

My first night, I'd suffered food poisoning and vomited for hours. My mother never woke to check on me, get me a glass of water, nothing. I spent the following day watching television while she worked the day shift at the casino. Her roommate came home with bags of greasy fast food and gave me a cheeseburger and French fries.

That was the one and only time I'd visited my mother. She'd called me every few months since the dark night, but her voice sounded distant, as if she watched TV or scrolled her phone in the background, as if she only half-listened.

She couldn't fathom that I hadn't left my apartment in nearly two years. She assumed I exaggerated the level of my agoraphobia. The idea of staying shut in her condo for a full twenty-four hours gave her hives —she'd told me as much on multiple occasions.

"She's lived in Las Vegas since I was seven," I told Webb.

"When's the last time you spoke to her?"

I bit my cheek. "Umm… I guess Christmas. Yeah, she called me the day after on the twenty-sixth."

"Okay. Is your relationship volatile at all?"

"No. There's really no relationship."

"All right. What can you tell me about things happening in the weeks leading up to the music festival? Dorian mentioned Wren feared someone was following her."

26

———

I frowned, picked at a string that had pulled loose on my athletic pants. "Well… I mean, the bouncer who had a thing for her—Bryce—she thought he followed her after gigs once or twice. He acted pretty crazy at the festival and tried to drag Wren away from the crowd. Dorian told the police about him though."

"Yeah, Bryce Dobbs. Detectives have looked pretty closely at him. He's been spoken to and denies any involvement."

"Have *you* interviewed him?"

"No. Like I said, I only came onto this case with the disappearance of Kelly. You and Wren were attacked in a different jurisdiction, so we don't have the lead on your case. That being said, the sheriff's office in Ontonagon is happy for the help because their investigation stalled a long time ago. We're searching for anyone who knew you and Wren and also knew Kelly, which includes looking at Bryce."

I imagined the man with the scorpion tattoo and the dark eyes. He was not Bryce Dobbs, but if there'd been another man, one who'd stayed in the shadows to avoid being identified… he might have been the angry bouncer.

"I have a highlighted section here where Dorian and you mentioned to police early in the investigation that Wren observed someone outside your apartment. It spooked her."

"Oh, wow, yeah…" I struggled to remember, to walk back into the time before the night that had shattered us.

"Glo, look out the window," Wren had announced one night, slipping into our apartment and turning off the lights.

"Hey," I grumbled. "I nearly snagged this hat I'm knitting for you."

"Just... come, look." She hurried to the window, but hunched down and peeled back the curtain.

I joined her. "What? Mr. and Mrs. Bigfoot going at it in the camper again?"

Wren said nothing, but pulled the curtain open more, pressed her forehead almost to the glass. "He's gone," she murmured.

"Who? Who was out there?"

"Some guy. He was in the shadow of that big tree over there by Mr. and Mrs. Bigfoot's house. I heard him move when I got out of my car. I think he was wearing a mask."

"Well, that's creepy."

"Yeah."

"You sure it wasn't Mr. Bigfoot in some sick role-playing game?"

Our neighbors across the street, whom we'd nicknamed Mr. and Mrs. Bigfoot thanks to no fewer than six Bigfoot statues and signs adorning their property, had four young children. When the weather had started warming up, we regularly spotted them sneaking from their house after dark into the camper in the driveway, which would then shake for several minutes before the duo snuck back into their house. Sometimes they left the camper light on and we got quite an eyeful.

"It wasn't him," Wren insisted. "Mr. Bigfoot's like five feet seven inches tall. This guy was over six feet. Before I saw him... I felt him."

"Come again?" I said, pulling away from the window.

"That sense when someone is watching you. The hairs on my neck stood up and I turned and he was there."

"Did he say anything?"

"No, just stood watching me. He knew I saw him and he just stared back at me."

I walked across the room and double-checked that our door was locked. It was. "Weird. Probably just some jerk out to scare people."

"Yeah, maybe."

"She saw a guy watching her outside our apartment," I said, focusing on Webb, the memory of Wren sliding away. "It happened twice. The first time he was in the yard across the street. We'd nicknamed those neighbors Mr. and Mrs. Bigfoot. I don't know their actual names.

"The second time she saw him from our window upstairs. He stood near these big shrubs at the side of the house. He wore a Halloween mask that almost looked human, like a normal face, but sort of distorted. She saw him at night both times and he was kind of hidden."

"Did you ever see him?"

"No. The first time she tried to show me, but he was gone when we looked out the window. The second time she was home alone."

"Did she ever report it to the police?"

"No. We figured he was just some asshole who liked to spook people."

"The man who abducted you also wore a mask, didn't he?"

"Yeah, but he wore a balaclava—a winter mask. The guy Wren saw wore a costume mask. At least she thought he did."

"Okay." Dan made a few notes and then set his pen down. "I have a few notes here about calls you've made to the police about strange noises. Have you ever been threatened here?"

Color climbed into my face at the memory of those panicked calls. "No. I… I've been paranoid since the attack. If I hear or see something, it's hard to shake it. I've gotten better. I haven't called the police in months."

"Is there anything else you can think of, Gloria? Anything that has come back to you in the years since it happened?"

I glanced toward my laptop and nodded. "There is something." I stood and walked to my desk, picked up the three printed photographs Leslie had taken. I returned them to Webb.

He shuffled through them and looked up. "I'm not sure what I'm looking at here. This is you and Wren at the festival?"

I pointed at the man in the background—Scorpion. "I saw these for the first time recently and… there's something about this guy. I feel like he's the one."

"The one who attacked you?"

"Yes."

Webb scratched his jaw, frowning at the picture. "Can you send me the original? We have a photo guy who might be able to blow this up, get a few more details."

"Yeah. Write down your email and I'll send it to you."

He took out a business card and scrawled his email on the back.

"Do you have any suspects? Any leads at all?"

"We have a lot of leads. I wouldn't call any of them suspects yet." He rubbed at a line of puckered pale flesh on the back of his left hand.

"What happened?" I asked, nodding at his hand.

Dan tilted his hand back and forth. The shiny flesh reflected the light. "Someone tried to kill me."

I widened my eyes. "In the line of duty?"

"No, not exactly. I was on leave from the force and started looking into a missing person's case. The murderer got wind of what I was up to and tried to silence me."

"But you survived."

"Yep, a little worse for the wear, but I survived."

"With no... like inner stuff, mental stuff?" I was thinking panic attacks, agoraphobia, PTSD.

"To some extent a job in law enforcement prepares you for such things. By the time you face your own mortality, you've been brushing up against the violence long enough that it's hardly a shock. It's different for"—he gestured at her—"people who haven't lived that kind of life. You survived the night, Gloria. That feat alone makes you stronger than you realize."

I started to argue, but he cut me off. "I get it. You're afraid now and that makes you feel weak, but I can't tell you how many people in your shoes that night would have lain down in the woods and bled to death. They would never have tried to run, to jump in a river, to get away. They would have given up rather than face what you went through. At some point, you have to acknowledge the courage it took to do that and have faith in yourself again. Only you can do it."

Anger flared in my chest, but I didn't retort. He didn't get it, not really. But then my eye caught his hand and I wondered how many times he'd nearly died and yet here he was working the same kind of crimes, putting himself in the path of murderers time and again.

I found the prospect horrifying, and yet... some tiny spark lit in my brain. It was also exhilarating, the thought of turning the tables, facing down the bad guy with a gun gripped in my hands.

"Are you a Marquette native?" I asked him.

He shook his head. "I'm from the Lansing area in Michigan. My wife and I moved to Marquette a couple years ago. She's a fly fisherman who hails from West Virginia. She still goes down there for a month every year to lead fly-fishing excursions."

"Wow, really? That's great. I love fishing, but I've never tried fly-fishing." I caught my statement and backtracked. "I loved fishing. It's been a long time."

"She'll take you when this is all over, show you the ropes. Her name's Cass. She keeps us stocked in fish year-round."

"Thanks," I said, desperately wanting to believe I'd someday take him up on the offer.

"I've got to get going," he said, standing and picking up my file. "I'll let you know if we identify the guy in the photo."

As he was leaving, Dan turned back at the door. "One more thing. Do you have a personal item I could borrow? Something of yours and ideally something of Wren's."

"A personal item?"

"Yeah. A piece of clothing, a knickknack—anything would do."

"Would do for what?"

He scratched his jaw and studied me as if trying to decide what answer to give. "In investigations as complex as this one, I try to keep an open mind. There's a woman I work with sometimes on difficult cases. She's a psychic."

I frowned. "A psychic?"

He chuckled. "I know. It's not the usual line of inquiry for detectives, but I prefer to consider things from every angle."

I stood and walked to my coat closet. I pulled out a scarf I'd knitted. From the shelf above my coats, I grabbed a shoebox and carried it to the table. I removed the lid and studied the jumble of contents. A guitar pick that had belonged to Wren, a pair of her balled-up socks, feathers she'd clipped in her hair and a stack of wrinkled papers in varying sizes on which she'd scrawled song lyrics and music notes.

It was all Wren's stuff that had been in my car. I had boxed it up sometime after I'd left the hospital when I'd been trying to return to a normal life before I'd shut myself away.

I took out one of her songs. Of everything, those surely had the greatest essence of Wren. At the top she'd scrawled a working title: "The Golden Hour of the Flower," a song about wildflowers.

"This is a scarf I knitted and this is a song Wren wrote." I handed the items to Dan.

He held up his hands. "Any chance you could slip them into a plastic bag? I don't want to taint them in some way."

Seriously? I didn't ask the question, but I was sure it showed in my expression as I grabbed a plastic bag and slid the items inside.

"Thanks, Gloria." He glanced beyond me at my bedroom door, opened a crack. He blinked towards it. "Is there anyone here with you?"

A tremor of dread crept up my spine as I shook my head. "No. Why?"

He shifted his gaze back to me. "I thought I saw something move. Probably a shift in light. Sun goes behind the clouds, changes the shadows." He stepped back into my apartment. "Do you mind if I do a quick sweep?"

"Not at all."

He moved through my apartment, opening closet doors, crouching to peer under the bed in my room. He pushed clothes aside in the closet. I followed him knowing full well what he'd seen but saying nothing.

Back at my front door, he shrugged. "I hope I didn't spook you. I wouldn't have been able to sleep tonight if I hadn't checked."

"No, I appreciate it. Thanks, Detective Webb."

He glanced past me toward the open bedroom door and nodded. "I'll be in touch."

27

Two Years Ago
    June 21, 2012

For the entire two-plus hour drive to the Porcupine Mountains, Wren and I talked. Despite having been friends for the entirety of our lives and living together for the last year, we never ran out of things to chat about.

"Whatever happened to Marty?" Wren asked. "The first love of your life."

I guffawed. "That'd be the day. Gosh, I can't believe I lost my virginity to him."

She smiled and shook her head. "Poor Marty. I think he really expected you guys to get married and live happily ever after."

"Hardly. He moved out of state. His mom came into Black Rock a few weeks ago. He's definitely moved on."

"Really? New girlfriend?"

"He's dating a guy."

Wren looked at me, eyes wide. "No way. Marty is gay." She returned her gaze to the road, face thoughtful. "I guess now that you say it... I could see that."

"Yeah, me too. He always felt so... tame. When he kissed me, it was like making out with a mannequin. Apparently, he wasn't into it."

Wren nodded. "Good for Marty. He's even told his mom. That couldn't have been easy. Isn't she kind of a religious fanatic?"

"Going to church once a week does not a fanatic make, but I'm sure it was a blow, anyway. She was trying to plan our wedding junior year. She once told me she couldn't wait to have five grandchildren. I still remember Marty turning ten shades paler than he already was."

"Impossible. He was practically a ghost."

I laughed, remembering Marty, skinny and bone-white, trying to catch a tan each summer and only burning himself the color of a radish.

I didn't have much of a dating record. Marty and I had gone out during my junior and senior years of high school, but it had been far from young love. We'd both been busy. I played volleyball and soccer. When I wasn't busy with sports, I was hiking, learning to rock climb. Marty likewise had been engaged with the debate team and running track.

Something about Marty had always felt... bland. We'd made out, done some heavy petting, but I never saw fireworks, never lay in bed daydreaming about him. The one time we'd had sex had been so clumsy and passionless, I'd never wanted to repeat it. When he'd gone off to school in Indiana, I hadn't shed a tear.

I thought about Tom then with his mountain-man looks, tousled blond hair and beard, body chiseled from spending summers working as a lumberjack with his dad. During the school year, he was studying at Northern to become a game warden. We were both in the fish and wildlife undergraduate program and had met when we'd been paired up in a plant physiology course. He was the exact opposite of Marty Burks.

"He's dreamy," I said, propping my feet on the dash, knees bent, which caused my skirt to slide so high on my legs, my white underwear stuck out. I yanked it back down.

"Marty?" Wren made a face.

"No, Tom. Obviously."

Wren tilted her head. "He's all right. I guess if you're into that forest man thing."

"Which I am."

She laughed. "I like my guys a little more emo than that, but to each their own."

Wren had never had a boyfriend for more than a few months. She'd dated musicians and poets and one guy who insisted he was writing a novel and was forever carrying around a battered notebook, which he never seemed to actually write in.

Wren rarely dated guys who attended our school, instead meeting boys at open mic nights and concerts and dating from afar, which often consisted of phone calls and social media chats. She'd see the guys once a month when they had a gig in Marquette and after a few months the romance would fizzle out.

"Oh, yeah," Wren shouted when the next song came on. She cranked the volume.

Laura Branigan belted out the lyrics to "Gloria."

"Why do you have this song on an indie playlist? It's like thirty years old."

"Which means it's a classic," Wren cut in. "'Calling Gloria!'" she sang.

I shook my head and laughed, irritated as my skirt crept up yet again.

"Screw it," I grumbled, twisting around in the seat to unzip my duffel bag and pull out a pair of shorts and a blue t-shirt that said *Take a Hike* above a mountain landscape.

I shuffled out of the skirt and pulled on shorts, replaced my push-up bra with a sports bra, and my sexy top with my t-shirt.

Wren side-eyed me, shaking her head. "Not bad. You lasted almost an hour in that outfit. That might be a new record for you."

I leaned back, stacked my hands behind my head, and kicked my feet up on the dash with no underwear reveals. "Ahh. That's better."

"We're almost there," Wren announced, gesturing at a large wooden sign mounted on the side of the road. *In Five Miles You'll be Dancing with the Dead* it said in enormous white letters against a black backdrop.

When we arrived at the gate, twenty cars lined the forest road. People milled about. Some climbed from their vehicles and sat on the hoods smoking joints or drinking from plastic cups.

Beside us, on the fifty-plus acres where the festival was held, campers and vendor tents and food trucks had been erected. The stages were set back from the road, but through our rolled-down windows, music drifted in.

"The Black Cat Band," Wren said, bobbing her head. "Hear that? It's Zena Bracht playing the fiddle. Man, she kicks ass."

I grinned. "It sounds like she plays a mean fiddle."

Wren put the car in park, and one of the gate guys walked over. "Need tickets, or have you got them?"

I handed her the tickets, and she gave them to the guy who wore a t-shirt that said, *Ain't nothing bristly about the Porcupine Mountains.*

"Cool… cool. Follow the other cars in. Most of the campsites by the stages are gone, but if you follow the signs, you'll get into the sites that are more wooded. Take a left up there if you want to be closer to the porta-johns. Go right if you're trying to get lost in nature. Here's a map. This little brochure has the line-up of events and you each get one of these nifty purple wristbands. Enjoy."

"Thanks." Wren took the packet and dropped it in my lap and eased the car forward behind a little blue Toyota so trunk-heavy its back bumper scraped the ground when it pulled from the road onto the grassy trail that led toward the campsites. "Definitely musicians," she said.

When we came to the fork, she glanced at me. "Bathrooms or deep woods?" she asked.

"Definitely deep woods."

"I knew you were going to say that. What happens if I wake up in the night and have to pee?"

"You step out of the tent and squat behind a bush."

"And if a Sasquatch drags me into the forest?"

"Then I'll run out, snap his picture and we'll be millionaires."

She laughed. "I was hoping for something more like you'll rescue me."

"Oh, well, I'll do that too after I take his picture. Plus, do you remember the Mad Jammin' Music Festival? Waking up to the smell of the porta-potties in the morning?"

"Ugh…" She grimaced and made a gagging face. "Don't remind me. I don't think they'd ever emptied those things."

After we set up camp along a section of old-growth hemlock trees, we headed for the Pine Stage, spread a blanket out, and sat down to listen to the band.

Wren dove in front of me and curled into a ball, pulling part of our flannel blanket over her.

I leaned toward the opening, where she peeked out.

"What?" I asked.

"Over there. It's Bryce."

I looked over my shoulder, scanning the crowd, and finally spotted him near the beer tent. "Oh, no! He's coming this way," I whispered.

Wren pulled the blanket so hard over her, she nearly flipped me off it.

I laughed and steadied myself. "Jesus, Wren. I'm joking. He's going… and he's gone. Headed off toward the Aspen Stage."

She poked her head out of the blanket like a meerkat from its hole. "Are you sure?" She squinted toward where he'd been.

"Yep. He's gone."

"Damn," she muttered, emerging from under the blanket and smoothing it back out. "I wouldn't have come if I knew he'd be here."

"Oh, come on. He's not that bad. Right? There are hundreds of people. You probably won't even run into him again."

"He is that bad. I swear to God, he followed me home the other night."

"Really? When?"

"After I played that gig at the Avenue Pub. He was working the door and when I left, I dropped Miranda off at her place and I noticed this car behind me, but staying kind of back, so I took a detour and just looped through town and the guy followed me the entire way."

"What makes you think it was him?"

"I don't know. He drives a little dark car. I couldn't see it clear enough that night to say it was definitely him, but… I felt like it was. You know? The same itchy, gross feeling I get when I'm on stage and suddenly I know he's watching me and sure enough, if I look out in the crowd, he is. For all I know, he's the creepy dude who's been outside in the mask."

I frowned. "God, I hope not. That takes the creepiness to a whole other level."

Wren nodded and folded her arms across her chest.

"Hey, birthday girl." I reached behind her back and gave her a half-hug. "Are you okay? This is really bothering you?"

Wren smiled faintly and touched the earring in her right ear, a tiny silver leaf. "I just have a bad feeling."

"You do? About Bryce?"

Wren smoothed her fingers over a dandelion poking from the grass, her expression uneasy. "I'm not sure. It's probably nothing."

"I'll keep an eye out for him. If he comes around, I'll pester him with dumb questions and you can make a run for it."

"Deal."

28

———————

Less than ten minutes after Detective Webb left, Dorian arrived.

He appeared frazzled, his hair woolly from the humidity. Sweat stains dotted his gray t-shirt and beaded at his hairline.

"You okay?" I asked as he hurried to my kitchen and filled a glass with water and ice.

"Yeah." He wiped an arm across his brow. "It's hot out and I've spent the last two hours mowing the property on Fern Street because the lawn guy didn't show up and there are vacationers checking in tonight. I'll be happy when this weekend is over. What'd the detective say? Any developments on Kelly?"

"No developments. We went over my and Wren's case, mostly. He showed me the file."

Dorian leaned against the counter, sipping his water. He pressed the glass to his forehead. "Anything significant in that?"

"Not really, no."

Dorian frowned, set the glass on the counter and paced to my window. "I wish I didn't have all these rentals this weekend. My mind feels like it's split in two, trying to deal with work but wanting to go back over everything—see if I can find the link between you and Wren and Kelly."

"Focus on work. I have faith in Detective Webb. I really do. I think… he might be the one to solve this."

"He didn't have any suspects at all with Kelly? No eyewitnesses who saw a guy hanging around the apartment? Nothing like that?"

"Not that he told me, but who knows? Cops don't usually like to spill the details. He said one thing I found really curious, though."

"What's that?"

"He works with a psychic. He's going to take her to the trail where Wren and I were abducted."

"A psychic?" Dorian looked skeptical.

"It can't hurt, right?"

He shrugged. "I guess not." He lifted his glass and gulped the rest of the water. "I've got to run, but… the day after tomorrow is Wren's birthday."

I sucked in a little breath. In the tumult of activity, I'd somehow forgotten, and now it was here.

"I thought… if you're up for it, we could move the celebration to your apartment? It's nothing big, just my parents, Rylie and I. My mom ordered Wren's favorite food."

"Beef with broccoli?"

"You know it. With a hefty side of fried rice. My mom and Wren are making a cake. Rylie, I mean. My mom and Rylie are making a cake. What if we brought it here?"

I sat on the arm of the couch. I hadn't seen Wren's parents in months. They'd visited at Christmas with Dorian and Rylie. They'd given me gifts, including a velvet bath robe and a set of aromatherapy candles. I'd knitted them both hats and scarves. "I don't want to make Wren's birthday about me."

"You guys always shared your birthday. Yours is two days after. Plus, my parents miss you."

"Okay…" I said after a moment, surprising myself. "Let's do it, but only if your mom is totally comfortable with the idea. If she has any hesitation—"

"She won't," he said.

"What about Val? Isn't she coming?"

He shook his head. "Val and I are done."

"Really? Just like that?"

"Yep, just like that. I'd like to do something on your birthday too. Just me, you and Rylie. Virgin piña coladas, pineapple and bacon pizza, *Gilmore Girls* marathon. What do you think?"

"That sounds like a perfect day," I said.

"Good. I'll try to stop by later. Text me if you need anything."

~

A knock at my door broke my concentration as I completed the last of the mermaid tail for Rylie.

I peered through the viewing hole to see Nicki in the hall. I unlocked the bolts and let her in.

She triumphantly held up a laptop. "I logged into Kelly's Gmail account."

We sat shoulder to shoulder on the couch, Nicki's laptop open before us. She clicked the Gmail account and opened Kelly's location history.

"Here's her locations the day she went missing. From ten in the morning until five, she's at the parking garage working as an attendant. It literally traces the route she drove home. Then her location is at our apartment. And then…"

Nicki's finger moved over the highlighted route, which showed Kelly's phone leaving the apartment near midnight. It travelled out of Marquette to Highway M-28 running west. In Covington Township, the phone stopped and its location remained at that point.

"She ended up in Covington Township," Nicki said, triumphant.

I stared at the screen. "Her phone did, at least. But see, there's no signal after four a.m., which means the battery died or…"

"Or it was turned off."

"Do you know anyone in Covington Township? Anyone along that route? Friends or family she might have had out that way?"

"No one I can think of."

"You gave this login stuff to the police?"

"Yeah. I stayed up last night trying to get the password, finally got in around ten and Kelly's mom called the police right away, so they should be tracking this stuff too."

"Good," I said. Detective Webb hadn't mentioned the discovery to me. I wondered if he'd already been in Covington Township searching for Kelly Rice.

I leaned over Nicki and scrolled to the icon that offered all the Gmail apps. "Did you check her email?" I asked.

"Yeah. Nothing stood out. She had a few emails applying for internships at police stations, but nothing that seemed important."

I clicked on the email icon and read the subject lines of her incoming messages, but discovered nothing odd. I moved over to the sent folder.

The first four messages were correspondence between her and police stations, but the following three piqued my interest.

I opened the first and read the message, which essentially asked if a person could get life insurance without the insured knowing it and if higher premiums were paid if the death was violent.

"Look," I told Nicki. "She emailed three insurance companies about life insurance claims, specifically about violent death policies."

Nicki leaned over, scanning the emails. "Huh, that's weird."

"Would someone have taken life insurance out on her?"

"I doubt it. I mean… her parents have a lot of money."

"She doesn't give any details, just asks these open-ended questions about how life insurance works," I murmured, not sure what, if any, relevance the emails had. "Let's look back through her history."

"Here." She handed me her laptop. "I need to use your bathroom. Is it down here?" Nicki stood.

"Yeah. First door on the left."

I scrolled back to the days leading up to Kelly's disappearance, peering at the locations she'd visited. She mostly moved between her apartment on Franklin, NMU, and her job at the parking garage.

I paused at a location listed five days ago. It was the address of my childhood home.

"What the hell?" I murmured.

Nicki reappeared, her face pale.

"What?" I asked her.

She looked behind her, lips pursed, and shook her head. "Nothing… I just… I thought I saw someone in your room, like looking at me through a crack in the door. Is there someone in there?"

"No, it's just me."

"Creepy," she said, rubbing her hands up and down her arms.

"Do you want to double-check? We can go together," I suggested, oddly unafraid. The man in my apartment couldn't hurt us. I was sure of it now.

She nodded. "Yeah, otherwise I'm going to be jumping at every sound."

I stood, set the computer on the couch and walked past her down the hall. I pushed the door open all the way and flipped on the light.

Nicki hovered behind me in the doorway. I peeled back the curtain, crouched and looked under the bed, performing the very tasks Dorian had done for me on so many occasions and that Dan Webb had done less than an hour before.

I opened the closet, and a terrible smell rolled out. I recoiled and put an arm over my face.

Nicki's face wrinkled in disgust and she clamped both hands over her nose and mouth. "Oh, my God, what is that?" She stared into the closet. We both did, but there was nothing save my rack of clothes and the jumble of boots, hiking gear and blankets beneath it. And beneath that...

"There must be something dead in the ceiling," I grumbled, though I knew there wasn't.

29

___

I closed the door firmly behind us and we walked back to the couch.

"Did you find anything?" she asked. "In her history?"

"Maybe," I admitted, pointing at the location, 71 Brook Lane, my childhood home. "This is where I grew up. My dad and stepmom live there."

"Really? Hmm, that's weird."

"Maybe she was trying to find me?"

Nicki bit her lip and shook her head. "Possibly," she agreed.

The laptop pinged and Nicki clicked on the Facebook icon. Someone had commented on a recent post she'd made about Kelly's disappearance.

I didn't mean to look, but my eye caught on the name of the poster: Tom Russell.

"Tom Russell?" I asked, leaning closer.

He'd posted the comment: *Sending prayers that she's found safe.*

"What?" she asked. "Do you know him?"

"Yes. I went to school with him. How do you know him?"

Nicki didn't answer but scrolled to Kelly's page and opened her photos. A photo of Kelly, arms linked with Tom, appeared on the screen.

"Kelly knew Tom?"

"Yeah, they dated for… I don't know—six months maybe."

I studied Tom, who'd changed in the two years since I'd last seen him. He was clean-shaven, no longer the mountain man I'd been so drawn to. He wore khaki pants and a red button-down shirt. Kelly stood beside him, nearly his same height in heels. She wore billowy black pants and a strapless black and white top.

"He looks different," I said.

"Like a banker?" Nicki asked. "He works at Chase Bank. That's how he and Kelly met."

"He works at a bank?" I shook my head. "He was going to school to be a game warden. How did he end up doing that?"

Nicki shrugged. "Beats me. His grandfather maybe? I remember Kelly mentioning his grandfather was a higher-up at Chase."

"Bizarre," I murmured, remembering that weekend, that one sweaty night in Tom's tent and how quickly the romance I'd fantasized about for months had been snuffed out. Clearly the Tom in my head in no way matched the Tom in real life.

"I haven't seen him in a while," Nicki said. "You don't think he could have been involved?"

I shook my head. "I doubt it. But… did Kelly or you know a guy named Bryce Dobbs?"

Nicki bit her lip and then nodded slowly. "Yeah, yes. Bryce sometimes hung out with Wyatt, the guy across the hall. He came to a few parties there."

"You're kidding?"

"No. I didn't like him, Kelly either. He'd get super drunk and make lewd comments. One time a guy I was seeing threw him out of the apartment building, like literally dragged him down the steps and shoved him out the front door. I was scared shitless he'd come back later and murder us all."

My heart slammed against my breastbone and sweat trickled from beneath my arms. "How long ago was that?"

Nicki scrunched her face. "In the spring right after classes ended, so not that long ago."

"Does Detective Webb know that?"

"Yeah. He asked about Bryce." She bit her lip.

"What?"

"He also asked about your friend, Dorian."

"That's standard. I mean he just met Kelly the other day." I said the words, but something in Nicki's face troubled me.

"Did you get the sense he suspected Dorian of something?"

She fiddled with the ends of her long hair. "Maybe… he pushed pretty hard about whether Kelly and Dorian had ever gone out. If Dorian had ever come by the apartment."

"But they hadn't, right?"

"No. I mean, not that I know. When she met him she told me all about it. How cute he was and how adorable his little girl was. But that was it."

~

After Nicki left, I lifted weights and did fifty push-ups followed by one hundred sit-ups. I thought again and again about the information Nicki had discovered. Kelly had dated Tom Russell. Both girls had had an altercation with Bryce Dobbs. It all felt significant and yet I wasn't sure how.

One thing was certain, Kelly had visited my dad's house less than a week before she vanished and I wanted to know why.

I dialed my dad's number.

"Gloria? Hi! I'm so happy you called," my dad answered cheerily.

"I'm sorry about the other day, Dad."

"No, no. I'm sorry. I shouldn't have brought them. It was a stupid thing to do."

"It's fine."

"Water under the bridge, then? Shall we reschedule our visit? Me and Hercules on our own this time. I promise."

"Sure, but first, I have a question. Did a girl come by your house last week? Tall and thin with long blonde hair. Her name is Kelly."

"Not that I'm aware of, but you know I'm off to work during the day. Got to keep Janice in purses and jewelry." He chuckled, but I suspected neither of us thought it was funny.

"So, if she stopped by Janice might have met her."

"More than likely. She or Jeff. He's home a lot during the day as well."

"Isn't he working?"

"Oh, no, Janice wants him to enjoy his summer. He's working so hard during the school term and all."

"Yeah, right. Could you ask her for me?"

"Ask Janice?"

"Yes."

"Right now?"

"If she's home."

"Oh, sure, sure. Yeah, hold on."

I heard him set the phone down and I waited. Minutes passed and then he came back on the line. "No such luck. Janice said no one has come by on her watch. Who is this person?"

"Just a girl I know," I lied.

"How's tomorrow for a visit, hon? Lunchtime? I could bring Reuben sandwiches from Donkers. You always loved those."

"Okay, yeah. Let's plan for that."

I ended the call and my phone buzzed. A text from Dorian.

Dorian: *Hey. I can't stop by tonight. The driver I hired to take the tourists to the concert has strep throat and just canceled, so I'm playing chauffeur. FML! I am so ready for this weekend to be over. Text if you need me.*

I texted back. *No worries. Good luck.*

Outside a horn honked and I slipped to the window and peered out. A few houses down three teenagers piled into a van and drove away.

Behind me a door slammed and I jumped.

I turned and stepped cautiously toward the hall that led to my bedroom. The door was closed, though I knew I'd left it open after Nicki and I had searched it earlier.

A week ago, I'd have called Dorian, hysterical. I would have strongly considered calling the police. Now, I did none of those things.

I walked slowly down the hall and reached for the doorknob. It felt cold beneath my palm. I twisted and pushed it in, cringed at the smell— the smells.

The stink of decay and the heady smell of cigarette smoke, the headache-inducing cologne, the stomach-turning sweat smell.

It rolled over me in a gust, wet and icy, and beyond it I saw the voodoo doll, eyeless with its red slash mouth, resting in the center of my bed.

30

———

The following day, I opened the door to my dad and Hercules.

Hercules bounded through, jumped up and put his paws on my legs, tail wagging wildly.

"Is that my good boy?" I gushed, kneeling and leaning in to his sloppy kisses. "Oh, goodness, that's the very best boy, isn't it? Huh? Come here, let me rub your belly."

Hercules plopped down and rolled onto his back, exposing his pale belly.

My dad walked in, grinning, a tinfoil-wrapped casserole dish in his hands. "You've just made his day," he told me. "Poor Herc's not been getting nearly as much lovin' since Liza came along."

I looked up at him. "Who's Liza?"

"Our new dog. Janice bought her last month for a small fortune. Apparently she's some sort of hyperallergic or hypoallergic—"

"Hypoallergenic?"

"That sounds right. She won't make us sneeze, apparently. Not that I've ever had an issue with that, but Janice has been saying Hercules' fur and saliva is giving her a rash." He sighed and slid the dish onto my table.

"What does that mean? You're not getting rid of Hercules?" I tried to keep the edge from my voice, but it came through.

"No... no. I mean, if it gets too bad, we might have to move him into the shed, but—"

171

"What about the winter? He'll freeze."

"Let's not get into all that right now. I haven't seen you in… weeks, at least." He gave me a one-armed hug and pointed at the casserole. "I skipped Donkers because Janice made you barbecue brisket and baked beans."

I pulled away from his hug and gazed at him, wide-eyed. "Are you serious?"

He frowned as if unsure how to answer. "Well… yes. She thought you might like it."

My stomach rolled with fury and I shook my head. "She thought I might like it? The last meal I ate the night I was attacked. The meal she made three nights after I returned from the hospital, despite my telling her just days before that the thought of it made me sick to my stomach."

My dad opened his mouth, took a faltering step toward the casserole. "Oh, shoot, okay. I forgot, honey, and obviously Janice did too. She didn't mean any harm."

But it wasn't true, not remotely. My dad likely had forgotten because that was his personality. He took unpleasant things and tucked them in some black box far back in his mind, never to be retrieved, but Janice kept those things at the forefront. They were ammunition in her war to dismantle me, to push me completely out of my father's life.

"I'll get rid of it," he said. "I'll take it back to the car."

I put my hand on his arm, forcing my breath to even out. "No, it's okay. Stay."

He nodded and walked to the couch, sat and crossed his legs. "You've changed your hair." He smiled. "Reminds me of that purple wig you used to wear of your mother's. Remember the one? She bought it for a fairy Halloween costume."

I sat beside him, lifting Hercules into my lap and scratching his neck. "I forgot all about that wig. I wore it outside so much you threw it away."

He laughed and slapped his knee. "It was full of burdocks! And you fished it out of the trash and went right on wearing it."

I laughed too, remembering tromping through the woods with Wren, me in that snarly purple wig and Wren in a white cowboy hat poked through with wildflowers.

"How is your mom?" he asked. "Talked to her lately?"

I shook my head. "Not since Christmas."

He frowned. "That's too bad. I wish... I wish it was better than that for you, that you could confide in her and whatnot."

"Yeah." I sighed. "You can't pick your family."

I wished I could take the words back the instant I said them. My dad's face fell, and he reached a hand to Hercules, patting him on the back. "That's true," he said.

"So, what's new?" I asked. "You and Janice been up to anything?" I didn't really care what Janice had been up to, but I wanted my dad to feel like he could talk to me about his life, even if I inwardly cringed whenever he mentioned his wife.

"Oh, you know, the usual. Workin' like a dog." He laughed and patted Hercules. "I'd like to know who came up with that saying because Hercules has never worked a day in his life."

"That's not true," I crowed to Hercules. "Think of all the holes you've dug in the backyard. There must be a million by now."

My dad chuckled and scratched the dog's ear. "Don't even get me started on those holes."

"Business is good, though? Anything new in the world of elevator manufacturing?"

"Nothing much of note. Paulie retired a few months back. We did a big farewell party and Tawny made him a cake shaped like a trout. Good times."

"Paulie retired? That's sad. He's been your best friend for... well, forever, right?"

My dad shrugged. "Yes and no. We've grown apart these last years. He's a bachelor and I'm a married man. I think he got tired of me never going on the fishing trips and hunting trips."

"You used to love to go on those."

My dad stared at the floor, his mouth turned down. He perked up, shifting his gaze back to me. "Just so happens I'm going on a hunting trip in a couple of weeks. Jeff and I are going elk hunting in Canada."

"Jeff? Since when does he hunt?"

"His dad taught him as a boy. He never took to it all that much, but he's ready to give it another go. He planned the whole thing. Rented us a lodge, mapped out the best spots. I think it'll be a hoot."

I said nothing, amazed for the umpteenth time at my dad's complete inability to read people.

Jeff was not a hunter, not a 'cabin in the woods' kind of guy. He wore ironed slacks and silk golf shirts, hair gel, cologne. He drove a sports car, whitened his teeth so often they glowed. Nothing about Jeff matched the persona of an ideal hunting partner. They were probably staying in a posh condo in downtown Toronto, and Jeff's idea of hunting elk included dinner at a fancy restaurant decorated in taxidermied elk heads.

"Janice is letting you out of her sight for an entire weekend?"

"Five days, in fact," he said, his excitement lacing every word. "I can't remember the last time I went hunting. Gosh… years at least."

"Probably about nine," I said, my sarcasm leaking through.

"Nine, huh? Could be." He'd missed the point of the comment, that nine years ago he'd met Janice and she'd quickly put a stop to his doing anything that didn't include her. "Enough about me. How have you been, honey?"

I thought of the previous days filled with the apparition of Wren's murderer, my witnessing another woman's abduction, stepping outside on my own for the first time in over a year. I should have shared these things with my dad, but I didn't. "I've been good. Just doing the usual."

"I'm happy to hear that. And you're still regularly talking to Dr. Fry?"

"Yep. Once or twice a week."

"Well, that's just great."

My cell phone rang, and I glanced down to see Detective Webb's name. "I've got to grab this real quick," I told my dad, stood and walked to my bedroom.

"Hello?" I answered.

"Hi, Gloria, it's Dan Webb. Is this a good time?"

"Yeah, my dad's here, but I can talk for a minute."

"Great. I wondered if I could swing by this afternoon, chat about a few additional things."

"Did you find something? Kelly or—"

"No, but we're working around the clock until we do. Can I come around three?"

"Sure, that's fine."

I returned to the living room. My dad no longer sat, but stood near my desk gazing down at the photograph of Kelly Rice Detective Webb had left at my apartment.

"Who's this?" he asked.

"Her name is Kelly Rice, and she just disappeared a few days ago."

He looked up, his face pale. "Disappeared? Here in Marquette?"

"Yes." I knew I should say more. Tell him that not only had she disappeared, but she'd been living in my old apartment, looking into Wren's and my case, that I myself had probably witnessed her abduction.

"Why do you have a picture of her?"

"Because the detective working the case came to see me. That's who just called."

"But why? Why is he contacting you about this?"

"Because they're considering the possibility that our cases are connected."

He rubbed his forehead, averting his eyes from the photo. "That's very concerning. Gloria, you should move home. If this madman is still out there, has abducted another woman, you're not safe here alone. And you know what!" He stood, clapping his hands triumphantly. "I just installed security cameras. Nearly every room in the house has a camera, plus four outside the house."

"Why? You've left the front door unlocked forever. Since when are you worried about security?"

He wrung his hands, a little frown on his lips. "No reason. Well... that's not entirely true. Things have gone missing—little things, but still... I've been far too lax with security."

"What things have gone missing?"

He shook his head. "That's the problem, you see? I'm not sure I didn't just misplace the items... but, well, a few of my golf clubs. I had some cash on my dresser that disappeared, but... maybe I spent it." He laughed.

"Did you ask Janice and Jeff?"

"Oh, sure, sure, but they didn't have a clue what I was talking about. Looked at me like I'd gone a tad loopy." He chuckled. "Can't argue with them there."

"And yet you think I'd be safer coming to live in your house?"

"Oh, yes, most definitely. You wouldn't be alone there. That's the thing, Gloria. You're all alone here."

"I'm not moving home, Dad, okay? I appreciate your concern, but the answer is no."

He nodded. "I figured as much, but... it's my job to try, isn't it? I think it is, yes, but perhaps I could get you cameras. The same I've gotten myself. Here... look, you can log in right from your phone and check every room."

He walked to me and showed me his phone. I stared at the house, my former home. He clicked from room to room. It looked nothing like it had in my childhood. Stiff modern furniture and ugly abstract art had replaced all the warmth. It looked like a house in a magazine, not one where people lived.

"You put a camera in Jeff's room?" I asked, surprised.

"Sure, sure," he said. "In all the rooms. There are windows in there, after all. Could be someone is crawling through a window and stealing stuff when no one is home."

"That's pretty disturbing."

"Well, you know your old dad. It's just as likely, more likely, that I misplaced things, but better safe than sorry."

31

———

After my dad left, I spent an hour working out with the weights, reminded of how pitifully weak I'd become in the previous two years. Twice, I walked out my door, down the hall, descended the stairs and pushed through the front door. The first time I made it to the sidewalk, the second all the way to the garage before the quickening of my breath urged me back to my apartment.

When Dan Webb arrived, I was coated in a layer of sweat and my hair was plastered against my head.

"Hi, sorry," I said, opening my door so he could walk in. "I meant to save time for a shower."

"No shower necessary on my account. I can't stay long, but I had a few things." He sat at the kitchen table and took out a large photo. "Our photo guy blew this up with a lot more clarity. Do you recognize him?"

Scorpion's face was large and clear. I could see the outline of his scorpion tattoo in more detail, his off-kilter nose, his dark, shifty eyes.

"No, but I'm… I'm almost positive it's him."

"Okay, that's good. That's progress. I'm going to send it out to all the precincts, shoot a copy to the sheriff's office over by Porcupine Mountains, see if anyone recognizes him."

"And if they don't?"

"The next step will be to share this image with the press. Request anyone who recognizes him to call in with his name."

"Okay."

"I took Sally, the psychic I told you about, to the trail yesterday evening where you and Wren were abducted. Do you mind?"

I stared at the little black device he'd taken from his pocket. "What is it?"

"A voice recorder. I recorded everything she said. I wanted to play it for you and see if it jogs your memory."

"Okay, sure."

He rested the recorder on a stack of paperbacks I had ready for Dorian to return to the library.

Webb hit play and muffled sounds emerged. "We're walking here so it's a little distorted," he explained.

I listened as they moved, tried to distinguish between the crunch of leaves underfoot and the shift of fabric as they walked.

Dan: *This is Detective Dan Webb walking with Sally Mitchell on June twentieth, at a trailhead in the Porcupine Mountains. Sally, please speak up so the recorder picks up anything you say.*

Sally: *I'll do that.*

More shuffling and then a long moment of eerie quiet as if Dan and Sally as well as the forest itself had gone still. Sally began to hum, a melody that sent a shudder from the top of my head to my tailbone. I stood abruptly from the chair and stared at the recorder.

"What?" Dan reached forward and hit pause.

The song stopped, but it picked up in my head. It was one of Wren's songs, "Glow"—a song she'd written for me, both about me and about the sunrise—a play on words, she'd told me triumphantly the first time she'd sung it.

"She's humming one of Wren's songs."

Dan frowned at the recorder. "Okay… well, that's sort of how Sally works. She picks up fragments of… energy, memories, other things."

"What other things?" I couldn't smell the cigarette smoke or the cologne, but the presence of the thing that had taken up residence in my home was never far from my thoughts. The ghost of the man who'd murdered my best friend.

Dan picked up the recorder, turned it over in his palm and returned it to the books. "Spirits. She calls them spirits."

"You're saying she could hear Wren's ghost?"

He gazed at me as if gauging how much I believed in the possibility of that. "Something like that, yes."

I looked from him to the recorder, my heart pumping faster, the tremors of panic trying to get hold. The song echoed in my mind. I could picture Wren in a wooden chair, guitar on her knees as she flicked the strings and sang about the first light that broke the darkness at dawn.

"Play it," I said, returning to my seat, using my thumbnail to push down the cuticles on my opposite hand.

He hit play and Sally's humming returned and then abruptly stopped.

Sally: *I'm sensing a new energy here, a young woman. Oh!*

Sally cried out, and I heard rustling sounds, muffled voices.

"She fell," Dan explained. "Well… just listen."

Sally: *I felt…*

Sally's voice was breathless.

Sally: *As if someone shoved me and I was falling from a great height. I'm hearing the name Gwen, but… she's slipping away.*

Dan: Gwen?

"Sounds like Wren," I murmured.

"I thought so too," Dan agreed.

Sally: *Falling star…*

I stared at the little black box and tried to remember if that had been printed in the papers. We'd walked away for a meteor shower. *Look, Wren had said, a falling star.*

Sally: *So dark… and then a light, bright, narrow, right in their faces.*

I heard a sniffing sound from Sally.

Sally: *Smoker… he smoked cigarettes. He smoked while he was following them. There's probably an old cigarette butt on this trail somewhere—maybe a few.*

More rustling.

Sally: *I'm seeing money. A stack of one-hundred-dollar bills covered in blood. Blood money. I'm seeing… a shack, a cabin. There's water running. Pain here in my throat, terrible pain, like fire at the front of my neck.*

The recording ended and though there were no images emitting from the little black box I stared at it just the same.

"You're bleeding," Dan told me.

I jerked my head up, had half-forgotten he was there.

He gestured to my hand. Blood trickled from the broken skin along my thumb. Red and bright and instantly mingled with the blood from that dark night. My blood splashed down the front of my shirt. Wren's blood.

"Oh, God." I slid off the chair and onto the floor, crawled to the sink and wrenched open the cupboard. I pulled the wastebasket out and bent over it, salivating, nausea rushing up and over me. I vomited my breakfast, toast and coffee into the trash.

Dan stood and walked to the counter. He opened drawers and then turned on the faucet. A moment later, he squatted beside me, dabbed at my face with a cool wet rag. "Think you might puke some more?" he asked.

I shook my head. The sensation had passed, the need to evacuate my body. I trembled as he helped me to my feet and guided me to the couch. I sat down, and he lifted a blanket from the chair and whooshed it over me. It blew my hair back and for a single suspended moment I was a child again, Wren and I lying on her bed as her mother lifted a blanket and fanned it over top of us. Soft, it had tickled our faces as she'd pulled it off and sent it flying a second time.

I clenched my eyes shut until I felt Dan's hand on my own.

"I'm just cleaning this up," he said, taking my thumb and wiping it with a wet paper towel. "Where are your Band-Aids?"

"The bathroom," I said, my voice weak.

He stood and disappeared, emerged a moment later with a single Band-Aid. He unwrapped it and took the little bandage—decorated in sloths, a gift from Rylie—and wrapped it around my thumb.

"Does Sally know all the details of the case? Has she read my file?"

"No. She doesn't know anything about it. She doesn't live in the U.P., and she assured me she'd never read any articles about what happened to you."

"And you trust her?"

"Completely. I don't pay her. She does this work because she believes she was called to do it. There's nothing in it for her except the hope of justice for the victims, for you and Wren. What stood out to you in the recording?"

I sighed and rubbed my eyes. "All of it. She knew Wren's song. The falling star, the cigarette smoke."

"I didn't see that anywhere in the original report, that the perp was a smoker."

"I... I think I blocked some of it, but it came back. His smell... it still makes me queasy, but yes, he smelled like cigarettes."

"And how about the money comment? Does that ring any bells?"

I shook my head. "There was no money that I remember, but… we had those sacks over our heads for a lot of it."

"And neither of you had cash on you that night?"

"Maybe fifty dollars between us."

"Okay. And what about the shack? She mentioned a cabin or shack."

I frowned. Something struggled to get through. Had there been a shack? Some moment where the earth beneath us changed, hard, hollow-sounding? Or had that been part of the nightmare, the distorted images that had flooded me in the river?

"I don't know. Maybe. I'm… it's almost like there's a memory of something like that, but after I got away and ended up in that river… I had dreams or hallucinations. I kept thinking I was back there. I was dead and Wren had escaped. All these weird things that have mixed with reality and it's hard to separate them."

"I understand that."

"Nicki said she sent you Kelly's Google login. Have you checked the last location on her phone?"

"Yeah, and to be clear, I don't think Nicki should have showed you that. It's important to not get too deeply into this thing with Kelly. For your own protection, it's safer to not appear to be involved in this investigation in any way. If the man who abducted her was involved in your attack and suspects you might be able to identify him, you could be in danger."

"I'm not telling anyone."

"Okay. To answer your question, yes, we visited the last location. Covington Township. There's a church, a fuel station and a lot of woods. We showed the guy at the gas station a picture of Kelly. He didn't recognize her. We left fliers and there's a few officers knocking on doors, but…" Webb sighed. "Nothing useful has come out of it yet. It's possible that whoever took her tossed her phone out of the window in that area."

"You searched for her phone?"

"Yeah, we went up and down the road there, looked on the shoulder, but like I said, it's wooded. There's tall grass right up to the road edge in some areas. It could be three feet from the concrete and we wouldn't be able to see it."

"And Bryce? Nicki told you about him?"

"Yes. We're trying to track him down for an interview."

"You don't know where he is?"

"No. His most recent phone number is disconnected. His mother says he was working for some guy doing construction out of town, but we haven't verified that. In the meantime, be vigilant."

"Nicki told you Kelly was looking into our case?"

"Yeah, she did, and unfortunately whatever she found appears to have disappeared with her."

"Did you take Sally anywhere connected to Kelly? To our old apartment?"

Dan's phone buzzed and he looked at it and frowned. "I have to go, Gloria. We'll talk again soon. I promise."

32

Two Years Ago
June 21, 2012

"Seriously?" I muttered, inclining my head toward the Pine Stage where Janice's son—technically my stepbrother, though I rarely called him that—stood talking to a gaggle of girls wearing cut-off jean shorts and matching tank tops that proclaimed 'Let's Get Toasted,' above images of marshmallows over a fire.

Wren followed the tilt of my head. "Huh, that's bizarre. This doesn't seem like his scene."

"It's not. I don't know why he's here."

"This festival has turned into a high school reunion, except instead of our former classmates it's literally every creepy dude we know," Wren said.

I laughed and took another drink of the lukewarm jungle juice a friend from NMU had given us a half hour before. I grimaced at the taste. It was overly sweet and didn't entirely mask the alcohol taste beneath it. I was by no means a prude when it came to underage drinking, but I never understood how people enjoyed the taste of alcohol.

On the opposite side of the grassy clearing, I spotted Tom Russell.

"He's here," I told Wren, hip-checking her harder than I intended and nearly sending her sprawling onto the grass beside us. She ran into the back of a tall, thin guy who managed to keep his balance.

"Jeez, Glo." She scowled at me and turned to the guy. "Sorry. My friend's dancing is comparable to fighting geese."

The guy grinned and ran a hand through his blond hair. He had a Kurt Cobain look about him—shaggy hair, ripped jeans and a black t-shirt that proclaimed 'Reality is None of My Business.'

"No problem. Are you a musician?" He nodded at the guitar case on the ground.

"Yeah. I mean not here. I'm not playing the festival, but I lug this thing around and play with people I run into."

"Come play then." He gestured toward a group of tents near the woods. Four people sat on stumps in the center playing instruments.

"Are those your friends?" Wren asked.

"Friends, band members, all of the above."

"You're in a band? Which one?"

"Chasing Monkeys."

"Oh, wow, I've heard of you guys. You're from where? Wisconsin?"

"Illinois."

I turned away from their conversation to watch Tom, who stood near the Birch Stage where the band was warming up. His best friend, Rob, walked up and handed him a cup.

"Glo, this is Kai." Wren tugged my sleeve until I turned back.

"Hi," I told him. "I'm Gloria."

"Do you play?" he asked.

"Music?" I snorted. "God no. I'm still recovering from the humiliating recorder solo I had in elementary school."

He laughed. "Well, you've got ears. You can listen. Come on." He turned to walk toward his friends.

Wren grabbed my hand, but I pulled it free. I pointed toward Tom. "Tom's here," I said. "I'm going to head for the Birch Stage."

"Okay. But watch those hips." She hip-checked me, but much more gently than I'd done to her.

"You too." I winked and headed across the grass, pulled my blanket from my shoulder bag and spread it on the ground, close, but not too close to Tom.

The band hadn't yet started, and I felt awkward sitting on the blanket alone. I took out my paperback copy of *Into the Wild* and tried to read, but the words did little more than cross beneath my eyes, unperceived by my brain. I'd never had a crush of the magnitude I had on Tom Russell.

I'd liked boys over the years, but never found myself reduced to the pining chaos monster I'd become at the thought of him. Wren thought it was hilarious. More than once she'd witnessed my near-ineptitude in his presence, the way I suddenly started fumbling over my words and whipping my hair around like a wild horse.

For an hour I sat, sipping my drink that had gone from warm to downright hot and re-reading the same two paragraphs fifty times.

Eventually Tom's gaze drifted my way and I held up a hand and waved. He walked over.

"If it isn't Gloria, the Queen of the Sugarloaf hikes."

"Queen?" I asked, standing. "That's a new one. Where's my crown?"

He leaned down and grabbed a few dandelions, clumsily wove them together. He plopped it on my head.

"What did I do to deserve this glorious accessory?" I asked, touching the dandelions with the tips of my fingers.

He grinned. "I saw you on the Black Rock website. You've been leading the Saturday hikes, huh? I need to start doing those."

"You should. It's a beautiful trail."

"With a beautiful guide."

My face grew warm, and I took a drink from my cup, realizing too late that a giant moth had landed in the sticky alcohol. It swooshed past my lips and stuck in the back of my throat.

"Ugh!" I bent over and spit, hacking as the moth fell from my mouth and flapped feebly in the grass.

Tom slapped me on the back, laughing. "Whoa. Are you okay? About swallowed a bird there from the looks of it."

I stood up, wiped the stickiness from my chin and wished vaguely that the ground would open and swallow me whole.

"Tom!" Rob yelled from near the stage. "We're going to check out the Gin Boys, come on."

Tom gave my shoulder a squeeze. "I'll see you around, Gloria." He started off toward his friend, and I stared after him, wanting to tag along, but equally wanting to disappear into the forest to escape my shame over having coughed a moth up right in front of him.

I found Wren sitting on a stump near the kids' tent painting a mermaid on a little girl's cheek.

"There you are," I said, dropping onto the stump beside her. "You're face-painting now?"

Wren smiled. "I thought I'd offer myself up. Apparently two of the girls who volunteered never showed up. They had about ten kids standing around waiting."

The little girl with dark frizzy curls turned and grinned at me, revealing a gap where one of her front teeth had been. "Do you like mermaids too?"

"Sure, yeah, what's not to like? Goddesses of the sea and all that." I winked at Wren. "What happened to Kai?"

"He had to get ready to play. We could go watch them. They're on the Birch Stage in…" She pulled out her phone. "Forty minutes."

"Sounds like a plan, but first I'm going to hunt down some food. Hungry?"

"No, but I could use a water. How'd the Tom encounter go?"

I grimaced. "Don't ask. I'll be back in fifteen minutes—tops."

I left Wren and made my way to the food trucks.

"Moonshine. Made it myself. Come on, have a swig." A guy named Rex held the large glass bottle in his hands and jostled the dark liquid inside.

"You first," I told him.

He tilted the growler back, his Adam's apple bobbing with the enormous gulp. He righted himself and wiped an arm across his mouth. "Damn, that's good."

I took the bottle, sniffed it and winced. My eyes watered from the astringent alcohol. "Fuck it," I murmured, tilted the bottle back and took a drink.

The first taste was sweet, followed immediately by a roar of fire that streaked down my throat into my belly. "Here," I gasped, handing the jug to Wren. "Holy shit, that's strong."

Wren wrinkled her nose and pressed the opening to her lips, lifted and let the dark liquid slide into her mouth. Tears streamed down her face when she handed the bottle back.

"Good God, is that gasoline or moonshine?" she rasped.

"That's the finest apple pie moonshine north of the bridge, my dear lady," he said.

"I'll be coming to your tent for aspirin in the morning," I grumbled, eyeing the moonshine. The aftertaste wasn't too bad. The sweetness and a touch of cinnamon lingered on my tongue.

"You can come to my tent right now if you'd like," he told me, winking.

"Ooh, yes," Wren announced lifting her arms and swaying. "The Crow Maidens. I love them. Come on." She grabbed my hand. "Let's go dance."

"Thanks for the moonshine, Rex," I called over my shoulder.

He saluted us and carried his jug to a group of girls sitting on a flannel blanket.

"Ladies!" I heard him bellow. "Can I interest you in some moonshine?"

Tom twirled me around and the world spun, and I fell sideways. He caught me, laughing, gripped my waist and pulled me close. He leaned in. I could smell whiskey on his breath and then I tasted it. I registered the other voice then, the man's voice—gruff, angry.

"Come on, come here, I just want to show you something. Stop pulling away. I just want to show you something."

I twisted my head, and Tom's lips grazed my cheek. I caught sight of Wren near the edge of the woods. Bryce, the bouncer, had his hand on her wrist and was tugging her toward the trees. His face was red. Wren looked around wildly, caught my eye. "Gloria!" she shouted.

I jerked away from Tom, stumbled and righted myself. "Hey!" I yelled. "Get away from her."

I ran up to Bryce and shoved him as hard as I could. He stumbled back and released Wren's arm.

"What the fuck?" he spat. "What's your problem, bitch?"

"What's *your* problem?" a voice snarled behind me. I turned to see Tom had followed me. He towered over Bryce, who was solidly built, but stocky.

Bryce's lip curled, but he tossed his hands up. "Whatever. Good seeing ya, Wren." He stomped into the woods, kicking a folding chair in someone's camp and knocking it over.

Wren threw her arms around me. "Thank you, thank you. Gosh, he just came out of nowhere."

Tom stepped closer to us. "Are you okay?" he asked her.

"Yeah, thanks." She tucked her pink hair behind her ear.

"What was he trying to do?" I asked. "Drag you into the woods?"

Wren stared into the trees where he'd disappeared. "I don't even know. He said something about his tent. He had something to show me. What a weirdo."

"Yeah, you better watch out for him this weekend," Tom said. "He about lost his shit. Why don't you move your tents closer to me and the guys? Probably not a good idea to be on your own."

"Yeah," I agreed quickly.

Wren smirked at me. "Sure. I would feel better doing that."

After we moved our tents, we danced until nearly two in the morning.

"We could share a tent tonight?" Wren suggested when we decided to turn in for the night.

Tom snaked an arm around my waist and whispered in my ear. "Stay with me."

I opened my eyes wide and grinned. "How about I'll sleep with you tomorrow night, Wren?" I suggested.

She winked and ducked into her tent, zipping the flap closed.

"Come on," Tom murmured, his breath boozy.

"Mmm-hmm," I agreed, following him into his tent.

The tent was hot and we fumbled out of our clothes and had drunken sex on his sleeping bag, which clung to my sweaty legs and back.

I'd never had casual sex and before that night, I'd only slept with one person—Marty, a stiff encounter that I think had more to do with us both no longer wanting to be virgins than any actual physical desire for each other.

I fell asleep with Tom's large arm draped across my stomach and the sound of his snores filling the air.

33

───────

In the evening, armed with the taser, I left my apartment, walked down the hall, descended the steps, and pushed out the front door. I strode to the garage, slipped into the cool, musty interior and climbed in my car, which I hadn't driven in nearly two years.

I didn't start it, but sat with both hands on the wheel staring at the back of the garage door. The space beside my car was empty, which meant Earl was travelling.

My cell phone rang. I didn't recognize the number, but answered it. "Hello?"

"Hi, this is Levi Foley, you called me a few days ago about a guy with a scorpion tattoo."

My breath caught. "Hi. Yes, thanks for calling me back. Did you find his information?"

"Yep, I've got it right here." I heard papers shuffling. "His name was Dominic Sitz and his address is here in Houghton. I have a phone number too."

"That'd be great." I fumbled a pen and old receipt from my glovebox.

Levi gave me the number and we ended the call. I stared at the man's name, but nothing about it rang familiar. I hadn't known him.

Now I had a name, an address and a phone number, but I had no intention of calling. Instead, I climbed from my car and hurried back upstairs to my apartment.

I sat at my laptop and opened up a search bar on my computer and typed 'Dominic Sitz, Houghton, Michigan.' The first result that populated was an obituary.

Dominic Francis Sitz was born on December third, 1986, to parents Kathy and Roland Sitz. He died Tuesday, April fifteenth.

He was dead.

I'd known he was, but somehow this obituary, this confirmation struck me with heavy finality. It was an end of sorts, though not the one I'd imagined.

I stared at the image in the obituary for a long time, an image likely painstakingly chosen by his mother, an image that carefully hid the evil concealed within. The Dominic immortalized in the death notice wore a pale blue shirt, buttoned high, and a black tie. He did not yet have his ugly tattoo. He smiled with his mouth closed, but his eyes remained as black as caves in the ocean floor.

I read the obituary a second time, contemplating each detail revealed within the short write-up.

Dominic—Dom to friends and family—attended Escanaba High School. He worked in various jobs around the Upper Peninsula.

Dom loved to ride ATVs and dirt bikes.

He is preceded in death by his father, Roland Sitz, and survived by his mother, Cathy Sitz, and his sister, Lara Sitz Pennington.

It was a bare-bones memorial and I wondered if his mother had struggled to find positive things to say about her son.

I returned to the search results for Dominic's name and found an article published in the Mining Press titled 'Body Found by Railroad.'

Two boys were startled Friday when they discovered the decomposing body of a man near the railroad tracks just before the Jumbo River Railroad Bridge in Trout Creek. Initially police suspected the man had been hit by a train, but an autopsy revealed he'd been bludgeoned to death.

The man found deceased has been identified as Dominic Francis Sitz of Escanaba, Michigan, though his residence at the time of his death was Houghton. There is an open investigation into the death of Sitz, though law enforcement has stated that drugs may have been a factor.

The photo that accompanied the article showed a wooden railroad bridge cutting through a patch of dense pines.

I found another article about Dominic. This one described Dominic's arrest for burglarizing several houses. He'd been with two acquaintances, who'd escaped when the homeowner caught them and the police were called. He refused to give up the names of his fellow thieves and was ultimately convicted and sentenced to eight months in jail.

I thought about Bryce Dobbs, the bouncer who'd been arrested years earlier for the same type of crime Dominic Sitz had been arrested for. Could Bryce have been one of Dominic's co-conspirators even then?

Who could connect them? Who would know if they were friends?

A sister had been listed as having survived Dominic. I typed her name into the search bar, Lara Sitz Pennington. I found a few listings, several of which included a Lara Sitz Pennington who worked at a company called Superior Long-Term Care as a human resources manager.

I dialed the number.

"Superior Long-Term Care. How may I direct your call?"

"Lara Pennington, please, in human resources."

"One moment."

Smooth jazz crawled through the phone, interrupted by an advertisement for the facility, stating it was the best in long-term care for aging parents.

"Human Resources, this is Lara," a woman said.

My breath hitched and for a moment I said nothing.

"Hello?"

"Hi, sorry," I quickly started. "Lara, my name is… Brenda and I work sometimes on… uh, cases, crime cases." I fumbled over my words, realizing I should have thought them through before I picked up the phone.

"What's this regarding, please?"

"Umm… your brother, Dominic Sitz."

No response.

"I'm just following up on the investigation and hoped to ask you a few questions about Dominic."

"This really isn't a good time."

"Please, it will only take a minute."

She sighed, and I sensed this was a topic she preferred to stay well away from. "I'm sure I can't help you. Dominic and I were not close."

"That's totally fine. I'd still like to ask, if that's okay."

She didn't answer, so I forged on. "Can you tell me anything about who he was spending time with when he passed? Did he have a girlfriend?"

Another loud sigh. "A girl showed up at the funeral with mascara running down her face and threw herself on the casket like an actress from a bad movie. If I remember correctly, she called herself Dom's girlfriend."

"Do you remember her name?"

"Hardly. Polly or Patty. My mother would know."

"Do you think she'd mind if I called her?"

"She'd probably be overjoyed if you called her." Lara's voice was hard.

I suspected her relationship with her mother was strained. "Was your mother close with Dom?"

"Oh, sure, as close as you can be to a person like him. He could do no wrong in her eyes."

"But in yours?"

"He was not a good person. I don't know why, but… he never was. He was cruel even when we were young. I know saying this makes me sound like the bad guy, talking about my dead brother in such a negative way, but he hurt a lot of people and I'm not surprised someone finally hurt him back."

"Who did he hurt?"

"Everyone. Me, my mother, my father before he died. He hurt our pets, the pets in the neighborhood, the kids where we grew up. He was arrested in high school for rape, kicked out of college for robbing his roommate, arrested for drugs, for battery, for sexual assaults. I seriously never understood why they kept letting him out of jail, why they didn't lock him up and throw away the key. But you must know all of this. I'm sure you've seen his rap sheet."

"Yes, that's true," I lied. "I just wondered if you knew of anything he'd done that he didn't get caught for."

"I don't doubt there's a line of victims no one ever knew about. Did you know that eighty percent of rapes and sexual assaults go unreported? And with good reason, because people like Dom get a slap on the wrist and then they're free to come back and take revenge on you for turning them in. The system is sick."

"It is…" I murmured, remembering how hard it had been to share those details, how dirty I had felt, still felt.

"I have to go. I have a staff meeting in ten minutes and after this conversation I need a cigarette."

"I understand. Would you mind giving me your mother's number?"

She rattled it off. "Good luck, but honestly, I don't care if you never find out who did it."

I wanted to set the phone aside, lie on the couch, turn on *Gilmore Girls* and numb out, but I couldn't, not now, not when I'd finally begun to dig out of the grave I'd buried myself in.

I dialed Cathy's number. A woman's gravelly voice answered. "Hello."

"Is this Cathy Sitz?"

"It sure is. What are ya sellin'?"

"Nothing. I'm calling about your son, Dominic."

Cathy made a sound like she'd taken a pull on a cigarette. "It's about time somebody called me back. I've left half a dozen messages. You're with the police over there in Trout Creek? You sound too young to be a detective."

"I'm not a detective… yet. But can you tell me anything about his friends at the time of his death? In particular I'm wondering if he knew a man named Bryce Dobbs."

"Bryce? Hmph… nah, not that I remember, but Dom wasn't no baby anymore. I didn't know all his friends."

"Did he have a girlfriend?"

"She called herself that, but that's on account of her wantin' Dom's automobile, which she didn't get. Not a chance in hell I was givin' that to some trampy thing who'd been seein' him for all of a month. Nah, I sold it for funeral expenses. I didn't exactly have three thousand dollars layin' around."

"Okay," I murmured, suspecting I wouldn't be getting a phone number for the former girlfriend from Cathy Sitz. "This may sound strange, but did he ever spend any time near the Porcupine Mountains?"

"Yes, of course. That was the only thing his deadbeat dad left for Dom and Lara, not that Lara ever appreciated that property. She's not the kind of girl to get her hands dirty, if you know what I mean."

"Property? Your son owned property there?"

"He and Lara. Just Lara now," she said bitterly. "Probably sold it before the ink was dry on his death certificate."

34

I'd only just ended the call when my phone rang—Dorian.

"Hey," I answered.

"How's it going?" he asked.

"Good. Getting ready to eat something."

"I could bring pizza or subs? Rylie and I?"

"No. I appreciate it, but I'm really tired and… I think I'm going to eat some cereal and go to bed."

"Are you sure?"

I wasn't sure if it was surprise or hurt I heard in his voice. I didn't think I'd ever once told him not come over when he'd suggested it.

"Yeah. Plus, you guys are coming over tomorrow for… Wren's birthday and you probably have things to do for that."

"Yeah, that's true. Don't hesitate to call, Glo. For anything."

"Thanks, Dorian. Say hi to Rylie for me."

I didn't eat cereal, or anything for that matter. I sat at my computer searching tax records in an attempt to locate the Porcupine Mountains property owned by Dominic and Lara Sitz. By midnight, I'd found nothing and my eyes had grown gritty and strained.

I turned off my laptop and shuffled to my bedroom, too tired to consider whether I'd feel safer on the couch. I climbed beneath the comforter and gasped, threw off the blanket and jumped from my bed.

My mattress was soaking wet. An enormous dark stain spread out from the center of the bed as if someone had poured a bucket of cold water onto it.

For more than a minute I stared at the wetness, blinking, shivering. I thought of the doll and something akin to hopelessness crawled through me. I didn't know what to do, how to make it stop. Even as my strength, my self was returning, my familiar world was unraveling around me.

I returned to the couch, slipped on my headphones and curled onto my side, gradually falling asleep to a relaxation hypnosis.

~

The morning arrived with the blaring of my cell phone. I sat up, disoriented, and saw an incoming video call from Dr. Fry.

I wanted to ignore it, but Dr. Fry was the kind of man who'd get in his car and drive over, assuming my not answering was a cry for help.

"Hi," I said groggily when his face slid onto the screen.

In the corner of the video chat I saw my own reflection and cringed. The skin beneath my eyes looked as purple as my hair.

"Gloria, good morning. Did I wake you? It's nine o'clock." He considered me, surprised.

I yawned, quickly covering my mouth. "Yeah, I went to bed late. I totally forgot about our call."

"Well, today is Wren's birthday, as I'm sure you're aware. I thought it best that we connect and make sure you start the day off in a good place."

"Mmm-hmm," I grumbled. "Do you mind if I make coffee?"

"Not at all."

I stuck a filter in the pot and poured in the grounds, spilling half the cup on the counter. "Shoot," I muttered.

"How have you been sleeping, Gloria? Still having some trouble there?"

You don't know the half of it.

"It's been better," I lied.

"Really?"

I glanced down at my phone, at his skeptical expression. "Well, not last night but before that."

"Okay. And what about last night made sleep difficult?"

The pool of water saturating my bed.

"There's been some stuff going on, possibly some developments in Wren's and my case."

"Really? That's interesting to hear, and… is that good news?"

"A girl disappeared from my old apartment. They think she was abducted."

Fry's eyes widened. "It's not good news then. The police suspect this girl's disappearance is related to what happened to you and Wren?"

I leaned against the counter and watched the coffee drip agonizingly slowly into the glass carafe. "Yes."

"They believe the same man is behind it?"

"Possibly," I said.

"That is disturbing news that we could easily spend a good deal of time on, but first I'd like to know how you're feeling about this day in particular, Wren's birthday."

I pulled the carafe from the maker and stuck a mug beneath the stream of coffee, then quickly maneuvered the pot back into place, spilling only a little. I carried the mug and my phone to the couch. "I'm okay. Dorian and his family are coming over later and we're going to celebrate."

"That's good, very good. Perhaps that's why you're so tired this morning? Up late thinking about—"

His words were cut off mid-sentence when my phone battery died. I sighed, grateful for the conversation to have been cut short.

After I drank the entire pot of coffee and charged my phone, I sent Dr. Fry a text assuring him I was fine and I'd call him the next day.

Then I dialed the phone number for Lara Sitz.

"Lara, hi. We talked yesterday about your brother, Dominic."

She released a frustrated sigh and then spoke low and angrily. "Listen, I told you I don't give a shit about Dom. Okay? Don't call me again."

"Wait, please—"

"What?" she snapped.

"Your mom said you owned property, you and Dominic, in the Porcupine Mountains."

"Yeah, so?"

"I'd like to know where it is. The address."

Lara released a harsh laugh. "The address? There isn't an address. It's a shack surrounded by trees with no road in."

"But there must be… like coordinates."

"Jesus Christ. Why? Why do you want to know about it?"

I held my breath, considered my next words carefully. "My name is Gloria Cline. I was viciously attacked at the Dancing with the Dead Music Festival in the Porcupine Mountains two years ago. My best friend was murdered and she's never been found. I think your brother attacked us. He may have taken us to that property."

Silence. When she spoke, her voice wavered. "You're Gloria Cline?"

"Yes."

"I read about you in the paper, you and Wren. I'm… I'm so sorry."

"It's okay, it is. I just… I need closure. Wren's family needs it. If Dominic was behind it, it's too late to… hold him accountable. But if we could find Wren, bring her home…"

"Oh, God," she groaned. "Okay… I'm sick just thinking about this. But… okay. Do you have a pen and paper? I can tell you how to get there."

"Thank you. Yes, I'm ready. Go ahead."

She described the route, a tangle of turns without road names, known only by landmarks.

"Once you're on the two-track," she continued, "the cabin is another five miles. It's rough terrain. Four-wheel drive is the only way you'll get there. I haven't been in years. If the shack still stands, I'd be amazed."

"You didn't sell it after Dominic passed?"

"No. Oddly I had a guy reach out to me and want to buy it about a month after Dom died. I have no idea how he even knew the property existed or that it belonged to me."

"Do you remember his name? The man who wanted to buy it?"

"No, I'm afraid I don't, but I have it somewhere. I wrote down his name and number, told him I'd think on it and call him back. I never did call him back, but I'm sure I hung onto the note."

When Dorian and Rylie arrived that night, I was lost in thoughts of Dominic Sitz and specifically the cabin in the woods near the Porcupine Mountains.

"I thought we'd go in the backyard," I announced.

Dorian looked at me, surprised, and Rylie jumped up and down.

"Really?" she asked. She looked at Dorian for approval.

"You're sure?" he asked me.

"Yep."

As we walked out the door, Dorian's parents, George and Lee arrived. Lee held a three-tier cake decorated in turquoise frosting with purple and pink mermaid scales adorning the side.

"You're outside!" Lee exclaimed, handing the cake to George and hugging me. "My goodness, and your hair is purple. How lovely. We've missed you, Gloria. How have you been?"

"I've been good," I said. "Getting better."

"I'd say so," George agreed, giving me a hug after Lee had released me.

"We're taking the party to the backyard," Dorian told them.

"Oh, wonderful. It is such a beautiful evening," Lee said. She took the cake back from George. "I wonder if we could put this in your apartment, Gloria, I'm afraid the frosting will get weepy in the heat."

"Of course. I'll take it up." I took the cake.

"I can run it up," Dorian suggested.

"Nope, I've got it. I'll meet you out back."

When I walked into the backyard, Lee and Dorian had set the picnic table with mermaid-themed paper plates and napkins. George scooped beef with broccoli onto plates, and Rylie ran to me and handed me a gift.

"This is from my grandpa and grandma," she chirped. "Daddy and I got you a gift, but we have to wait until your birthday to give it you."

I took the present wrapped in mermaid paper. "Thank you," I told them, sitting at the table. "You didn't have to get me anything."

Lee kissed the top of my head. "Nonsense. Open your present."

I peeled off the paper to discover a large green blanket.

"It's a weighted blanket," Lee explained. "They say..." She glanced at Dorian as if she shouldn't finish her sentence.

"It's supposed to help with anxiety," Dorian cut in. "It's okay to talk about it, Mom. Glo is fully aware that she suffers from panic attacks."

Lee blushed and slapped his arm playfully. "I know that, Dorian. I only meant…" She gestured at the yard. "Here you are. I didn't want to make you feel as if you haven't made progress. It's so wonderful you're out here."

I leaned over and hugged her. "I love it and I appreciate it. Really. Blankets are my happy place these days."

We ate and talked. Rylie dominated the conversation, filling us in on the 'wicked cool' fort she and her friend Jolene had built in the woods behind Dorian's house.

"Those clouds look like rain," George said, and as if on cue a few drops fell, splattering our heads and the table.

We gathered the food and hurried inside and up the stairs.

As we reached the hallway to my apartment, Lee wrinkled her nose. A terrible odor filled the space—cigarette smoke, cologne, sweat and death.

"Good Lord," George said, sniffing at the air. "What is that smell?"

"Gross!" Rylie pinched her nose.

Dorian glanced at me. "Yeah, that's bad. Where is it coming from?"

I shook my head, cupping my hands over my face and breathing through my mouth, trying not to let the scent into my brain where it might trigger a reaction that would ruin everyone's evening.

I moved toward the door on stilted legs, but Dorian held an arm out. "No, let me open it. This is weird. Stay back."

George ushered me, Rylie and Lee behind him and stepped closer to the door with Dorian.

They opened it and the smell gusted out, a wave of stench that even as I blocked my nose overwhelmed my senses. My stomach clenched and my eyes watered.

Rylie clutched my hand and fumbled toward her grandmother. Lee took Rylie's other hand, frowning toward the open door that Dorian and George had walked through.

"What the hell?" I heard Dorian say.

"What is it?" I called.

"George?" Lee asked, her voice wavering. "What is it, honey? Should we… call the police or something?"

"Let us search," Dorian called back.

Several minutes later, George appeared, face ashen, his expression tense.

"There's no one in here," he said, and his eyes drifted to me. I couldn't read his expression, but he looked uneasy.

"Glo." Dorian appeared, his mouth in a line.

"What is it?" I whispered, afraid to go further, but needing to see what lay inside.

I stepped past him into the apartment and blinked at the kitchen, where all my cupboards and drawers stood open.

Dorian watched me and then looked beyond me. I followed his gaze to the cake his mother had made. All of my kitchen knives were stuck into the top and sides of it, destroying the mermaid decorations. Huge chunks of cake had broken loose and fallen onto my kitchen floor.

"What…?" I stepped closer to it, scratched at my neck.

"What happened?" Dorian asked quietly.

I turned to look at him and my eyebrows shot up. "I didn't do this. You can't think I did this."

"What is it, Daddy?" Rylie asked, pushing into the apartment despite Lee's attempt to hold her back. She noticed the cake and her mouth turned down. "Oh, no! Wren's birthday cake is ruined."

"Honey," George said to Lee, "why don't you take Rylie down to the car, okay? We'll get this figured out and I'll be down. Maybe we could stop for an M&M blizzard at the ice cream shop instead."

"But what about Gloria?" Rylie demanded, tugging away from Lee and moving toward me.

Dorian lifted his arm, as if he wanted to stop her, but let it fall to his side. She clung to me, wrapping both arms around my waist.

I swallowed, unsure what to say, how to explain this terrible moment away.

"I made you a gift, Rylie," I said finally, forcing a smile and moving toward the living room.

Rylie ran ahead and snatched something off the couch and held it up. "This?" she asked, wrinkling her forehead. "Is it a doll?"

She held the voodoo doll in her outstretched hands and I stepped back so quickly I bumped into Dorian, who braced his hands on my back.

"Why don't you guys go on," he told Lee and George. "We'll be fine here. I'll grab a cake on my way home. Okay?"

They exchanged a glance, and then Lee walked to me and gave me a stiff embrace. "It was good to see you, Gloria."

"Thanks, Mrs. Ashby." My words were filled with unshed tears and when George hugged me as if I were too delicate to touch, tears rolled down my cheeks.

I watched them go, felt Rylie and Dorian's eyes on me. I wanted to run into my room, shut and lock the door, crawl beneath my bed and scream.

Breath held, I took the poppet from Rylie's hands, and, fingers trembling, sat it on the coffee table. I lifted the gift bag from beside the couch and handed it to her. She reached in and took out the mermaid tail blanket.

Her face brightened and she squealed. "Oh, my God! It's a mermaid tail. Daddy, look. Did you make this, Glo?"

I nodded. Rylie hopped on the couch, extended her legs and pulled the blanket up to her waist.

"How about a movie?" Dorian suggested. "*The Little Mermaid* to mark the occasion?"

"Yes, please. Do you like *The Little Mermaid*, Glo?"

"I sure do."

Dorian lifted the remote, maneuvered to the right streaming service and turned on the movie.

I stepped toward the kitchen, staring at the cake with its chocolate and vanilla marble interior exposed. The turquoise and pink frosting had been gouged and stabbed. I saw smears of it on the table.

Dorian followed me. "I don't understand. There was no one in here, Glo. No one could have gotten in and done this."

"Let's go in the hall," I whispered, nodding toward Rylie, My eyes stopped on the doll. I didn't want to take it with us, but I couldn't leave it behind with Rylie.

Biting my lip, I hurried over and grabbed it by its leg. I stuffed it into a black trash bag and carried it from the apartment.

Dorian eyed the bag, but said nothing.

In the hall, I closed the door and dropped the bag on the floor, tempted to jump up and down on it, to run it from the house and stuff it into the trash bin at the end of the driveway. Instead, I leaned back against the wall and closed my eyes.

"I..." Dorian started then stopped, pulled off his ballcap and brushed a hand through his curls. "I don't know what's happening. Should we call Dr. Fry?"

"I told you I didn't do it," I snapped.

He hardened his jaw and stared at me. "Who did it then, Gloria? There was no one in your apartment."

I looked at the trash bag, scratched at my neck, and then moved my hands up to my ears and picked at the lobes.

"It was the doll," I whispered.

He leaned toward me. "What? Did you say—"

"It was the doll," I repeated, louder.

He clutched his hat tighter. "I don't know what to do here. I'm... you're scaring me. I'm scared."

How did I explain it? How did I make him believe? I couldn't. It was that simple and yet I had to try.

"Hold on." I returned to the apartment and walked to my desk, sifted through papers until I found the copy of *Blue-Eyed Dropouts* where I'd originally read about poppets.

"How's the movie?" I asked Rylie as I started back toward the door.

"So good," she said. "Ariel just missed her big performance and Sebastian is so mad." She giggled.

In the hall, I flipped to the page about the dolls and handed it to Dorian. He put his hat back on and leaned closer, scanning the words. "The doll in the bag is a poppet? I'm still not making sense of this."

"I sewed it in the likeness of him, the man who attacked Wren and I. I looked up a banishing spell and I... drowned the doll."

"You drowned it?"

"I tried to. I put it in the bathtub and that evening he appeared to me in the mirror."

"The doll?"

"The man, Scorpion."

"Wait. Who's Scorpion?"

"The guy who murdered Wren!" My voice was shrill and Dorian winced. I lowered my voice. "I made this doll and that night the man who abducted us at the festival appeared in my mirror. I recognized his eyes. He had a scorpion tattooed on his neck. I saw him, Dorian, I've seen him. I've been seeing him ever since I made this fucking doll." I kicked the doll and the bag flew into the opposite wall.

Dorian leaned heavily against the wall, rocking his head back. "You're saying what, then? You made this doll and... and..."

"And now the monster is in my apartment. He's..." I almost said "he's dead," but I suddenly couldn't tell the whole story, not all of it, not yet.

If I told Dorian about Dominic Sitz and the property in the woods, he'd insist we call the police, that we go there right now, but I couldn't go with him. I had to go alone.

Once the thought took root, I couldn't yank it free. It grew and bloomed. It was an oak tree—unshakable.

"It's him, Dorian. Somehow, he's haunting me or whatever. I didn't do that to the cake. I swear to you, I didn't. I would never, ever do that."

Dorian sighed, crouched and pulled the bag to him, peeled it open. He took the doll out and held it in his hand. "I know you wouldn't," he said. "But what you're saying… it can't be real."

"It is real. The smell when we walked up here, that doll is causing it. It's his smell. I remember from that night—cigarettes and cologne and sweat. The decay smell…" I shook my head. "I don't know why that's there, but I know the doll is creating it. Stuff has been happening to me, Dorian—crazy stuff that I haven't told you about because of the look on your face right now."

"I'm sorry." He sighed and pinched the bridge of his nose. "I don't want to make this worse. What do we do with this thing?" He waved at the doll. "How do we destroy it?"

"I think I've figured it out, but not tonight, okay? Tonight, I'd like you to buy a cake and go celebrate Wren's birthday with Rylie and your parents."

He shoved the doll back into the bag and stood. "Maybe I should take it with me and burn it in the firepit behind my house. If it really did do that to the cake, it's clearly dangerous." His voice was low, his face unreadable.

I didn't know if he believed me. I suspected that he wanted to, but that deep down he feared I'd begun to lose my mind.

"No," I told him. "I know how to get rid of it. You just have to trust me."

35

Two Years Ago
 June 22, 2012

I crawled out of the tent at daybreak and found Wren emerging from her tent. She grinned and started to speak, but I put a finger to my lips. "Let's go get coffee," I whispered.

She snaked an arm around my waist as we walked. "Tell me everything," she said.

I sighed dreamily and tried to call up the memories of the night before. Unfortunately, the alcohol made the encounter quite fuzzy.

"It was good," I murmured, and the bits I could remember *had* been good. Tom's slick body on top of mine, me kissing him, rising up against him. The bristles of his beard as he kissed me everywhere.

"He couldn't have been better than Marty." She laughed.

I elbowed her lightly. "That is so not funny. Wow… I cannot believe I did that."

"I can." She smirked. "You've been fantasizing about Tom Russell for a year. It was bound to happen sooner or later."

"Think so? I didn't know if he was even aware I existed."

"He's aware now." She giggled.

We got in line for coffees and breakfast burritos and found a fallen tree to sit on while we ate and talked.

"Thank God Bryce didn't come lurking around last night," I said.

"Yeah, I know," she agreed. "I hate to say this, but a part of me just wanted go home last night. He really spooked me."

W e had one of those perfect festival mornings. Coffee and breakfast followed by a gentle yoga class on the grass. Afterwards, Wren found a tent where the Crow Maidens were practicing and they invited us to sit in and listen. At one point, Holly, the Crow Maiden who played the guitar, offered the instrument to Wren and she joined them for a song.

After they finished, the Crow Maidens and a group of friends hiked to a river to swim. Wren and I joined, holding hands and screaming as we leapt from a cliff into the icy water below.

The deep pool swallowed us. The breath sucked from my lungs, blissfully refilled when I broke through the surface and gulped air. Wren trod water beside me, her gaze fixed on the shore and the impenetrable trees.

"Did you see that?" she asked.

I followed her gaze, blinking. "No, what?"

She continued to stare, mouth turned down. "I thought I saw someone watching us."

"Really?" I scanned the trees, but saw no pale face leering from within them.

"Come on, you two," one of the Crow Maidens called. "Time to show us your cannonballs and front flips."

For an hour we swam, climbing out frequently to warm up. The water was frigid from the winter run-off. It likely wouldn't warm up until later summer, if it did at all, but beneath the scorching June sky, it was perfect.

As I backstroked and gazed up at the cliffs and the forest beyond, I longed to pull on my hiking boots and disappear into the woods for the afternoon. I wouldn't for Wren's sake, but I thought it might be time to plan another long hike somewhere. Maybe a weekend back here at the Porcupine Mountains by myself.

I toweled off and slipped into my canvas shorts and a t-shirt. Wren had pulled on a long tie-dye dress and flipflops.

"You're going to have blisters if you wear those all weekend," I told her.

"Nah. I'm going mostly barefoot anyway. I just wanted these for the rocks." She gestured at the outcropping of cliffs we'd been jumping off of.

We walked back to the festival and I searched the crowd for Tom. My feet slowed and stopped.

"Well, that sucks," I muttered, nudging Wren who followed my gaze.

Tom Russell stood near the Pine Stage, making out with a petite redhead who wore a deerskin fringe skirt and red top that barely covered her large breasts.

"What a total dickhead." Wren planted her hands on her hips. "Let's go tell him so."

"No." I tugged her away. "Let's go find something to drink."

I painted on a smile, but my belly felt hollow and tears bubbled behind my eyes. I'd spent half the day imagining some scenario that included Tom and I leaving the festival as boyfriend and girlfriend. In a matter of seconds, the fantasy had been destroyed.

My memory of the previous night now felt painful and ugly. It hadn't been special. Just drunken sex at a musical festival. I could have been anyone.

"Hey." Wren squeezed my hand. "He's fake. Not who you thought he was. Better to learn it now than after you've dated him for a year."

I smiled, swallowed the saliva building in my throat. "Yeah. What a jerk."

"A colossal jerk," she agreed.

❧

"Let's go listen to the Black Cats," Wren suggested after we'd moved our tents away from Tom's and his friends' into a little patch of woods on its own.

"Sure," I said, forcing an enthusiasm I didn't feel. The shock of seeing him, of having this pristine dream of Tom Russell extinguished so quickly had really messed with my head and I was struggling to think of anything except him kissing the redhead.

Wren hugged me from behind, resting her chin on my shoulder. "I know it hurts," she murmured. "I do. How can we make it a little better?"

"Beer," I said, wrinkling my nose at the thought of it.

She laughed. "Okay then. Beer and music."

"And a night hike," I added.

She groaned. "A night hike? Do you want to get eaten by a wolf?"

I laughed. "There's a meteor shower tonight. I know the perfect viewing spot up on this hill where there's a break in the trees. Please?"

"Well, I can't say no now that you're heartbroken." She kissed my cheek. "Beer first though. So I'm not screaming every time I hear a rustle in the trees."

"For a Yooper you are awfully afraid of the woods."

"The woods at night," Wren corrected. "In daytime, I'm all about the woods, but at night…" She shivered.

36
___

I opened my eyes and stared at the ceiling, at the tiny cracks in the plaster.

Two years. Today marked two years to the day since Wren and I had walked into the forest to watch a meteor shower and met the end of life as we knew it.

I had expected to spend this day in bed. Sleeping pills or couch medicine or something else to knock me out, to keep me sedated, to ensure I passed the day with minimal thought.

I threw off the blankets and stood, slipped out of my night clothes and rummaged through the closet for hiking pants, boots and a long-sleeved dry-fit shirt.

Coffee brewed and in a to-go thermos, I added two protein bars to my hiking pack and filled a large water bottle. Before I left my apartment, I walked to the closet, took out the doll, and stuffed it in my backpack.

Today I would bury it.

I opened the garage, pulled my car into the driveway, and shut the garage door behind me. I didn't want to risk Dorian driving by and seeing the empty space where my car should have been.

For the first five minutes, my heart raced. My hands slid sweaty on the wheel and the voice in my head released a steady torrent of fear propaganda. *I might have a panic attack and crash. The second man might be following me at this very moment, waiting for his chance to finish me off.*

I refused to listen, focused on the white line that ran at the edge of the road. At fifteen minutes, my pulse steadied and slowed. I'd done this a thousand times before, this easy drive along Highway M-28, woods on either side, sun shining, blue skies.

The next two and half hours alternated between muscle memory, all the times I'd driven this exact route, and moments of sheer panic where suddenly the road sloped and tilted and black shadows edged into my vision. When those moments arose, I performed the tapping exercises and took deeper breaths, gripped the wheel, and counted down from one hundred.

Twice I nearly pulled to the side of the road, but I feared if I did, if I stopped the car, I'd never start driving again. The moment I'd seized upon waking would flutter away, a leaf in the wind, and once out of my grasp, it would be gone forever.

I had to get there. This was the moment, the pivotal moment that could shift the trajectory of my life. Dr. Fry would disagree with me. *No single moment changes it all,* he'd say. *It's a series of small things.* But he was wrong.

It had been a single moment that had ripped me out of my life before, a single moment that had ended Wren's life forever, and it would be a single moment, this one before me, that decided my future.

I turned onto the rutted two-track, bumping over roots and divots. *Five miles to the cabin,* Lara had said. I watched the odometer, thankful it hadn't rained the night before. Muddy, this trail would have been impossible with anything short of an all-terrain vehicle.

At four miles, I spotted a large tree down on the path. It crisscrossed the two-track. I stopped, turned off the engine, and stared at the path ahead. I'd have to walk from here.

I pulled out my pack, took a final swig of my coffee, and stepped from my car.

The sounds and sights of the forest overwhelmed me and I braced a hand on the hood of my car. Birds cawed and crickets chirped and a soft breeze rustled the trees and carried the scents of pine resin and the earthy smells of fungus and fallen trees.

I closed my eyes and inhaled and no terror swept through me. After several minutes of relishing the smells and sights and sounds, I started forward.

The mile walk taxed me, but felt surprisingly good. Muscles pumping, I followed the overgrown path until I spotted the derelict shack largely hidden by foliage.

I moved toward the cabin and then a spot of color off in a grove of trees caught my eye.

37

I stopped and stared, aware of what lay before me and yet...

Her bones were faded, yellowed. A single scrap of clothing was discolored, the pattern of black cats was now a blur of dark blobs, and yet, in my mind's eye, it was crystal-clear. Bright yellow shirt, cut to hang off one shoulder, scattering of jumping cats, sleeping cats, hissing cats.

Wildflowers called goldthread grew through her eye sockets, delicate and white with tiny yellow shoots. More flowers—marsh marigold and trillium—protruded through the spokes of her ribs.

"Wren..." I murmured, staggering to where she lay, my once-best friend. I sank into the grass—fragrant, beautiful, even as the horror of finding her tried to break into my thoughts.

I touched her skull, ran my fingers down the smooth slope of her forehead, and I could see her as she'd been with her pale porcelain skin, her bright green eyes, and her baby-pink hair.

This was supposed to be an ugly moment, a horrible moment filled with despair, but I felt only peace sitting there beside her—hearing the river sifting stones and sand as it cut an ancient path through the trees, a blue jay loud and cawing somewhere above me, the rustle of foliage as the squirrels chased one another.

This was the place—the final place she'd stood. My own final breaths had happened here before I'd stumbled blindly through the forest and into the river. A baptism by blood and terror. The water had washed me clean, not of my sins, but of the person I'd been. I'd emerged on the other side as this new me, a Gloria who'd been instilled with a fear so powerful it painted ugly everything I'd once found beautiful.

In the dark, Wren and I hadn't seen the flowers here or the enormous beech tree just behind me.

Sun slanted through the awning of leaves and it felt like the warmth of Wren when we'd sit in the car and listen to the White Stripes. The way it felt when we stayed up all night watching movies, when we sat together after class at NMU and plotted the summer—camping and festivals and road trips.

As I lingered, a tiny voice tried to yank me out of the moment, to remind me this was urgent—I'd found Wren's body. I should have been walking in circles, staring at the bars on my phone, and searching for a point where the signal grew strong enough to make a call—Dorian, the police, Detective Webb.

Instead, I stretched out in the grass and lay down beside her. I reached my hand until I felt a hard ridge of bone beneath my fingers, her own skeletal fingers entwined with mine.

Just now, all the rest didn't matter. We were together for our birthdays as we'd always intended.

"Happy birthday," I murmured and tears poured over my cheeks and watered the earth.

With the soft grass and the slope of the ground beneath me, I was transported back to childhood. Wren and I lying in her backyard on a summer day with the scents of honeysuckle from the flowering tree near the driveway and the smells of herbs growing in her mother's pots, rosemary and lavender. The sound of bees hovering and the darting glitter of dragonflies and the sun watching over it all like some too-bright God, always there but painful to look at.

One word had encased us in that former life, shrouded us, wrapped us in infinitely strong arms—safe. We'd been safe there in the grass and as we lay together giggling and plotting our next trip to the local pool, we'd had no concept of a future beyond that instant.

I'd come to realize that the real gift of childhood was complete immersion in the present moment, a singular focus on this second right now, the ability to take every moment that had come before and every moment that would come after for granted. Some people thought it was selfish. I might have thought so once too, but not anymore. Now I longed for that absolute devotion to the now.

I was a hostage to the past, a prisoner to one horrible, violent night.

I closed my eyes and clutched Wren's fingers and felt the tranquility sliding away as my thoughts nudged in. Thoughts of her last breath. Thoughts of my terrified running. How even in my adrenaline-fueled sprint, my mind had been throwing obstacles in my path. *What if you trip on a root? He's following you. He'll find you. You're being too loud. Wren is dead.*

There'd been an instant of absolute thereness—the moment I'd made the choice to run, all thought had left me. If I'd thought, pondered the decision, I would simply have lain there and died as Detective Webb said so many did. The fear would have been too great.

This is where it happened. This is where the worst night of my life happened.

"Shhh…" I silenced the voice. I thought of Dr. Fry then.

Breathe back from ten… nine… eight…

I felt Wren in my hands and the soft grass that smelled of a thousand summers and I blinked as more tears spilled from my eyes.

For a while, I did nothing. I lay beside her and I breathed. The outside world, in all its richness, surrounded us, just her and I once more.

When I opened my eyes, time had passed, more time than seemed possible. I'd fallen asleep, but I'd had no dreams, no terror had slipped in to rattle me awake.

Still, the light had changed. Daylight remained, but the sun now hovered above the trees to the west.

I stood, pained to leave her there, wanting to gather her bones in my backpack and carry her with me, which was absurd. I could not do that. Soon this tranquil sliver of forest would become a crime scene strung with yellow tape and trampled with the boots of men and women searching for a stray hair or fiber, some link between the savagery of that night and the man—men?—who'd orchestrated it.

Horror still had not crashed upon me. It was as if someone had ushered that terrified, panicked, traumatized part of me into another room. She was asleep in there, lying in the safety of her apartment, heaped with blankets, oblivious to having found Wren. I was not afraid, and I never wanted to be afraid again.

My cell phone had no service. I'd likely have to return to my car and drive out a way before I'd get enough bars to call, but it didn't matter now. I'd found her.

I set my backpack on the ground and unzipped it. Beneath my bear spray lay the doll. I took it out, set it in the grass and considered it. It did not look magical or evil. Its crooked red mouth didn't suddenly grin, the sun did not slip behind the trees, the world did not go dark.

With my hands I dug into the earth, savoring the sensation of the damp, black soil. An earthworm wriggled beneath my palm and I lifted it, watched its gray body squirm from my grip and land in the grass.

I set the doll inside the hole and I forced myself to imagine the man, the monster with his scorpion tattoo and his dark mask and his black eyes and his deadly blade.

"Dominic Francis Sitz.

"You are gone from my life.

"Your energy does not affect me.

"You cannot see me.

"You cannot speak to me.

"You do not exist.

"I banish you.

"I banish you.

"I banish you."

I repeated the words two more times and then I scooped handfuls of black dirt over the doll's face until all that remained of the hole was a little patch of uneven soil.

I stood and walked away, wiping my hands on my t-shirt.

I returned to the shack. Invasive vines snaked over the mossy, partially collapsed roof. A door hung on its hinges and when I stepped to the dark opening, a terrible smell seeped from the interior.

I closed my eyes and braced a hand on the frame. Beneath my palm the wood was splintered and soft, rotted. I suspected Kelly Rice lay in the cabin, but I couldn't bring myself to go in and look.

Behind me, in the direction of my car, a twig snapped and then another. Someone was walking in the forest nearby.

Without thinking, I shuffled into the dark cabin. There was nowhere to hide. It was a single room with a dirty mattress buzzing with flies in the corner. There was no other furniture at all. Some floorboards had rotted through and I could see a dark crevice beneath.

A small rusted metal loop stuck from a square trapdoor and I pulled it, revealing a root cellar. Cool, rancid air wafted up, and I leaned closer, peering into the darkness. The floor was dirt, and the space was compact. Not enough room to stand fully upright.

Beyond the cabin, I heard the crunch of leaves and branches. I climbed quickly into the cellar and eased the door closed above me. It had to be deer walking out there… maybe even a bear or bobcat, but just to be safe.

My eyes adjusted to the darkness, aided by the splash of light that came through the rotted floorboards. The smell in the cavern nearly brought me to my knees. My eyes watered and I bunched my t-shirt in front of my nose.

Something lay in the far back corner of the root cellar. I stared, horror trembling through me as I made sense of the tangle of pale hair, matted and dark in clumps, the shape of a head, her face turned away.

I'd found Kelly Rice.

It was her long body, pale arms and legs poking from shorts and a t-shirt, and though I couldn't clearly see the color of her clothes, I suspected Kelly wore what she'd had on the night I'd last seen her through the binoculars—terrycloth shorts and an NMU t-shirt.

A shaft of light from above cut a path across her pale legs. A cockroach scurried across her thigh and into her shorts.

I gagged and dropped to my knees. A stream of coffee, not yet digested, spewed onto the dirt floor.

Above me, the rusted hinge on the cabin door shrieked, followed by the sound of boots on the wood floor. Someone stepped into the cabin. Not a bobcat or a bear, a human being, a man based on the heaviness of his footfalls.

He walked across the decayed wood planks, raining dust into my hair. Through spaces where the floor had largely rotted, the shadow of the person, the man, moved. I crouched and slowly, so slowly, let my backpack slip down from my shoulders.

I found the zipper, and, cringing at the slightest sound, drew it open. I reached inside, gripped the canister of bear spray and pulled it free.

"Drop it," a voice commanded, and I froze.

Through a hole I saw the shadow of the man, but more prominently, the round cylinder of a gun leveled at my face.

I stepped quickly aside, clutching the canister tighter. I'd moved out of his line of sight, but there was nowhere to run to in the claustrophobic space. The only escape was the trapdoor. He'd shoot me the instant I poked my head through it.

"Gloria, there's no way out. If you hide down there, I'm going to dump gasoline on the floor and light this place up."

Very still, I moved again, peering up through the slats in the floor, searching for the face of a man whose voice I recognized.

38

Two Years Ago
June 22, 2012

Wren and I stood frozen in the flashlight's glare, the man hugely tall behind it. I could no longer hear the music from the festival. The lights were a far-off mirage.

"Put these on her," he barked, and something landed near my feet.

I couldn't see what, but he shined the light on black zip ties.

I crouched and picked them up, my mind moving a thousand miles an hour. When I stood and registered Wren's face, the terror in her eyes stopped me cold. I blinked at her, whispered, "It's okay."

"Shut up," he spat. "Five seconds and your friend will have a bullet between her eyes. Five, four—"

Wren thrust her arms out, her pale wrists tiny.

"No," he said. "Turn around. Secure them behind her back."

She turned and extended her arms behind her. They were shaking. I wrapped the ties around her wrists and threaded the plastic through the little opening. I left them loose.

"Tighter," he snarled.

I ratcheted the cable tighter. The man moved closer. His leg shot out and buckled the back of Wren's knee. She cried out, and I moved to help her.

"Don't fucking move!" he hissed at me. "Face down," he told Wren.

She did as he asked, awkwardly falling forward with no hands to break her fall.

His hands were on me then, forcing my arms behind me, twisting the zip tie so tight it bit into my skin. I realized I could feel both of his hands. He had set the gun down, but it was already too late. My wrists were locked in place.

I could run, but I'd be leaving Wren behind, helpless, facedown on the trail.

He leaned forward, grabbed the back of her t-shirt and yanked her to her feet. I still couldn't see him well, a hulking shadow with a black mask and equally black eyes. His hands looked huge and pale and it struck me as odd and scary that he wore no gloves.

"Go… walk," he told us.

We walked, our shoulders bumping. Wren cried quietly beside me. I searched the dark trail ahead of us where his light swept back and forth like the beam of a lighthouse.

His movements were manic, his breath heavy. He never held the light in any one place long enough to see what was there. He could easily miss someone on the trail ahead. But we'd walked so far from the festival, I doubted we'd encounter anyone who could help us.

We marched a few hundred yards and then he told us to stop. I turned to Wren, who peered at me fearfully before looking back at her feet as if the mere rebellion of looking at each other might cause him to kill us.

He yanked something rough over my head. Scratchy and dry, it felt like a burlap sack. I heard Wren whimper and thought he'd put a similar bag over her head.

A shrill beep broke the quiet, the automatic locks on a vehicle, and a new dread stole over me. He was taking us somewhere, not merely doing what he wanted on this dark trail and then leaving us behind.

"Please," Wren pleaded. "Please, we'll do anything you want. Please don't hurt us."

I said nothing. No words could possibly matter to this man. No begging would make him change his mind. Whatever happened from this point on would not come down to his sympathy, but our strength and luck.

He shoved me roughly forward and my shins cracked the side of the vehicle. I yelped.

"Lift your legs, ya dumb bitch," he growled.

I bent one knee, lifted my foot and stepped forward. He shoved me hard, and I plunged face first into the crevice between the seats. I struggled to sit back up but felt his fist in my hair, coiled, ripping.

"If you sit up, or so much as make a sound, I'll blow your friend's brains all over the front seat."

I didn't move, but let my forehead rest against the scratchy carpeting, dirty and stinking of oil.

Another door opened and closed. I heard Wren begging, breathing heavily. Another door slammed, and the engine started.

Wren continued talking, her voice muffled. "Yesterday was my birthday," she said. "I turned nineteen and Gloria turns nineteen tomorrow and… and we're here this weekend to celebrate because…" She hiccupped. "Because we celebrate together every year. We've been best friends since we were little girls and… please… please don't hurt us."

I wanted to sit up, find a way to slip my arms beneath me. If I could get them in front of me, they'd still be bound, but they'd be useful. I could sit back on the seat and kick forward, perhaps connect with the back of his head.

But then what? What happened if I managed to connect? Would he crash the vehicle? Doubtful. More than likely, I wouldn't incapacitate him at all, only enrage him.

And then he'd kill Wren and then he'd kill me.

I didn't move. I stayed face down, and I prayed that if God existed, he would save us. He would not let our lives end this way.

In the front, Wren continued, sounding breathless, terrified. "My niece is, umm… six, and she's really excited because I'm teaching her to—"

"I like 'em young," he interrupted, his voice deeper, huskier. "Is she pretty like you?"

Wren went silent, and I swallowed the scream bubbling in my chest. His words, not only the words themselves, but the way he'd said them caused the hairs on my arms and neck to stand on end.

The vehicle bumped and shook as we drove. We weren't on pavement, but a two-track or a very uneven dirt road. Not a road, I thought. The sharp scratch of branches against the windows and body of the car proved the path was too narrow to be a road.

Fifteen, maybe twenty minutes of driving and the vehicle stopped.

He turned off the engine and got out. It was quiet except my muffled breaths within the sack.

"Wren?" I called.

"Oh, God, Gloria, what do we do? What do we do?"

I wanted to have a plan, an answer ready, but my mind was suddenly as smooth as a river stone, not a ridge in its surface. I could think of nothing to say, no reassurances, no way out.

I blinked into the bag and swallowed. "I think... we have to go along with him. We have to hope he does what he wants and lets us go."

"Okay... yeah. Maybe he'll just let us go." Her voice was thick with tears.

Fear and helplessness and rage took turns seizing me, but none of it helped. I started to sit when the door at the front of the vehicle opened. I heard Wren gasp and though I couldn't see, I suspected he'd lifted her up. He was twice her size. She was little more than a doll in his enormous hands.

The door behind me opened a moment later. He grabbed my hair, and he yanked me back.

I shrieked and tried to twist away from him, but he didn't let go, pulling me out of the vehicle. My scalp was on fire. I scrambled to get my legs beneath me and found my footing, relieving some of the pain in my head.

Beneath my boots, grass and twigs crunched. Even through the bag over my head, I could smell his stink. Sweat and cigarette smoke. He smelled as if he hadn't merely spritzed on cologne, but had dumped the bottle straight over his head. He shoved me hard, and I tripped, plunged forward onto my knees.

"Face down. Now," he hissed.

A little way off I heard Wren crying again. I slumped forward. The cool grass tickled my neck and legs.

For a moment it was eerily quiet and then Wren cried out and I heard a sound, a ripping sound, clothes being torn. She screamed and white-hot fury raged through me as I understood what he was doing.

"No!" I screamed, struggling to push up onto my knees.

I heard him striding toward me. I stood and the force of him pummeled into me, sent me sprawling onto my back, knocking the air from my lungs. I turned my head just as his boot—steel-toed, I suspected—rammed into my face. My nose exploded, the pain like a bomb detonating between my eyes. I howled and swallowed a mouthful of my blood.

I rolled away, curled into a ball, pulling my knees toward my shattered face. Dark spots swam behind my eyes and the sound of the forest and Wren's cries and my own ragged breaths merged into a nightmare symphony.

Sometime later, he returned to me, tore off my shorts, and I lay numb and still. When he was finished, he wrapped his hands around my throat and squeezed and squeezed. I floated down and down into the murky black.

When I next awoke, the sensation beneath me had changed. Grass no longer tickled my bare legs. Something hard pressed against my spine—a wood floor, I thought—and far off came the voice of the man and then another voice. I strained to hear it, almost thought it was familiar, someone who'd come to rescue us, but then it too faded and I faded with it.

Fragrant, cool air rushed against my battered face. I opened my eyes. The sack had been removed. I lay on my back, my arms numb beneath me. The stars overhead blinked against the black void, so enormous, that world out there, and us light-years away, our lives being snuffed out just as the spark in those stars might have burned out centuries before.

Tears leaked from my eyes and I listened for Wren. After a time, I heard her. No longer crying or pleading, just the gusts of her breath. I lifted my head, and the moonlight cut a shaft through the trees and there she was, oddly on her knees, and the monster stood behind her.

So swift I did not at first understand, he swiped his arm across her neck. Her pale throat opened and darkness poured out.

I screamed and screamed until I too was jerked to my knees by my hair and a sudden flash of heat tore across my throat. I slumped forward, warmth spreading beneath me.

I was dying, or perhaps I had died, and yet still I felt the coolness of the grass and a breeze ruffling my hair and causing my nose and face to throb harder. Somewhere were far-off voices, men's voices, angry, arguing. I dug my forehead into the ground, struggled to get my knees beneath me, somehow managed it, and then my feet.

I stood and ran.

39

———————

Jeff stared down at me through the opening in the rotted floorboards, the gun in his outstretched hand.

"Come up," he said. "I won't shoot."

I stood, mouth sagging, and stared. For a moment, all had gone still within me. My heartbeat, my breath, my mind—it all ceased its movement.

"Now! Come on. Hurry up," he spat. "Or don't." He stepped closer, pushed the gun lower. I sensed the tension of his finger on the trigger. One little pull and I'd be gone.

"Okay…" I breathed.

I moved toward the trapdoor, bear spray growing slippery in my hand.

"Drop the can first," he said. "Now. I can see you're holding something. Leave it."

I considered my options. I could try to spray him the moment he opened the trapdoor, but I had no clue where he'd be standing and he had the gun.

No, there'd be a better moment. There had to be.

I dropped the can of bear spray and hoisted myself through the trapdoor, climbed to my feet and watched him warily. He stood between me and the cabin door, the gun raised and pointed at my face. Except for the gun, Jeff looked as he always did. Dressy dark jeans and a button-

223

down shirt, aviator glasses at his collar, not a blond hair out of place. It was surreal.

"Why?" I murmured. "It was you? I don't…" My head swam as I tried to fit the pieces together. Dark spots, sweat, heart thumping. It was starting—the body wanting to shut down, curl up, hide. "Why Wren? Why me?"

Jeff sighed. "Wren was an accident—well, not literally. I made a mistake with Dom, plain and simple. You were supposed to be alone."

"With Dom… You put him up to it? You were the reason—"

"Gloria… this will not end well for you. Okay? You're not going to walk out of here. What's the point, anyway? Look at your life, at what you've become. I'd be doing you a favor. I have something…"

He kept the gun in one hand and reached into his pocket with the other, pulled out a bottle of pills and shook them at me. "It could be so easy. We'll sit by Wren if you want. Take the pills and go to sleep. No one will question it. Everyone's amazed you haven't already done it. The alternative is going to be scary. It's going to be just like that night. You remember that night, don't you, Gloria?"

I blinked the sweat from my eyes, swayed on my feet.

"Except it's going to be even worse because I'm going to shoot you and leave you to bleed to death under this cabin, down there with dead Kelly. It could take hours, maybe days."

"Why Kelly?" I whispered, wishing I hadn't seen her down there, left in that dark, dingy little room beneath the floor.

"Because she was smarter than the cops."

"She found out it was you?"

"Close enough."

"And you killed her?"

"She's no longer with us, yes."

"And now you're going to kill me and just carry on as if nothing happened? They're going to find out it was you. If Kelly found out, it's only a matter of time before the cops discover what she knew."

"Don't count on it. Everything she knew went up in smoke."

Sweat dripped into my eyes and burned. I lifted my hand to swipe it away.

"Don't," he said. "Or the next thing you'll feel is a bullet in your stomach."

He watched me through flat, dark eyes. A half smile curved his lips, but his eyes were void of anything, of humanity, of soul.

"Just... okay..." I swallowed the thickness gathering in my throat, a desire to vomit churning in my stomach. "I'll do it, I'll take the pills, but first... I need to know why."

I wanted to stall him, but I also wanted to know, had to know. This man had stolen my best friend, shattered my life, Wren's family's life. "Why did Dominic take us that night? Or if it was only meant to be me, why me?"

Jeff studied me. "I met Dominic at school in Escanaba. He was a senior. I was a junior. He got kicked out a lot. Big troublemaker. We became friends and, well..." Jeff shrugged. "You needed to die, Gloria, simple as that, and I had a friend capable of killing you. What better time than an isolated music festival? I knew you'd be wandering off on your own because that's how you are. Like you're fucking invincible." He smirked. "Apparently not."

"Why did I need to die?"

He held my gaze. "If it's any consolation," he said, "I didn't condone"—he gestured a hand—"all the other stuff Dom did. I only realized once he got you both here how out of control he was. Drunk, high on God knows what and just... intent on doing what he was going to do. Royally fucked everything up, might I add. I made a mistake bringing him into the fray. None of us got what we wanted. Well, Dom did. But I made him pay for that."

"You killed him?"

Jeff nodded slowly. "I had to. Dom had a big mouth. Sooner or later, he was going to get inebriated and brag to someone about what he'd done. Just so happened, he fell asleep on some train tracks. Nasty way to go." He frowned and shook his head. "I've never enjoyed the sight of blood and the smell of it, that metallic stink and..." He shook his head. "Anyway..."

"The police know he was murdered."

"They also know Dominic Sitz got what he deserved. I promise you they won't be wasting many resources to find his killer. I thought you'd thank me. You know what he wanted? To finish you off. He even went by your apartment a few times, considered ambushing your little boyfriend, Dorian, to get inside. Be grateful I got rid of him before he did that."

I cringed at his words, at the thought of the monster sitting outside my apartment, me oblivious inside. "You're going to spend the rest of your life in prison, Jeff," I told him. "They're going to love you in there. Pretty boy who thinks he's better than everyone."

I don't know what compelled me to goad him, sheer fury perhaps. What I really wanted was to attack him, tear the eyes from his head. Most of all, I wanted to convert my rising terror into anger. I could not afford to break down. If I did, it was over.

"Last chance for the easy way, Gloria." He shook the bottle of pills.

"There is no easy way, Jeff."

I looked past him and widened my eyes as if I'd seen something behind him. He turned ever so slightly, and I darted forward, smashed my shoulder into his. He swung the gun around, but he'd lost his footing, stumbled.

I lunged through the flimsy cabin door and fled into the woods. Behind me, the gun went off, deafening, spooking a flock of birds into the trees.

I tripped over a root and nearly fell. Jeff caught me around the waist, dragged me down. I fell, gasping, kicked my legs out. My foot connected with the gun and it skittered from his hand. I slithered away, but he clutched my ankle, yanked me back toward him.

I kicked with my opposite foot, caught him in the jaw. He yelped, and I scrambled back to my feet and hurtled away from the cabin toward the river, the path that had saved me once before.

I lay beneath a pile of brush for an hour, maybe more. I'd heard nothing, no footsteps, no rustle of branches, but still, I didn't dare move. If Jeff left me behind, prison was a certainty. I didn't think he'd risk it, but I also knew I had the advantage. Jeff wasn't a woods guy. If one of us was going to get lost out here, it was him.

Still, I waited longer, waited until the sky grew dark. I pushed the leaves and branches off and I climbed to my feet, wiggling my legs and arms, all achy and tingling from my prolonged position on a nest of sticks.

I'd lost my cell phone, couldn't call for help if I wanted to. My car lay to the west, but if Jeff intended to finish me, that was where he'd be, waiting at my car.

I couldn't risk it. Slowly I walked, straining through the night sounds for the water. Eventually it came to me, the soft rush, and I moved toward it, pausing often to listen and ensure no one followed.

I found the river's edge, and I stayed along the bank, but hidden in the trees where the moonlight wouldn't give away my location.

I walked for hours, limping from a thrum in my right knee. I must have twisted it when I'd escaped from Jeff.

My watch read three a.m.

I was officially twenty-one years old.

40

"Dorian, it's Glo."

"Oh, my God. It's her," he called. "She's on the phone. Holy shit, Glo. Everyone's been flipping out. We thought you got abducted by the same guy who took Kelly. Then your car was gone and… and…" His voice cracked.

Detective Webb came on the line. "Gloria, it's Detective Webb. Where are you?"

I swallowed, my throat desperately dry. "In the Porcupine Mountains. I broke into someone's cottage. Thank God they had a landline. Detective, it was Jeff, my stepbrother. He was behind the whole thing, what happened to me and Wren."

"How do you know that?"

"He followed me here. He tried to kill me."

"Okay, we'll go pick him up now."

"One more thing…"

"What?"

"I found Wren… her body. I know where she's at. And Kelly too."

"Is Kelly alive?"

"No." My voice caught. "Kelly is dead."

"Okay." He sighed. "Are you okay, Gloria? Do you need medical help?"

"No. I'm all right."

"I'm going to give you back to Dorian. Tell him how to find you and we'll reach out to the sheriff's office in the area and get deputies over to pick you up."

～

"No sign of Jeff," Dorian murmured, taking my hand and squeezing. "I cannot believe you came out here by yourself. What were you thinking?"

I stared through the window where the sky had begun to brighten. I'd been sitting in the sheriff's office for over four hours. I'd ridden with deputies to the trailhead where my car was parked and told them where to find Wren and Kelly.

After that, I sat and stared and drank gritty coffee until Dorian arrived with my oversize afghan and my kitty stress balls and hugged me so hard, he lifted me off the ground.

"I was thinking it was time," I told him. "Time to… face it."

He leaned over and braced his elbows on his knees. "And you found her? Wren? She's up there?"

I nodded. "She is."

He wiped at his eyes and then bent down, drew something from a paper bag. "Happy birthday," he told me. "I didn't get a chance to wrap it."

I stared at the box, which depicted an image of strange, futuristic-looking goggles. "What is it?" I asked.

"It's a VR headset. Virtual reality. It comes loaded with all these places. I thought… since you don't—or didn't—leave your apartment, this was a way you could experience the world again."

I smiled and leaned my head on his shoulder.

～

The police had searched my dad and Janice's home, but Jeff was gone. Eighteen hours after I'd escaped him in the Porcupine Mountains cabin, they found him.

Jeff's black sports car sat on an isolated dirt road that led to a derelict farm just outside of Marquette. He was slumped over the wheel, dead of an apparent suicide.

～

The hours that followed were a blur of questions and tears and long, numb silences where I could think of nothing and feel nothing.

I dreamed of Wren and Kelly and Jeff.

~

A knock came on my door and I opened it to see my dad.

"Gloria." He hugged me, squeezing me so tight I lost my breath. "My God, I was so scared when Dorian called and said he couldn't find you. I... I thought... it doesn't matter. You're here."

"Yeah." I sighed. "I'm here."

My dad's face fell. "I just cannot believe that Jeff... just don't understand why."

"And Janice? How'd she take it?" For all my dislike of Janice, my heart hurt for her, too. She'd loved her son so much and now he was gone, not only him, but the memory of him destroyed by the revelations about what he'd done.

He scratched at his chin. "She's... keeping it together. Very calm, scary calm," he admitted. "I fear when it really sinks in, she may... come unglued."

"Well, I can understand that," I said. "Dad, did you tell the police about the surveillance cameras you set up?"

"Oh, yes, sure. They're picking up the footage this afternoon."

"Did you watch it?"

He pursed his lips and shook his head. "No... I doubt there's much to see. Jeff must have come home after... after he followed you to the Porcupine Mountains. A few of his things were gone, but..."

"I want to watch it. Can you pull it up on your phone?"

"Oh, gosh, Gloria. I don't think that's a good idea."

"You don't have to, but I need to. Okay? Let me see your phone."

He looked like he might argue, then handed it over.

I plugged it into my laptop and scrolled through the surveillance history, clicked on the block of time I suspected Jeff had returned.

I fast-forwarded until I saw Jeff's car pull in the driveway just after seven p.m. So, he hadn't stayed and searched the woods. After I'd escaped, he'd made a run for it. That was the only way he could have gotten back to Marquette so quickly. Janice's car was also in the driveway.

My dad stood and walked behind me, watching over my shoulder.

Jeff jumped from the driver's seat and ran into the house. I clicked another camera that showed him rushing into the kitchen, talking to Janice, his hands waving as he spoke.

"Where's the volume?" I asked.

My dad reached for his phone, clicked on a little gear symbol and changed the volume setting from mute to on.

Jeff had disappeared from the frame. I clicked until I found him in his bedroom. He had a duffel bag open on the bed and stuffed clothes into it.

Janice walked in and stood in the doorway. "You left her then? You left her to tell the police everything?"

"She got away. If I'd stayed to find her, I'd be sitting in jail by tomorrow. I have to go."

"Why did you follow her out there? Why, why, why? God dammit!" She picked up a pillow from Jeff's bed and squeezed until her face was red.

"I had to. She was going to find Kelly. I…" He sat heavily on the bed, buried his face in his hands.

My father had grown very still behind me. I too sat frozen, eyes glued to the screen.

"We were done with her." Janice said. "The hunting trip was weeks away. Jeffrey, you've ruined everything. You realize that, don't you?"

Jeff looked at his mom, his face pleading, the man gone, replaced by a scared little boy. "You have to help me, Mom. There's still some money, isn't there? From Gwen?"

Janice released a high-pitched laugh and snapped the pillow at Jeff's face. It hit him and landed on the floor. "Money from Gwen? My God, I overestimated you. Why do you think we got the life insurance on Gloria to begin with? The money from Gwen was gone before I ever met Edgar Cline. Why do you think I chose him rather than the podiatrist from Mackinaw City? Because he had a daughter."

Jeff stood suddenly, his eyes darting around the room.

Janice stepped in front of him, put her hands on his shoulders. "Jeffrey Francis Calder, you will stop that right now. Calm down. Okay? I will help you. Now, we don't have money from Gwen, but I have a little nest egg I can dip into. Pack only the essentials. I will buy you a bus ticket and you'll get on a bus leaving town tonight."

"They'll be waiting with handcuffs at the first stop."

"Let me finish," she said sharply. "You will board the bus and then get off before it leaves. I will drive you to the storage unit. There's a mattress in there you can sleep on tonight. Tomorrow, I'll get money out of the account and buy an old car from someone online and bring it to you."

"Mom, they're going to be watching every move you make."

"I wasn't born yesterday, Jeff. I know how to play the shocked, grieving mother. They won't give me a second glance. Once you have the car, don't head for Canada, they'll expect that. Go south towards Mexico. Switch out the plate regularly. I can give you enough to last a few weeks."

"And then what?"

She sighed. "And then we'll have to speed up our plans with Edgar."

"You're going to go on the hunting trip?" Jeff asked.

She snorted. "Of course not. People die of all kinds of things. This situation"—she waved a hand at Jeff—"may play to our advantage. The stress of discovering you attacked his daughter could possibly cause a heart attack."

"Okay…" Jeff said after a long moment.

"Move along then," Janice told him. "We don't have much time."

They said nothing else.

My dad and I watched Jeff finish packing his bag, sling it over his shoulder, and walk out the door.

I clicked each screen as Janice left Jeff's room. She reappeared in the kitchen and took a plastic tumbler from the cupboard. From the refrigerator she grabbed a two-liter bottle of Pepsi—Jeff's drink of choice—and filled the cup.

From her purse, she drew out a small clear bottle. I couldn't read the label. She unscrewed the cap and emptied the bottle into the cup, snapped a lid on top and walked out the front door.

I turned in my chair and looked at my dad, whose lips were slightly parted, his eyes fixed on the screen, on the empty kitchen. Finally, he blinked and backed away. He sank onto my couch.

I stood and went to him, sitting so close our thighs touched. "Dad?"

"Oh, God," he murmured, his expression filled with disbelief morphing into horror. "Oh, God," he repeated.

I took his hand and squeezed it. "We need to call Detective Webb."

They arrested Janice two hours later, interrupting her at a women's luncheon. She did not go easily, but screamed and attempted to shake the police off, demanding her friends call her husband and ask that he summon an attorney immediately.

The following evening, after she'd been interrogated, Detective Webb met Dorian and me at my apartment. The three of us sat at my kitchen table.

"Did she confess?" I asked.

Webb shook his head. "No. She refused to speak, demanded an attorney. She expected your dad to hire one, but... she ended up with a public defender."

"She didn't admit to anything, then?"

"No, but... she might down the line once she knows about all the evidence. She had no idea your father put those cameras up."

"I wonder why he didn't tell her," Dorian murmured.

"Because he suspected Jeff was the one stealing," Webb explained. "I talked with him for a long time this afternoon. He installed the security system when no one was home and he placed the cameras so they were concealed. He knew if he mentioned them to Janice, she'd tell Jeff and the jig would be up.

"He's... pretty destroyed by the whole ordeal. He expected to discover Jeff was stealing money, not that his wife and stepson were plotting his murder and had already tried unsuccessfully to kill his only child."

"This is insane," I murmured.

Dorian was oddly quiet, and I wondered if he was thinking about Wren and the fact that she'd died because my greedy stepmother wanted to collect life insurance on me. It had nothing to do with Wren at all.

"Why... why this Dominic guy? Why did Jeff hire him?" Dorian asked.

"We have a big investigation ahead," Webb admitted, "but from what Jeff told Gloria, he didn't want to do the dirty work. I'm sure he agreed to pay Sitz some portion of the life insurance payout. He knew Sitz was a criminal, figured the guy wouldn't blink an eye at shoving Gloria off a cliff or whatever the original plan was, but clearly, he didn't have a clue who he was getting involved with. Dominic Sitz was a bad man and once Jeff let him out of the cage, he had zero control."

"So Jeff killed him," Dorian muttered. "Do you know for sure he killed him?"

"I do," I said. "He told me he'd done me a favor."

"Yeah, I suspect we're going to discover that Sitz was blackmailing Jeff. That might explain why Jeff started stealing from your dad. There'd never been any insurance money because you survived that night. Jeff and Janice had to find other ways to pay him off."

"Who was Gwen?" I asked, remembering Jeff's comment in the video about the money from Gwen.

Webb gave me a significant look and rubbed at the scarred skin on his hand. I suspected he too was thinking about the psychic's experience at the Porcupine Mountains trail when she said she'd been pushed and mentioned the name Gwen.

"Janice had a daughter," Webb said. "Gwendolyn Harper. She died ten years ago when she was fifteen years old from an apparent fall off a cliff during a family vacation in Yellowstone National Park."

"You're kidding me," Dorian said. "Do you think Janice killed her?"

Webb nodded slowly. "Yes, I do think that. Will we ever prove it? Unlikely. She had a hundred-thousand-dollar life insurance policy on Gwen, which she called to collect less than twenty-four hours after the girl died."

"Was Janice alone with her on the trail?"

"No. Jeff was there."

"What about their dad?"

"He and Janice were already divorced."

"Did Jeff and Gwen's dad know about the life insurance money on Gwen?" I asked.

"No, but he told me an interesting story when I spoke to him. A few months before their divorce, he became violently ill after Janice served him a milkshake. He went into the ER. They couldn't figure out what was wrong. He got better and then a few weeks later it happened again after he'd eaten something Janice gave him.

"He suspected Janice was poisoning him. Then he got a call from a friend of his who sold life insurance. The guy said Janice had tried to increase her policy on him for half a million dollars. She'd forged his signature on the document and this friend of his suspected as much and tipped him off. He moved out of the house right away and filed for divorce."

Dorian rubbed his eyes and took off his ball cap, turning it in his hands. "She murdered her own daughter for life insurance money."

"I think she did, yes."

"Why didn't anyone realize there was a policy out on Gloria? I mean, after the attack, don't police usually look into that?" Dorian asked.

"It depends on the detectives working the investigation. In Gloria's case, she survived, so the focus was on Wren and they looked for life insurance and there wasn't any. The attack looked like"—he glanced at me and his voice dropped—"the motive was sexual. The police believed Wren was the primary target. They had no reason to look at Janice or Jeff. I've been a detective for a long time and, to be honest, I wouldn't have looked at them either."

"But Jeff was at the music festival that weekend," Dorian argued.

"I know. In a way, it's a problem of classism. He doesn't look like a criminal. No criminal record, no violent assaults against women, no run-in with the law whatsoever. Dominic Sitz, on the other hand, fit the profile, but no one ever put him at the festival. He's not anywhere in the file for Gloria and Wren's cases. Police looked pretty deeply at Bryce Dobbs and truth be told they thought he was their guy. They just couldn't prove it."

"But it wasn't him," I said.

"No. He had nothing to do with it. Ultimately, the mastermind was Janice. Jeff was guilty, but his mother set the whole thing up. I think she had a lot of control over her son. She manipulated him and he… was groomed to become the person he was. I wouldn't be surprised to learn he witnessed his sister's death—maybe he even pushed her."

"I hope you're not trying to say he's a victim," Dorian muttered.

"No, not a victim, but… a product of a very manipulative, abusive mother. He murdered Kelly Rice. He had every intention of killing Gloria. Like his mother, Jeff did not value human life. The other issue with that insurance is that it wasn't recent. She took the policy out on you two years after she married your father."

I stared at him. "She did?"

"Yes. You would have been fourteen."

I frowned and pushed down the cuticle in my thumb thinking back to my freshman year in high school. I'd fallen terribly ill-vomiting and a high fever. My father had called an ambulance because I'd been unable to stand. Janice had insisted he was overreacting, that it was a stomach virus.

"I got really sick when I was fifteen," I said. "I still can't eat pudding."

"Pudding?" Webb asked.

"Janice made me chocolate pudding. I still remember it because it was so random. She never did spontaneous nice things like that. I came home from school and she greeted me at the door with a glass bowl of chocolate pudding and whip cream. I devoured it. I'd just finished with volleyball practice and I was starving. Within an hour I was throwing up."

"Did you go to the doctor?" Dorian asked.

I nodded. "To the emergency room in an ambulance. They couldn't figure out what was wrong. I spent three days in the hospital on I.V. fluids."

"Oh yeah..." Dorian said. "I remember now. Wren missed a day of school to sit with you at the hospital."

I smiled, remembering her reading quizzes to me from Seventeen magazine: *Does Your Crush Like You?* And *What's Your Friendship Style?*

Webb considered me. "Did they test you for any poisons?"

"I don't think so."

"She tried to kill you six years ago," Dorian said, incredulous.

"It's impossible to say that for certain, but she may well have," Webb agreed.

I clenched my hands together in my lap and closed my eyes wondering if there'd been other times, instances more elusive than the pudding. Had there been moments when she stood behind me and imagined shoving me in front of a car? Had she watched me sleeping at night and wanted to smother me with a pillow?

When I opened my eyes both Webb and Dorian watched me.

"Are you okay?" Dorian asked.

"Yeah." I massaged my temples. "I'm fine. It's just... a lot to think about."

"It is," Webb agreed.

There'd been so much collateral damage all stemming from Janice's greed-Wren, Gwen, Dominic, and Jeff-all dead.

"How did Kelly die?" I asked, though I wasn't sure if I wanted to know.

"Not peacefully."

"How did he get Kelly out of the apartment, though, without… leaving evidence of what he'd done?"

"We suspect, though we can't prove it yet, that after he extinguished the lights, he approached her with a weapon, likely the same gun he tried to use on you, and forced her into the bathroom. We think he tried to strangle her there, but she fought back and they struggled.

"Luminol revealed some blood on the bathroom floor and walls. He likely got her in the tub and beat her with something and then drowned her. She had water in her lungs. A blanket was missing from the closet. He must have wrapped her up and carried it out."

"And no one saw a thing," I whispered.

"If he had a gun, why didn't he just shoot her?" Dorian asked.

"Because it would have been loud."

"Wasn't the struggle loud?"

"No one else in the building heard anything."

"What about Wren's necklace?" Dorian asked. "How did Kelly get it? Do you have any idea?"

Webb nodded. "We've watched a lot of surveillance video from your dad's house, which included the day Kelly went there. Jeff was home. He invited her in. At some point, she excused herself to use the bathroom, but she bypassed it and snuck into Jeff's room and rifled through drawers. In the video, she stuck something in her pocket, but we couldn't see what it was. We suspect it was Wren's necklace and when Jeff realized it was gone, he must have connected it to Kelly and—"

"Killed her," I finished.

"How did she find out?" Dorian wondered. "What made her think Jeff was involved?"

"She found the insurance company where Janice had a policy on Gloria. The beneficiaries were Janice as primary and Jeff as secondary. Kelly spoke to an insurance agent at that company the day before she went to your dad's house. She may not have known, but suspected it and went to the house hoping to find some proof."

"And she found it," Dorian said.

"He took the necklace then," I murmured, thinking of Wren in those woods. He had stripped the bloodstained necklace from her throat and taken it with him.

"Why?" Dorian asked. "Why would he take it?"

Webb leaned back in his chair. "We're always curious about why, but… we'll never understand people like Jeff and Dominic and Janice. Their whys are incomprehensible."

"Is there any chance she'll get off?" I asked. "Janice?"

Webb tapped his fingers on the file before him. "I'd love to say absolutely not, but there are no guarantees. Still, the video surveillance is powerful evidence and I think once we start digging, we're going to find a mountain of evidence against her. If we're lucky, it will never go to trial. She'll take a plea deal and that will be that."

"What kind of plea deal?" I demanded. "Not some slap on the wrist?"

Webb leveled his gaze at me. "She masterminded the attempted murder of you, which resulted in Wren's murder. I'm nearly one hundred percent certain she murdered both her children. I think the toxicology report will prove Jeff's murder—not to mention the surveillance."

"She poisoned him," I said.

"But how?" Dorian asked. "I thought it looked like suicide? Won't they just assume whatever he took was self-inflicted?"

"When we searched Janice's car, we found an empty Visine bottle in her purse. My working theory is she poisoned Jeff with eye drops, put it in his pop."

I pressed my face into my hands. "That's it then, I guess. It's finally over."

EPILOGUE

Two Months Later

"Nutella s'mores," Dorian announced, holding up a paper grocery bag and striding into the backyard where Rylie and I sat by the campfire I'd built.

That afternoon Dorian and I had set up a large tent and filled it with our sleeping mats, sleeping bags, battery-powered lanterns, snacks and bottled water. It was a tad excessive considering we were camping only fifteen feet from his back door, but as Fry liked to say, it was a baby step toward the real thing.

"Flying school tomorrow?" I asked Dorian as he slid marshmallows onto sharpened sticks.

He grinned. "Yep, trying to ignore those first day jitters."

"Maybe we can fly to Mo-hair to visit Glo on her big hike next summer," Rylie suggested.

"It's the Mau-Har loop," Dorian corrected. "But who knows. Maybe we will." He winked at me.

～

Rylie lay draped across Dorian's lap, snoring softly.

"I'm going to carry her into the tent," he said.

I nodded and continued to watch the flames.

He emerged a moment later and sat in his chair. I looked up to find him watching me, something in his face, his eyes.

"What?" I asked.

He looked away, shook his head. "Nothing…" He looked back at me. "You just look… so beautiful."

Color rose into my face and I tucked a strand of hair, grown out an inch and dyed back to its natural dark brown, behind my ear.

"Thanks," I whispered and for a moment I thought he might move around the fire, might kiss me, but he didn't.

Instead, we sat in silence and watched the flames.

~

I woke around midnight and lay still, listening to the frogs and crickets. Quiet, so as not to wake Rylie and Dorian, I slipped from my sleeping bag and unzipped the tent. I stepped barefoot in the cool grass and tilted my face up.

The sky was a labyrinth of stars. As I watched, a star fell, dropping diagonally in a flash of white and then vanishing into the void.

~

Eight Months Later

It's the melting season, late April giving way to May. The snow is flowing in rivulets down the hillside, merging with the yellowed grass and mud. The snow that remains is wet and dense and slippery.

I watch that river in the woods, the one where I both died and was reborn, the one that carried me out of the dark night into the new dawn. I see it now as snow melts down its shores.

The water is running swift. It's as high as the muddy banks. It's whispering through the forest, singing its song of awakening. It tells the roots that line its banks that it's nearly time, that their slumber has almost come to an end. Soon they can reawaken, the flowers and trees and cattails, the insects and birds and bears.

In a month, the brown grass will be green and ankle-high. The birds will scatter across the fresh earth each morning and pluck twigs for their nests and worms for their breakfast. Some of the creatures of the forest will not emerge from the long winter. Some will die in the months ahead.

I'm not afraid to be here in the midst of all this life and all this death. Mist clings to the grass like the ghosts of a thousand trees and flowers and beings who have fallen here and remain, whispering their secrets to the next generation and the next after that.

It is a ritual for me now, coming to this place, to the Porcupine Mountains, to the land that held Wren and I, that absorbed our blood and our tears. The land that saw fit for reasons I still don't understand to save me. The land that took Wren home.

THE TRUE STORY THAT INSPIRED
FLOWERS IN HER BONES

On October 6th, 1997, two teen girls in Bega, New South Whales, Australia, set out on a night walk leaving the camp they were spending the weekend at to visit a friend several miles away. While walking on an isolated rural road, they were picked up by two men. For the following twelve hours the girls were assaulted. Ultimately the two men drove the girls to a remote location and murdered them.

The crime shocked the small community the girls were from, and forever altered the lives of their families. In particular the brother of one of the girls spoke extensively about his grief following the murder of his sister. In many ways, it was his story that first sparked the idea for Flowers in Her Bones.

The two men who abducted and murdered the girls were arrested and convicted of the murders.

You can find the full story in detail at http://jrericksonauthor.com/2022/06/true-story-inspired-flowers-bones.html/.

ALSO BY J.R. ERICKSON

The Troubled Spirits Series

Dark River Inn

Helme House

Darkness Stirring

Ashwood's Girls

Still Falling

Flowers in Her Bones

Black Hollow Hideaway

Or dive into the completed eight-book stand-alone paranormal series:

The Northern Michigan Asylum Series.

Do you believe in ghosts?

ACKNOWLEDGMENTS

Many thanks to the people who made this book possible. Thank you to Team Miblart for the beautiful cover. Thank you to RJ Locksley for copy editing Flowers in Her Bones. Many thanks to Will St. John for beta reading the original manuscript, and to Emily H., Saundra W., Jennifer H., and Debra G. for finding those final pesky typos that slip in. Thank you to Kelly Rice for offering up her name as a victim in this novel. Thank you to my amazing Advanced Reader Team. Lastly, and most of all, thank you to my family and friends for always supporting and encouraging me on this journey.

ABOUT THE AUTHOR

J.R. Erickson, also known as Jacki Riegle, is an indie author who writes ghost stories. She is the author of the Troubled Spirits Series, which blends true crime with paranormal murder mysteries. Her Northern Michigan Asylum Series are stand-alone paranormal novels inspired by a real former asylum in Traverse City.

These days, Jacki passes the time in the Traverse City area with her excavator husband, her wild little boy, and her three kitties.

To find out more about J.R. Erickson, visit her website at www.jrerickso-nauthor.com.